the_fatum_club

By Kevin McDonald

For my family

three_weeks_ago

The air in the waiting room was thick with the smell of sterilizer and people. Samantha looked around at the many long faces that stared from each other to the floor, that all-too-familiar hospital stench thick in the air. Some of the faces were crying; others were consoling. Two of them had even managed to share a joke, their short, reserved laughter breaking the terrible silence.

It had been more than three hours now and there had been no word of how Ryan was doing. Two rooms away, his family was privately waiting for news. They promised they would tell Samantha what was going on as soon as they heard something. That made Samantha feel good. *I guess that means I'm officially his girlfriend, not that it matters much anymore.*

"They have to know *something*," someone said desperately, again breaking the silence. "Sam, do you want me to go in the private room and ask his parents if they've heard anything?"

Sam just shook her head and tried not to cry. She was the only one who knew there was no hope for Ryan.

"I'm sure he'll be fine," someone else offered. "We all need to stay positive."

It was too much for Samantha. She quickly gathered up her purse and cell phone and ran through the revolving doors of Christiana Hospital, her hand franticly wiping her eyes with a tissue.

"Sam," yelled Shelby, her best friend. "What are you doing? You can't leave. Ryan needs you."

Samantha kept walking, quickening her pace. Shelby pleaded with her. "What if he wakes up and asks for you? Stay here with us. We're all here for you."

Samantha tried not to sob and gasped for air. "Shelby, you don't understand," she said helplessly. "It's Thursday."

"What are you talking about?"

Samantha put both her hands in her hair and let her chin drop toward the shiny blacktop of the hospital parking lot. "Ryan is already dead, Shelby. Don't ask me how I know. I just do."

"Sam, you're acting crazy. Nobody from the hospital has said anything about Ryan. He'll be fine, okay? Now come back inside."

"I can't be here anymore, Shelby. I can't face his parents." She quickly turned and began walking toward her car. Shelby chased after her.

"Ryan's parents love you, Sam. You know that. Didn't they offer to take you to the mountains next week? They need you in that waiting room as much as Ryan does."

Sam shook her head furiously. "There won't be any trip to the mountains for me, Shelby."

"You don't know that. Maybe Ryan can leave tomorrow or the next day. You never know, Sam."

Samantha stopped crying and took out her car keys. She took a deep breath, looked at Shelby gravely and said, "Thanks for being such a good friend, Shelby." She stepped into her car, started the engine, and rolled down the window. Shelby looked on incredulously.

"It's not that I don't think Ryan will get out of the hospital in time for the mountains," said Samantha, now in tears. "I *know* he won't. He's already gone. And I can't go because I know that by this time next week, I'll be dead too."

And she drove away.

Newark High School student dies in car crash
Victim was a friend of teen who died last month

By Lester Holmes

NEWARK – A Newark teenager was killed in an automobile accident at the intersection of Rt. 72 and Old Baltimore Pike when her car apparently skidded out of control and collided with a utility pole.

According to police, Samantha Selby, 17, was driving east on Rt. 72 at approximately 10:30 p.m. Tuesday night when she lost control of the car while driving around a tight curve in the road. Paramedics who responded to the scene reported that she probably died on impact.

The fatal accident was the second in two weeks involving area teens. On Thursday, October 2, Ryan Chambers, also of Newark, was killed after losing control of his car while apparently swerving to avoid another vehicle. He was also 17.

Capt. Jim Fahey of the Newark Police said that even though the two teens were known to be close acquaintances, the two accidents were not related in any way and that he believed "the whole ordeal is a terrible coincidence."

one

It was raining and Billy decided to take the long way home from school. By most people's standards it was a decidedly unpleasant day - clouds, scattered showers, cold, windy. Billy loved it. Days like this deserved to be appreciated. Billy showed his appreciation with a nice long walk.

Most Newark High students hurried onto busses, piled into their friends' cars, or desperately dialed their cell phones in search of rides. But Billy never considered himself to be a normal high school student, and by his standards this was a perfect day.

Newark, Delaware had been suffering through a long period of rain, cold weather and heavy winds for almost two weeks now. For Billy that was two weeks of turning down gracious offers of rides and pulling on his dark blue raincoat. Even his father had offered to let him drive the Jetta, since he was carpooling to work. *No thanks; it doesn't get any better than this.*

And there was plenty to think about as he walked alone. Homecoming was a week away. It wasn't that he was at all interested in going to dances or building those stupid floats in someone's garage.

"Dude, we're going to Molly's tomorrow night to help with the junior class float," Kenny Alvarez, one of his closer acquaintances had said. "It's a giant bumble-bee eating a Viking ship, *tons* of girls there, dude. We're going."

A nice offer, but Billy politely turned it down. He had better things to do than work on halftime entertainment. In fact, Billy was concerned about everything *but* halftime of the homecoming game. He was much more concerned with how fast Christiana's strong side linebacker was, and whether he would have to outrun or outmuscle him. Billy was capable of both, but he loved preparing for the match up.

He would spend tomorrow night watching the film of Christiana High's last game, seeing how their linebacker took on an opposing tight end. Did he hit him at the line of scrimmage? Play a tight bump and run? Maybe he was savvy enough to give a receiver a little cushion, trying to lore the quarterback into throwing the ball his way, setting up an interception. By morning, Billy would know the guy's game better than the linebacker himself. He was sure the junior class would have a great float, but it would be nothing compared to the game he would have. By halftime, the opposing coach would be so frustrated with Billy that he would assign the strong safety to cover him.

Then the fun would really start. Billy would spend the rest of the night making the smaller defensive back look foolish...faking him out on pass routes, barreling through him on running plays. He couldn't wait.

Billy continued walking and soon came to the railroad overpass near Academy Street. It was almost dark now, and he savored the cold, wet air blowing in his face. From this spot on the pedestrian bridge he could see clear across town, all the way back to his high school - the track, the football field, even the dumpsters next to "The Bee Hive," the nickname for the large brick shed that the football and lacrosse teams used for a locker room. He could also clearly see the Newark Shopping Center, which featured the *Cue and Cushion Pool Hall* and *Tijuana Taco*, the two most popular places for his classmates to waste their nights. Billy felt lucky not to be part of that crowd.

Beyond Main Street, where the over twenty-one college crowd spent their nights, he could see St. John's Cemetery, where so many poor souls were laid to rest along the perfect path for drunken college kids to get back to their rented homes on Cleveland Avenue.

Billy squinted and saw a thin figure walking through the graveyard, a cloud of cigarette smoke following as it navigated its way through the narrow columns of gravestones. Draped in a long black overcoat, the figure wore old work boots and an oversized backwards baseball hat.

Billy smiled and shook his head. *It was Noah Lively.*

"You're going to kill yourself smoking those things," Billy shouted from across the cemetery, announcing his presence.

"And I suppose you think spying on the town from the railroad overpass is healthy behavior." Noah was always quick with his responses. He might be the smartest kid Billy ever met. The two smiled as they approached each other and shook hands warmly.

"I didn't know we were watching each other. How have you been, Noah?"

"Junior year is nothing to sing about, but what is? Will I see you at Molly's tomorrow night?" The two laughed out loud at the question. There was very little chance either of them would be there, much less both of them. One thing they had in common was their knack for being antisocial.

"Did you hear what they're making?" Billy asked with a wry smile.

"Of course - a giant bee eating a Viking ship, a *yellow jacket*, I should say. The creativity of the junior class knows no bounds. I think I'll sit this homecoming out, thank you very much."

"I believe I'll do the same, Noah," Billy answered, knowing this would warrant some pointed criticism.

Noah immediately took the bait. "So you don't plan to showcase your prowess in the mindless exhibition of testosterone you call a football game? What ever shall the Newark Yellow Jackets do?"

"I meant that I would sit the *dance* out. I wouldn't miss the game for anything. And football, Noah, is a thinking man's game," Billy countered. "Someone as smart as you should know that. It's a game of skill."

"Chess, my friend, is a game of skill," Noah said lighting another cigarette and having a lot of fun with the conversation. "Football is mindless. A bunch of knuckleheads who think they're important playing a game that will do *nothing* for them five years from now."

"Exactly what will chess do for anybody five years from now? At least football teaches teamwork, and keeps you in shape."

"Chess teaches foresight and caution. There's really no room in this world for teamwork. You know that as well as I do. That's why neither of us will be building a giant bumblebee tomorrow. Am I right?"

"Always, Noah," Billy gave in. "We know each other way too well." Billy looked down at one of the gravestones. "Second grade really doesn't seem like that long ago does it?"

"In the grand scheme of things, it's a blink. But let's not get into that." Noah blew a cloud of smoke. "I suppose it will be a pretty subdued celebration this year anyway, right?"

Billy looked up. "I guess so." They both stared at the gravestones.

"Damn shame about those two," Billy finally offered. "I heard they're going to skip the homecoming king and queen thing altogether because of it."

Noah shrugged. "That's the best news I've heard in months. Maybe something good will come out of this after all."

"What are you talking about?"

"What I mean is it takes a tragedy to do away with a superficial, degrading tradition like the Homecoming Court. Two kids who look like Ken and Barbie, both are all but guaranteed to be the Homecoming King and Queen, and they get killed in two separate auto accidents less than a week apart." Noah shook his head in disgust. "Two kids are dead, but I guess the important thing is that we have a big freaking insect eating a ship." Then with mock melodrama he said, "*Ryan and Samantha would have wanted it that way.* Makes me sick to think about it."

Billy thought about this for a long moment. He knew Noah well but they were not close friends anymore, not since fifth grade. He knew there were certain times that Noah Lively had to be dealt with very delicately, and this was one of those times.

"It makes me sick too, Noah. But you understand that this might be a way of helping the school move on after a tragic event. In a way, those kids might need to be doing what they're doing."

Noah looked in Billy's eyes for the first time since they began talking. He took a long drag of his cigarette, exhaled and finally said. "Billy, you're smarter than that too. You're swallowing all of that psychobabble crap they've been feeding us at school. And if it really made you sick you just might consider not playing in that game on Saturday. But you never really considered that, did you?" He let the words sink in. "Two kids are dead, and this whole town is supposed pretend it didn't happen. Well not me, no way. People wonder why I keep to myself. This is it. I can't stand *people*. A person I can deal with. *People*, no way."

Billy was silent. He knew he had pushed buttons he hadn't wanted to push. Noah did keep to himself almost all of the time, but so did Billy. The big difference was that Billy was never sure why he was so introverted, where as Noah seemed to have it all figured out.

"Noah," he finally said. "There aren't many people I consider friends, but Ryan was as close to being one as anybody at that school, and I *know* that the last thing he would want is for this *stupid* game to be canceled, understand?"

Billy knew his emotions were getting the best of him, but he continued. "So just maybe playing on Saturday is *my* way of dealing with it, my way of dealing with the fact that the guy I've lined up next to in the huddle for the past three years isn't ever going to be there again. Maybe those kinds of s don't exist when you're playing *chess.*"

Billy knew that what he had just said was uncalled for, and he regretted it instantly, but didn't show it. Noah took it in stride, unflinching. After a short pause he said, "I didn't know you two were close."

"I wouldn't put it that way..."

"I know," Noah cut him off. "This is affecting all of us, trust me."

Billy didn't ask, but he couldn't imagine how this situation could really affect a guy like Noah.

"It's just that you get to know people after a while. Like I said, Ryan and I weren't friends, and God knows he got on my nerves. He was part of *that* scene that I've always hated. But I guess when people are gone...you find reasons to miss them."

"Or you find out you really did like them," Noah said. "I talked to Samantha a few times. She was in my marketing class."

This was news to Billy, though he tried his best not to show it. He simply couldn't picture Noah speaking to Samantha. *What would they talk about?*

"I'm sorry, Noah. I'll miss them both."

Noah quickly produced a pair of sunglasses from his overcoat and put them on. "Well, don't be sorry for me, Billy. Be sorry for those poor dolts who will be decorating that float tomorrow. And be sorry for the two who..."

Not wanting to see Noah get emotional, or embarrassed, Billy raised his hood and signaled he was leaving. "The rain is coming again. I'm gonna' go. It was good seeing you again, Noah."

"Don't be a stranger, Billy. I'm glad you're not afraid to be...the guy who comes and talks to the weirdo in the graveyard."

"Weird is all relative," Billy said as he started to walk away.

"So you're really not going to be at Molly's tomorrow?" Noah asked.

"Definitely not, Noah. I need the time to prepare for the testosterone contest."

"Well, good luck Friday. I hear Christiana's strong-side linebacker is a monster."

Billy continued his walk, close to home now. He wasn't lying when he said it was good to see Noah. For as long as he could remember Billy was always fascinated with the way Noah's mind seemed to work. He would always look at a situation in a way that nobody else had.

This situation with the deaths of Ryan and Sam seemed to be a little bit different for some reason. A lot of people thought the town's behavior after the accidents was in bad taste. That was normal. But for Noah to react that way was just plain weird. Noah always did his best *not* to be normal.

Death can do strange things to people, and Noah was no exception. The idea of Noah socializing with Samantha Selby really threw Billy for a loop, but the fact that Noah was choked up over the whole thing was just unfathomable.

But to Billy, the strangest part of the conversation was Noah's mentioning the float being built in Molly's garage.

two

Mr. King was getting frustrated. Every year, his job seemed to get more and more difficult and his students seemed to care less and less. Shakespeare, he knew, was not for everyone, but in thirty-two years of teaching he had never seen anything like this. Most of his current class wouldn't even give the poor guy a chance.

He looked out over the seventeen young faces, all with their eyes buried helplessly in the pages of *Macbeth*, except one who was asleep. *How do you sleep when you're reading* Macbeth? But Mr. King knew that they shouldn't be reading it anyway. He thought of the young, energetic teacher he used to be, arrogantly proclaiming, "Shakespeare didn't write this stuff to be read, but to be *watched and performed.* He would roll over in his grave if he knew high school kids were *reading* it!"

But here he was, after three decades, watching as his honors English class read one of the greatest plays in history. Somehow it wasn't in these kids to get up and perform it, or maybe it wasn't in him anymore.

Mr. King remembered the days, too long ago, when he was turning kids away from his Shakespeare class. *Sorry, not enough room for you.* Now, he could only vaguely remember piling his Shakespeare class into his van and driving them to elementary schools to perform scenes from *Hamlet or A Midsummer Night's Dream.* Those glory days were long gone.

Everything these days was too fast, too black and white, instant gratification. Dissecting lines of Shakespeare no longer had the appeal it used to have. And he no longer had the energy.

"Wake up, Roberts!" Mr. King snapped. Andrew Roberts' eyes opened and darted left to right. Realizing where he was, he wiped the drool from his lip and started reading again.

"Okay, everyone stop for a few minutes," Mr. King said, finally rising from behind his desk at the front of the room. "I had asked you to think last night about the elemental differences between fate and free will. What did you come up with?" Five students dutifully raised their hands; eight others tried not to make eye contact, and the remaining four fumbled through their notes.

Mr. King let out a purposefully pathetic sigh. "Ms. Jenkins. What do you have?"

Lisa Jenkins took a deep breath and began reading: "Fate: an unavoidable and often adverse outcome, condition, or end. Free will: freedom of humans to make choices that are not determined by prior causes or by divine intervention."

"Thank you, Lisa, but I asked what *you* thought, not Webster." Mr. King shook his head and massaged the bridge of his nose. "Did anyone come up with something original?"

The sound of rain outside the open classroom window became more pronounced by the second.

Mr. King felt his neck turning red. "Seventeen members of the

13

Junior Class hand-picked by me to take honors Shakespeare because of your alleged brilliance, and not an original thought among you? *Someone* must have thought of something. Now let's hear it!"

Silence.

Mr. King let out a groan that was way too loud to be genuine and the class responded with reserved laughter. He looked around the room and realized it was inevitable. If he were going to get his point across, he would have to call on Noah Lively, as usual.

"Mr. Lively," he said finally, as if raising a flag of surrender.

Noah shifted in his seat and fumbled with his pen. "I didn't raise my hand, Mr. King."

"But I'm positive you have a brilliant answer, and as you can see, I'm dieing up here." Again, the class laughed.

Noah was not amused, but respectfully offered what he could. "Well, I think fate means that whatever is *supposed* to happen will, no matter what. Like watching one of those stupid sit-coms, and knowing it's going to have a happy ending even if all the characters are miserable and depressed and there's only two minutes left in the show. You just know that it's going to turn out great in the end, because it's a sit-com. The end is *predetermined.*"

A few students chuckled at Noah's easy use of an unfamiliar word, but they were used to that from him.

"Continue, Mr. Lively."

"Free will is...free."

The class was about to erupt again, but Mr. King sensed it and immediately raised both hands in a grand, almost shocking gesture. The class stayed quiet. He looked intensely at Noah and almost shouted, "Continue!"

"What I mean, Mr. King, is that free will cannot be predetermined. Free will means that even if you already know the ending of the show..." he thought for a moment, "you turn it off and make your own ending. Instead of everyone being happy, all the characters die in a freak elevator accident."

Now everyone except Noah was laughing, even Mr. King. Noah's face remained as serious as ever. Mr. King, feeling a little bit of the energy he felt in those glory days of Shakespeare class, allowed the unrest, even enjoyed it. Finally he said, "So in other words, Mr. Lively, free will means you can make choices to determine a course of events, and fate means that no matter what choices you make, the outcome is already decided."

Noah finally cracked a smile. "I'd say it was *predetermined*"

"Of course, Noah. *Predetermined.*" Mr. King smiled back through his thick grey beard, looking happier than he had all year. "Have you finished reading the first act of *Macbeth*?"

"I already know this play, Mr. King. But, yes, I finished."

"Then tell me, Noah, did Macbeth suffer from fate, or was he blessed with free will?"

Noah thought for a moment and cracked another smile. It usually took him a little time to start enjoying the attention this class tended to bring, and he was becoming comfortable. "I'd say he was *blessed* with fate, but *suffered* from free will."

"Explain," said Mr. King, whispering now with an intensity this class had never heard in his voice.

"Well, Macbeth is leading a very happy noble's life. He has no complaints. But all of a sudden three witches tell him he's going to be king some day. He knows it's impossible, so he doesn't pay it much mind."

"Yes…"

"But then some crazy coincidence takes place so that it becomes possible that he *could* become king. So now he knows that all he has to do is make some really gruesome choices, like killing people, and his fate will be realized. He could have hoped for fate to take care of the killing for him, but Macbeth is no believer in fate."

Mr. King just stood with his eyes toward the floor, relishing the brilliant words coming from the trench-coated Noah Lively.

"It wasn't fate that ruined Macbeth; it was the free choices he made to make his fate come true."

"Wait!" Lisa Jenkins had to interrupt. It was a welcome intrusion since Mr. King was so caught up in the discussion he had almost forgotten the rest of the class was even there. "You're saying that if he hadn't been *told* by the witches that he would be king, none of the other stuff would have happened?"

"I'm saying that after he supposedly knew his fate, it was all the free will he exercised that ended up ruining him. He could have avoided all of it."

Mr. King was enthralled. "How, Noah? How could Macbeth have avoided his fate?"

Noah continued to take the questioning in stride. "How did he even know it was fate in the first place, just because three old ladies told him so? Maybe they were just crazy, conducting some weird experiment to see what they could make Macbeth do, see how far he would go. Who knows? But it wasn't fate. It was all free will."

Mr. King looked around at his newly enlivened Shakespeare class, some of them had even begun reading again to see what they were missing. As the bell rang to dismiss class, Mr. King took great pleasure in saying, "Tomorrow, class, we will act out the beginning of Act Two!"

After the class had finished leaving, Mr. King sat down on top of his desk for the first time in years, unable to stop smiling. *Maybe there is hope for the future after all, and it's resting uneasily in the hands of Noah Lively. If only he had been in my class last year!*

three

Billy looked down at the notes he had been scribbling for the past hour. He read them easily to himself, but his mother often reminded him that nobody else on earth would ever be able to read them. "That's okay. He'll be a doctor," his father would often say in his defense. *Thanks, Dad.*

But regardless of how they looked, the notes were good. Billy had been watching the tape of Christiana's last game and had outlined every defensive scheme the Vikings had shown. He had only watched one quarter of it, but that was really all he needed. He knew every strength and every weakness of this so-called All-State linebacker that he would personally face on Saturday, and Billy knew he would own him. Not only did Billy feel he was stronger and faster than his opponent, he knew he would outsmart him. Every week Billy's goal was to know what his opponent would do even before he knew it himself. And he always did. To Billy, football was much more than a team sport, it was a one-on-one contest for supremacy, and he loved it.

After more than an hour of watching and rewinding countless times, Billy knew something was wrong. He realized that for some reason he was trying harder than usual to concentrate. It wasn't that Christiana's defense was more complex than most, or because it was a big game. It wasn't even that Ryan, with whom Billy had played next to through so many football games, was dead. If anything, Ryan's death was cause for Billy to focus more than usual. He'd made that decision the day he heard the terrible news about Ryan, shortly after Samantha had stormed out of the waiting room unable to face the horrible truth. Something was eating away at his subconscious, and he had to figure out what it was. If he were going to dissect this tape the way he wanted to, he would need to identify whatever was holding his brain hostage and deal with it.

Noah Lively popped into his head. The messy-haired, chain-smoking chess player had gotten to him.

Could it be? Noah was as strange a character any Billy knew, but their conversation in the cemetery had really thrown Billy for a loop. Could any conversation that takes place in a cemetery ever be a normal one? He thought about their talk as he scribbled little footballs in his notebook. *What was it?*

Billy knew that as he sat and thought, with Christiana's defense suspended in animation before him, many of his classmates -*the in crowd*- were huddled in Molly Parson's garage drinking hot chocolate laced with vodka, stuffing a giant bumble bee with yellow tissue paper.

But what bothered Billy was that Noah seemed more than a little bit interested in whether or not Billy would be there. Shortly after their conversation Billy had considered for a moment that Noah might be planning to go himself, but he quickly dismissed the idea knowing that social gatherings were simply not part of Noah's nature. But Billy wasn't so sure anymore. Maybe old Noah was starting to come out of that intricately structured shell he had created. Maybe he *was* at Molly's house, and maybe he didn't want Billy to be there. Billy scratched his chin, feeling the beginnings of a stubble his mother would soon force him to do away with. *Noah specifically said he wasn't going to participate in any Homecoming activities. Why?*

Billy rubbed his eyes, knowing that this would bother him terribly. He felt he knew Noah better than anyone, and this mystified him. Something was going on with Noah, and he had to find out what it was.

He stood and walked to his dresser. Looking at his image in the mirror, he almost never liked what he saw. Having grown at least four inches in the last two years, Billy had to slouch his posture just to get a clear view of his face and hair. For as long as he could remember, he'd been told how handsome he was, how he was so lucky to inherit his father's good looks. But every time he heard this, all Billy could do was wonder why so few girls ever spoke to him beyond a polite, "Hi, Billy."

He ran a hand through his thick, dusty brown hair and thought of how Noah, even with his long, unkempt hair and sad eyes, always managed to draw the attention of females, even though he could not seem to care less. *What are girls looking for anyway?* Like most men, the question would always bother Billy.

The house phone rang once then stopped. Thirty seconds later his mother was shouting, "Billy! Telephone." Billy had to be the last junior at Newark not to have his own cell phone, and this didn't bother him in the slightest. He picked up the cordless phone that was lying on his bed.

"Hello."

"It's Kenny," came the familiar voice. "Turn off your VCR and get in the shower. I'm coming to get you and we're going to Molly's. *Tons* of girls dude."

Billy thought for a moment. "Alright, Kenny. I'll be ready in ten minutes."

"You serious?"

"Get over here. Ten minutes."

"Yes!"

four

The bee was huge. Its twisted barbed wire frame lay in two pieces, taking up all the room in Molly Parson's two-car garage. Half of the assembly had been covered in yellow tissue paper, carefully stuffed into the hexagonal openings in the barbed wire. They had started stuffing tissue paper squares at the head, using black for the eyes, white for the teeth, yellow and black for the body, and grey for the wings. The junior class had apparently decided that yellow jackets have teeth, and *big* ones.

In the backyard, protected from the elements by an impressively large tent, was the Viking ship, another mass of mangled barbed wire. It was fashioned in the shape of any classic Viking ship that might be seen on the History Channel; only it was missing a bite-shaped chunk where the giant bumblebee would sink its teeth, of course.

Shelby Cooper was a senior, and didn't really want to be there. Across town, the rest of the seniors were busily readying their float for the homecoming parade. Their brilliant idea: an enormous Viking ship being swallowed up by an even larger beehive. The senior's float was sure to win, but only because the senior's float *always* won. Shelby was sure the senior's float party was far more entertaining than this one, but that made no difference. As the Student Government Association Vice President, it was her official duty to make sure the junior class float committee was getting its job done. So she was here to smile, be as pleasant as can be and to act like she really cared. It could be worse, she thought. The SGA Treasurer had to go to the *freshman* float party.

And what did she really care about anymore anyway? Since her best friend, Samantha, had died, Shelby could hardly see the importance of any of this. Even going to school seemed like it was just a distraction, a way to keep occupied rather than face harsh reality. But reality always caught up one way or another. For Shelby, it was when she went to sleep. Samantha, her dead best friend, and those last words Shelby heard her say, haunted her dreams and turned them all into nightmares.

"By next week, I'll be dead too," Sam had said. *How could she have known?* It was a freak accident. Sam lost control of her car while coming around a tight curve and skidded into a utility pole. Actually, It was her friend Phil Margiotta's car, whom she worked with at Dairy Queen. She died instantly. But somehow Samantha knew it would happen. Shelby remembered their last conversation like it had only just happened. It was a terrible burden to carry, but Shelby knew she would never tell another soul that Samantha had predicted her own death. She knew nobody would believe her, or everyone would think she was crazy, another one of these poor children trying to cope with a terrible loss, making things up to compensate...she'd heard it all and did not want to be labeled. So the truth simply stayed within her, surfacing only in the quiet of the night when it invaded her sleep.

Shelby sipped her hot chocolate. "Want some vodka for that?" one of the float committee members had asked her, pointing to a backpack placed discreetly under a table. *Didn't anyone else think that was just a little bit disgusting?*

"No, thanks," Shelby had answered, flashing the beautiful smile that had helped her win this job. "I'm just stopping by to see that things are going smoothly. I won't stay long." *Wasn't that the truth?*

At least the vodka kid wasn't afraid to approach her, she thought. Shelby was amazed how most people had treated her since Sam died. People either avoided her, fearing awkwardness, or people were *overly* nice. *Can't people treat me normally anymore?* Shelby was learning a lot about life and death and the way people approached the subject, and she hated every minute of it. *If only they knew what I knew, then they'd* really *treat me like a freak.*

Even with everything going on, tonight had already been a little bit strange. When she first arrived at Molly's, some weirdo in a trench coat had approached her as she got of her car and just started talking. He said his name was Noah and that he had known Sam. *Noah?* If Sam knew him it was news to her, and there was very little she and Sam didn't tell each other. If Sam had been friends with a trench coat-wearing, cigarette-smoking outcast, Shelby would have known about it. *Wouldn't she?* He was probably just another guy who had a crush on her and was too afraid to tell her. That happened a lot to Samantha. Shelby's eyes started to well up.

"Shelby!" It was the friendly voice of Jackie O'Neal. Shelby and Jackie had been good friends ever since Shelby's sophomore year when Jackie joined the tennis team as a freshman. They got along well, and Jackie loved having a friend who was a year older, especially one of Shelby's status. The two hugged and kissed on the cheek. "I am so glad you could make it, Shelby!"

Shelby smiled, "Why wouldn't I?"

"Well, I don't now. I just thought with everything going on..."

"I know. Everybody thinks I should be home crying."

"No! That's not what I meant." Jackie was a little bit nervous now and Shelby could tell she had not turned down the offer of vodka.

"It's okay, Jackie. I'm used to the treatment. Change the subject, if you can."

Jackie hiccupped. "Okay...were you talking to Noah Lively before?"

Shelby chuckled. "I guess so. He said his name was Noah."

"I've never seen him anywhere but school before." Jackie looked at Shelby with wide, eager eyes that said she wanted every detail. "What did he say?"

"You know him?" Shelby asked without answering Jackie's question.

"I don't *know* him, but he's in some of my classes. He's really smart, and really...different. Today, he practically got in an argument with Mr. King about this Shakespeare story we're reading. It was *so funny!* These two are both using words none of us know, and we're all just watching, like...ok."

Shelby laughed, not at Jackie's story, but at how the vodka was affecting her.

"So what did he say to you, Shelby?"

"Not much." Shelby shook her head. "He just said that he knew Samantha, and that he was sorry. He said they talked a lot about stuff nobody else our age liked to talk about, and that he considered her a good friend." Again, the tears were coming.

"Well, that was really nice of him, I guess. But I don't think they were friends. I've never seen him out anywhere. Where could they have even hung out?"

"I don't know, but they weren't friends," Shelby said with authority. "He probably just had a crush on her."

"Did he leave already?"

"I don't know. I don't think he even came up to the garage. I spoke to him out in the street." Shelby turned her head toward her car. "It was like he was waiting for me."

"Weird."

"Yeah. Oh, and he mentioned how Sam told him last year that he should take that Shakespeare class, how she thought he'd enjoy it even though Mr. King was so burned out on it."

"I remember Sam saying how much of a kick she got out of watching Mr. King get so frustrated. God, she was a funny girl."

"Yeah. What the hell was she doing talking to that kid?"

Jackie ignored the question and launched into an imitation of Mr. King. "*Don't you kids understand? Shakespeare is timeless! Everything you need to know about life is in Shakespeare!*" Then she laughed hysterically, not realizing the joke was completely lost on Shelby, who had never even met Mr. King.

Shelby laughed courteously, realizing that Jackie's imitation probably was funny to someone in her condition. "How are you getting home tonight, Jackie?" Shelby asked.

"Oh, Mike Drummond's driving me. Don't worry. He *never* drinks during football season."

"Good."

Shelby squinted as headlights crossed the front of the garage. It was someone looking for a spot. The driver slowed and scanned the area, finally settling on a spot three houses down and across the street. It was Kenny Alvarez and Billy Wirth.

Billy climbed out of Kenny's Ford Escort and looked toward Molly's garage. He could tell right away that Kenny had been right: tons of girls.

"Hey!" Kenny said, ready to burst with excitement. "Jackie is here. Awesome."

Billy smirked. "Well, if I know her, you better talk to her soon.

She probably won't be awake much longer."

Kenny tried not to laugh, eager to put on his cool face. He stuck his chest out, and tried to look mean. He was sure that was what the ladies wanted to see. Billy tried not to laugh.

Kenny was tall and lean with classic good looks. He had full dark hair and intense brown eyes. But being the youngest child in his large family, he found it hard to be confident in his looks, having been the victim of seemingly endless ridicule by his older siblings. Like most youngest children, Kenny had been told by his parents to simply ignore his agitators, an impossible task. Eventually, Kenny began to believe that he was ugly and inadequate. It would stay with him forever.

"Hey, Billy!" Jackie shouted, to Kenny's displeasure. She ran to him and gave him way too big of a hug. "I didn't think you'd come! It's *so* good to see you!"

"Well, Kenny convinced me to come," Billy explained, trying to move away from the smell of her breath.

"Oh, hi Kenny!" I didn't even see you! It's good to see you, too!"

Kenny smiled, but wasn't convinced. "Hey Jackie."

Billy felt Kenny's frustration, and he felt for him. Billy remembered the summer after seventh grade, trying so hard to get the attention of a girl who lived on his street.

He would see her at the neighborhood pool, and he would agonize over finding excuses to explain why he never took his shirt off, embarrassed about his overly skinny frame and long, bony arms. Billy's body took longer to develop than most boys his age. Eventually he found it much easier to stay in his house in the summer time, or take a long walk by himself. When August came, he would walk to the University of Delaware sports complex and watch the football team practice. He quickly learned that he loved the game. And not just playing - he loved what one of the Delaware coaches called the *science* of the game. Soon, some of the players noticed him and began giving him little bits of advice. One of the quarterbacks even gave him lessons on how to read defenses.

When his body began to develop, the following summer, Billy kept going to watch the college practices, and started accepting invitations by assistant coaches to sit in on team meetings, *learn the science*. By the time he was in high school, Billy Wirth knew more about football than most of his coaches, and certainly all of his teammates. The coaches had wanted him to play quarterback so they could take full advantage of his football knowledge. But Billy preferred tight end, staying out of the limelight. Keeping to himself had paid off, so he stuck to it. Eventually he agreed to be a backup quarterback, in case the starter went down, at least Billy would have the know-how to step in.

As for girls, he still had no clue. They were completely foreign to him - enticing but incongruous. He had learned how to recognize an overloaded defensive backfield, how to take advantage of a nickel back, and how to completely frustrate zone coverage, but still had no idea how to strike up a conversation with a teenage girl.

"Do you guys want some hot chocolate?"

"Judging by you, we better not," said Kenny with just enough edge.

Jackie's face showed her embarrassment. "Well, I guess I'll see you guys around," she said, stumbling away as quickly as she could.

Kenny felt the look Billy was giving him. "What?"

"Why'd you say that? She's just having a good time."

Kenny did regret making the embarrassing observation, but didn't want to show it. He just shrugged, and Billy knew what he was feeling.

Looking around the float party, Billy observed an interesting conglomeration of people, most of whom he knew, but didn't particularly care for. Lying on his back stuffing the bumblebee's belly with gold tissue paper was Phil "Slim" Margiotta, a skinny track and field star who loved heavy metal, and was inwardly devastated by the loss of his car and his friend, Samantha. At the top of the ladder, working on the giant eyes, was Molly Parsons, the junior class president who convinced her parents to let her have twenty-three seventeen-year-olds in her garage for three straight nights. Little did they know there was a lot more going on than building a float for the homecoming parade. Coming out of the house, probably after using the bathroom, was Jeff Permar. Jeff's uncanny ability to play the guitar made him very popular with the girls, not that he cared that much. He was deeply in love with his girlfriend of three months, Shannon Rosenthal, who was at the sophomore float party. Helping herself to more hot chocolate was Jackie O'Neal, who by now was openly trying to drown out the embarrassment caused by Kenny Alvarez. Shelby Cooper was trying her best to comfort her. Finally, approaching from Billy's left was the quarterback, Mike Drummond, who was supposed to be driving Jackie home tonight. Mike was a senior, but as quarterback of the football team, no one was complaining that he was at the junior's float party. Billy and Kenny knew the only reason he was there was that, like Kenny, he had a major crush on Jackie O'Neal.

"Billy!" Mike shouted. "What's going on?"

Billy stepped back, the smell of stale vodka filling his nose. "Hi, Mike. Have you been drinking?"

Mike smiled sheepishly. "Guilty as charged," he answered, raising his coffee mug full of hot chocolate and vodka to his lips. It was no secret that Mike Drummond enjoyed a few drinks from time to time. But it was also no secret that the whole football team had a standing agreement that there was to be no drinking during the season. It had been that way since they were freshmen. This was a big surprise, mostly because Mike was being so open about it. For a guy the size of Mike, and with his fire red hair, it would be hard for him to do anything discretely, least of all underage drinking.

Kenny leaned close to Mike. "What are you doing?"

Mike flashed a guilty grin. "Kenny, Homecoming is once a year. What's the big deal?"

Billy was furious, but tried not to cause a scene. "The big deal is we have a game in two nights and none of us is supposed to be drinking. We all agreed on that. You're the quarterback. What's going on with you?"

Mike was suddenly more aware of the severity of his actions. Billy rarely spoke up like this. "It's okay guys. I know we're going to win Friday. Everything will be fine. I'll stop now, okay?"

Kenny shook his head in disgust. "You never should have started. Just because you're so confident doesn't mean the rest of us should have to watch our quarterback get blitzed." They both realized the pun, and couldn't help but share a moment of laughter.

Then Mike looked at the ground, his six-foot-three frame hanging in shame. "It's not confidence, Kenny. I *know* we're going to win." He tossed the contents of his coffee mug into the nearby bushes. "One for Sam and Ryan, right?" Nobody laughed. "I'm done, guys. I promise."

Billy looked around again, anxious to get away. Gatherings like these made him feel uncomfortable in his own skin. As luck would have it, Shelby Cooper was fast approaching. Jackie had run off to the bathroom out of shame and necessity, so she was free. Billy and Shelby had been close acquaintances. Since she was best friends with Samantha, Ryan's girlfriend, they spent quite a bit of time together, usually driving in Ryan's car to and from school.

Billy could see the terribly sad look in Shelby's eyes as she approached and their eyes simultaneously welled up with tears as they embraced warmly. Shelby whispered in Billy's ear. "I'm sorry I didn't get to say hi to you at the funeral."

"Which one?" Billy replied with the appropriate amount of sarcasm.

Shelby inhaled and shook her head. "I don't know. I can't believe this is all happening."

Billy closed his eyes, trying not to cry. Being with Shelby made Billy suddenly more aware of Ryan and Sam's being gone. Her sweet smell reminded him of riding next to her in the backseat of Ryan's cramped two-door Chevy. He thought of the last time they'd stopped at the drive through at McDonald's together, and Ryan accidentally spilled his orange soda in Sam's lap, and Sam was furious that Mike always had to ask for extra ice.

He still couldn't believe they were gone. "How are you holding up, Shelby?"

"I'm here, aren't I?"

Billy showed a half smile. "Yeah. Me too."

"You sure are, Billy. Why? You never come to these things."

"I know," Billy answered. "I'm not sure why. I just…"

"Please don't say you're here because Ryan can't be here. That would be too much for me right now." Shelby massaged the space between her eyes, trying not to lose it. She still looked very good. The past few weeks had taken a toll on her. She wasn't wearing any makeup lately, or paying much attention to her hair, but she looked as good as ever. Billy was always more impressed with natural beauty than with what makeup could do, and Shelby had no need for makeup anyway.

"I don't think it's that," Billy said. "I guess I feel a little bit closer to Ryan if I'm here. I also thought I might run into someone else."

"Well, you never know who's going to show up to these things anymore," Shelby said with just enough disdain to get the point across.

"Thanks *a lot*," Billy answered.

"Not you," she said gesturing toward the street. "Some kid in a trench coat. He was waiting for me when I got here. *Weird.*"

Billy knew immediately. "Noah Lively?"

"You know him?"

"We go back a long way. When did he leave?"

"He left as soon as I got here. We spoke for five minutes, then *poof.*"

Billy nodded and looked toward the street. "That's Noah. What did he want?"

"Who knows? He just kept saying how great Sam was and that he and she really got along, but he's full of it. She never spoke to him."

Billy was starting to think otherwise, but didn't say anything. He didn't see any reason to upset Shelby even more. Shelby seemed to be finding security in being the girl who was closest to Sam.

Billy changed the subject. "Sorry about Kenny. I know he upset Jackie."

"It's okay. She deserves it. She's so used to being carted around by boys. She could use the wake up call."

"I hope you don't mean Mike," Billy said. "He's not driving *anywhere* tonight."

"He's drunk?" Shelby quickly went from sad to angry. "How are they getting home?"

"I'm sure we can take them, if she'll get in a car with Kenny."

Shelby narrowed her eyes and said, "She won't have a choice. What's he thinking anyway? He's got a game coming up."

"Oh, not to worry," Billy answered sarcastically. "He already *knows* we're going to win on Friday."

Shelby quickly closed her eyes tightly, trying hard no to cry.

"What…" Billy wasn't sure what he had said.

"Nothing, Billy. Just make sure she gets home, okay?" The tears were coming now.

"Yeah," Billy said, wanting to ask what had upset her so much.

"I have to go, okay? Good luck in the game."

Billy thought about another hug, but he suddenly realized that they had been holding both hands through the entire conversation. The first hug never really ended. Shelby realized the same. She squeezed his hands tightly and said, "It's good to see you, Billy. Good luck." She hurried to her car, started it and drove away.

Yellow Jackets squeak past Vikings
Blocked punt seals victory for Newark

By Michael Talley

Newark – The Yellow Jackets narrowly averted what would have been a stunning upset by Christiana Friday night when a blocked punt was returned for a touchdown with less than three minutes remaining in the game. Newark won 14-10.

Newark's usually high-powered offense struggled throughout the night as quarterback Mike Drummond threw three interceptions, the most he has thrown in his three years as a starter. Newark's only offensive touchdown came on a 12-yard pass when Drummond managed to find tight end Billy Wirth in the back of the end zone late in the second quarter.

Newark finally got the break it needed with 2:41 remaining in the game. Trailing by five points, Newark forced Christiana into a punting situation from their own 23-yard-line. Sophomore Steven Banaszack blocked the punt and senior Nate Lemon recovered the ball and easily returned it for a touchdown.

The unlikely score spoiled Christiana's hopes for earning its second win of the season, but secured a homecoming victory for Newark, which advanced to a 7-0 record.

"I'd say we were lucky, but I think in football there is no such as thing as luck," said a relieved Newark Coach David Scott. "We're a good team, and Steven made a good play. It wasn't lucky; that's just what happens to good teams."

Newark might have felt lucky in the second quarter when Christiana blew two chances for easy touchdowns. The first opportunity came when Christiana wide receiver Travis Mix dropped a pass in the end zone. The second came on the same drive when running back Billy Hackett committed an unforced fumble on his way into the end zone.

"I don't know why we had such a tough time," Drummond said. "I was so confident going into the game, and I never had any doubt that we would win."

The truth was asleep, dreaming. His nightmares always reminded him of his inferiority. The world looked at the truth as someone of no importance or consequence. How wrong the world was. He was better than all of them, smarter than them, superior. Why didn't they treat him with the respect he deserved? They still didn't, even after everything came true and he was proven right.

In his dream the class turned to laugh at him, and pointed accusingly. It had been the same since he was very young. They laughed and drooled as they pointed, and got closer and closer. Except one boy who sat by himself, huddled in the corner. *Was that him or me?* He just looked on with that stupid smile on his face, but *he knew.*

And the others, they didn't know, but they kept pointing, and laughing, and getting closer and closer.

"Wake up!" It was his mother, saving him from the nightmare.

"I'm coming, mother," he called back.

"It's time for breakfast you lazy ingrate!"

He fell out of bed and looked at himself in the mirror. The truth was ugly, but he always had been. That was one of the reasons they laughed and never listened to his brilliant words. It tortured him every day and night that they didn't know what was inside him. If they only listened he would impress them and charm them, and they would ask him to sit at their table and tell them what he knew. But they never did. They just laughed.

But his job was almost complete. And when it was, they would all know the truth, and respect him. There would be no more need to hide, or to dream.

five

At a crossroads halfway between the great Chesapeake Bay and the Delaware River, which separates what is now New Jersey from Delaware, a village began to form. From prehistoric times until the 1700s, members of the Leni Lenape tribes would gather there to trade furs and other valuables. Sometimes they would travel to the hill just south of the village in search of metals used to make tools and weapons.

In the sixteen and seventeen hundreds, settlers from England, Wales, Scotland, and Ireland began to make the village their home, and by 1758 *NewArk* was home to so many settlers that King George II of England granted the small town its first official charter. These early Delawareans made their livings working in tanneries, mills, and brickyards.

In 1777, just after the colonies declared themselves free of the reign of King George, General Washington rode his horse to that same hill just south of the town, which was becoming known more and more as *Newark* (The people of this small town must have figured that one capital letter was enough for them). It was on the summit of that hill that General Washington and his French ally, General Marquise de Lafayette, watched as the British Army landed in the nearby Maryland town of Elkton.

A few days later a small group of soldiers from Washington's army, probably a scouting party out looking for food or supplies, collided with a similar group of Redcoats at a close by farm called Cooch's Bridge. A fight ensued resulting in many dead on both sides. What history would record as a skirmish, citizens of Delaware would always remember as the Battle of Cooch's Bridge, the only "battle" of the American Revolution to be fought on Delaware soil.

Whether the engagement was a battle or a skirmish or merely a brawl is not nearly as important as another event that proudly rests in the annals of Delaware history. During that collision of opposing forces, many believe that this was the first time the world saw the beautiful stars and stripes of the newly designed American Flag. It was the same color as it had been under the rule of King George, but was distinctly American. Washington's troops flew it proudly that day as they marched into battle, so say the people of Delaware. And many died defending it. Many more would die a few weeks later when the two armies met in force at the Brandywine River, just north of Delaware in southeastern Pennsylvania.

More than two hundred thirty years later, the farm and the hill probably looked a lot like they did when General Washington gazed upon the Big Elk River to see those hated British descending their boats. To Billy, who now stood at the crest of Iron Hill, few things were more fascinating than what might have happened in his town centuries ago. In school, he gave American and world history their respect as classes, though he was never fascinated with either. But the history of the ground he was walking on, *that* should be a subject in high school.

Looking in the direction of Elkton, Billy was sad that he could only see the boring sides of maple trees. Maybe in 1777 there were no trees up here. Maybe Washington had someone climb to the top of a tree to see Elkton. Maybe some local yokel made the whole thing up. Either way, Billy felt like he was a small part of history just standing here.

He walked in a large circle, like he had done at this same place since he was a small child and thought, maybe *I'm walking in the same exact spot as Washington.* He inhaled deeply. *Maybe I'm breathing the same air.* The possibilities were endless, and endlessly fascinating for Billy.

Brushing aside the temptation to ponder Washington's breathing a few more minutes, Billy continued his workout. He sprinted down the narrow path that led to the remains of Iron Hill Tower, which had been torn down a decade earlier. At one time it had been a fabulous monument with a terrific view, but after a few years, it turned into a major hazard with drunken high school and college kids making the tower the object of too many bets and simple tests of bravery.

Into the thick woods now, he quickly descended another trail building speed for the looming steep climb. *Quiet feet,* he thought. Part of being an effective receiver is being able to make your opponent think you're not there. This was rare among tight ends, who usually took pride in their heavy steps. But Billy had mastered this skill, and he took pride in the number of times he was wide open, creating a huge target for the quarterback.

Billy loved running the trails of Iron hill, and he was good at convincing his teammates to come with him. In July and August he had the entire receiving corps running the trails and even a few of the linemen. As the season wore on the numbers dropped. Today, just one day after Homecoming, he could only coax Kenny Alvarez and Mike Drummond into joining him. Kenny was easy, but Mike was still upset about his performance the night before, the worst of his career. Billy had convinced him that the hills were just what he needed to unwind. Mike finally agreed.

As he approached a steep incline, Billy's thighs began to burn in anticipation of the coming climb. This steep incline was known as Duncan Slope, and it was the best place on Iron Hill to practice those quiet steps. Anyone who could climb this hill at full speed without being heard could have his way with any safety in the state, and could turn a linebacker's game into a sixty-minute nightmare.

"Touchdown, Billy Wirth!" he yelled sending Kenny Alvarez and Mike Drummond jumping almost out of their shoes.

"Damn, Billy! I wish you wouldn't do that," Mike said.

Billy was laughing and catching his breath. "You didn't complain much when I was wide open in the back of the end zone last night."

"Well, save it for them. How do you do that anyway? You're two hundred pounds and quiet as a cat. Try making a little bit of noise."

"I'm one-eighty," Billy said, still catching his breath. "And you could be a little lighter on your feet yourself."

Kenny pulled at his Yellow Jackets t-shirt. He was getting impatient.

"It's getting dark. Let's finish. Race to the top. Incase anyone forgot, I've won the last three."

Mike smirked and said, "You've won the last three because you dog it on all the hills, saving it all for the end."

Billy added, "Just like practice, Alvarez. I think that's why you run so fast on game day. You don't run all week."

"Listen to this guy," Kenny said incredulously. "He makes one game-winning catch and all of a sudden he's the captain. I thought that was your job, Mike."

Mike's expression made it clear that the joking was suddenly over now and Billy knew it. Mike took a long drink of water from his sports bottle, dropped his head and said, "After last weak, I don't know if I should be the captain anymore." He looked at his friends. "I wish I weren't the captain right now."

"That game is history," said Billy, though he knew that would mean nothing to the quarterback.

"*This hill* is history, Billy. Last weak was a disgrace for me. I was totally irresponsible. I was drinking; I didn't pay any attention to film. We were lucky to win. All because..." He dropped his head again.

Kenny made eye-contact with Billy and asked Mike, "All because what?"

Mike stepped toward a nearby oak tree and furiously pounded his left fist into its rough, solid trunk.

"Hey!" shouted Billy. "What are you trying to do, miss the next game?"

"Maybe you're better without me, anyway," Mike snapped.

"If you really believed that, you'd be hitting that tree with your *right* hand," said Kenny. "What is this all about?"

Mike, too upset to even speak now, dropped to a knee and shook his head. Finally, he said, "I put the whole team at risk. I should have known it was all a bunch of bull."

"What are you talking about?" asked Billy.

Mike laughed and looked at his two friends. He wiped the sweat from his brow and said, "The whole thing is so crazy. You'll think *I'm* crazy." He shook his head and tried to laugh. Billy and Kenny just watched and waited. "Remember when I said I knew we were going to win?"

"Yeah."

"Well, I meant it. I wasn't just being confident." He looked blankly into the trees. "I *knew*."

"Mike. Are you alright?" Billy asked, noticing the tears welling up in his friend's eyes.

Mike continued to speak in the direction of the trees, addressing neither of his friends. "I almost was hoping we'd lose, just so I'd be wrong. And we almost did. But Banaszack blocks a punt and we win." He hit the tree again and inhaled deeply, absorbing the pain. He closed his eyes

29

as he winced. After a few seconds he looked toward the sky and opened them. Then he whispered intensely, "It came true. It was meant to be."

There was a long pause while Billy and Kenny looked at each other, completely confused, and Mike just stared at the giant trees, trying not to cry.

After a long minute, Billy asked quietly, "What do you mean, Mike?"

Mike just smiled painfully and shook his head some more. Finally he said, "Life is a tale told by an idiot, full of sound and fury, signifying nothing." Then he pounded the tree once more and took off for the summit of Iron Hill.

Kenny and Billy were totally befuddled, but took off after him.

"The streak ends now, Alvarez! I know I'll win this one!"

six

Shelby inhaled deeply and let out a sigh. It struck her as interesting that the hang-up button on her cell phone was much more worn than the call/answer button. Then she noticed the seven was worn almost down to being unreadable. That must be because it was the button she pressed to delete a voice message. Looking at the earpiece, she observed that there was a sticky, unclean substance that she hadn't seen before. It must be from her hairspray, she thought. Shelby wondered if the cell phone manufacturers were aware of all these intricacies one notices when staring at a cell phone for more than half an hour.

She put the phone down. Dropping her head facedown onto the desk in her bedroom, she put both hands in her straight blonde hair and let out a groan. *Ugh!*

Why was it so difficult just to make a simple phone call? The whole world was walking around talking on cell phones. People spoke more on cell phones than they did in person, yet here she was agonizing over making a simple phone call to Billy Wirth.

She had called Billy many times over the past year, but not once since the accidents. It had been almost a month and they had only spoken for a few minutes at Molly's party. The few minutes were nice though. It was really the only time she had felt really comfortable around another person since the whole thing started.

Call him! What was the big deal? He wouldn't even be surprised to hear from her, she was sure. She would suggest getting together just to talk. That was what she really needed. It wouldn't be much different than those afternoons after school. Just because Sam and Ryan weren't there didn't mean that much, did it? Of course it did.

Ugh! Shelby stood up and looked at herself in the mirror. She had lost weight in the last few weeks; she hadn't needed to. Her pale face was thinner than she was used to. She hadn't been hungry in a while, despite her mother's insistence that she was starving.

"I'm not anorexic, mom. I'm just upset," she had said more times than she could remember. "Can't you just let me be for a while?" Shelby was sure the next step was a psychiatrist if she wasn't careful. She would have to start eating again, and maybe even return to field hockey practices. That was if she could bring herself to be in public for more than a few minutes. *Billy could help me with that.*

She picked up the phone again and stared. She scrolled, once again, through her saved numbers and came to "B. Wirth." She pressed ever so slightly on the dial button, not to call him, but to remind herself what it would *feel* like. This was ridiculous. She took a deep breath and prepared to push the button when...

RIIING!

Shelby jumped and let out a stifled shout. She wasn't prepared for a phone call. It was Michelle Ramsey, a senior who was best friends with

31

Molly Parsons. What did she want? "Hello?"

"Hi, Shelby!" came the way too excited voice. "It's Michelle!"

"Hi, Michelle. What's going on?"

"I just wanted to thank you for coming to Molly's the other night."

"You wanted to thank me?"

"Yeah, I mean...I know it must be tough to come to those things, so...I just wanted to say thanks."

"Well..."

"Shelby, you know...I lost my dad when I was six."

"I know, Michelle." Shelby had known Michelle lost her father when she was very young, but didn't know how he had died.

"Yeah. I just...I know it's tough when you lose people. So thanks a lot. It meant a lot to see you there." Shelby felt a twinge in her stomach and her eyes filled up.

"Thanks, Michelle."

"Really, Shelby. If you ever need to talk, or just want to do something stupid for fun, please call me. I know we've never been close friends, but it doesn't matter. We could have a good time. We can talk anytime you want, okay?"

Shelby wiped her eyes and said, "That's really nice of you, Michelle. Thanks so much for calling. It's...it's nice to know someone cares."

"Of course I do, Shelby. Just let me know if you ever want to talk, okay?"

"I will. Thanks again, Michelle."

"Sure. Talk to you later."

"Bye."

It might have been the nicest call she'd ever received. Shelby put the phone down and sobbed. *I guess Billy won't be getting any phone calls tonight after all.*

The phone at Billy's house rang. "Hello."

"Dude, you *have* to get a cell phone." It was Kenny.

"You going to pay for it, *dude*?"

"Get on a family plan! Tell your parents this isn't 1990 anymore!"

"What do you want, Kenny?" Billy asked, sounding agitated.

"We need to go to Cue and Cushion."

"I don't need to go anywhere. I'm exhausted."

"No kidding, you're exhausted. You're the one who drags us to Iron Hill the day after a game. It's time for me to drag you around, so stop watching film for a change. It's Saturday night! I'll be there in fifteen minutes. Be ready." He hung up.

Billy slammed the phone down. The pool hall on Saturday nights was about as big a waste of time as there could be, and he had no desire to go. The phone rang again. Once again, it was Kenny.

"I think you should wear your letterman's jacket. You had a good game last night."

"Do I care what you think I should wear?" Billy shouted.

"Alright, alright. Calm down," said Kenny, knowing he was pushing it. "Just be ready in fifteen."

Billy shook his head, infuriated. "Wait!"

Kenny had almost hung up. "What?"

"What do you think Noah Lively was doing at Molly's?"

"Huh?" Now, Kenny was annoyed.

"Noah Lively," Billy repeated. "Shelby said he was there before we showed up. Why do you think he'd go to that? He never goes to things like that."

"Well neither do you, and why do I care about Noah Lively?"

"Never mind. I'll see you when you get here." Kenny hung up. Billy was about to take his shoes off when the phone rang a third time. *What could he want now?*

"Yeah," he answered, annoyed as ever.

"Billy?" It wasn't Kenny. The voice was female, soothing and familiar.

"Yeah. Sorry. I thought it was someone else. Who's this?"

"It's Shelby. How are you?" Billy bit his lip at the realization.

"Hi, Shelby. Sorry. Kenny's been calling me all night and I thought it was him again. You know how he is..."

Shelby tried to laugh. "Yeah, I know. He doesn't hold much back, does he?"

"He never has," Billy said. *Why was she calling?* "What's going on, Shelby?"

"Well, it's been a long time since we've gotten to really hang out, so...I thought you'd like to get together tonight if you're not doing anything."

Billy suddenly had the fantasy of throwing Kenny Alvarez off the highest point of Iron Hill. He sneered and threw a ball of socks at the wall as hard as he could. He was glad it made no sound. *The one Saturday Night I actually could go out with Shelby Cooper and I'm going to the freaking pool hall with Kenny!*

"Shelby, I would love to but,..."

Shelby tried to laugh again, very nervous. "I understand, Billy. I don't know what I was thinking, I..."

"No," Billy interrupted. "I'd love to hang out with you again. You're right. It's been way too long. It's just that I let Kenny convince me to go to Cue and Cushion tonight."

Now she really did laugh. "*You're* going to Cue and Cushion?"

"I know, I know," Billy said, laughing at himself. "I don't know what's getting into me. Can we do it another time? Maybe one day this week after practice is over, we can go for a drive."

"Definitely!" Shelby realized this was the happiest she had been in three weeks.

"Okay. It's great to hear from you, Shelby."

They hung up. Now there was knocking on his bedroom door.

"Yeah," Billy said, his signal that it was okay to come in.

It was his mother. "What's with all the phone calls? Are you the Secretary of State all of a sudden?"

Billy shrugged and shook his head. "Mom, if I can't have a cell phone, could I at least put the caller ID in my room? It would save me *a lot* of embarrassment."

It was raining again. Billy loved the rain, but not when Kenny was driving him in it. "So what's with Noah?" Kenny asked. "Why are you asking about him?"

"Just watch the road."

"What are you, my mother?"

"Shelby called right after you did."

"Really? What did she want?"

"I think she asked me out."

Kenny laughed, a deep belly laugh. "Dude, how do you *think* somebody asked you out? She did or she didn't."

"Well, I guess she did then," Billy answered unable to keep from smiling.

"That's great dude! She's hot!" Kenny shouted slapping Billy's knee.

"Watch the road, *dude*!" Billy said, gripping the door handle.

Of course Kenny was excited at the news. It wasn't so much that he was happy for Billy. He was happier that he didn't have to worry about Billy going after Jackie O'Neill, not that Billy had even considered that scenario. Kenny was right about Shelby being "hot." She always had been. Even since the accident, when she had noticeably let herself go a little bit, getting very skinny, no makeup, and simple hair. She still looked great. Billy loved when beautiful girls wore jeans and sweats, and that seemed to be all Shelby wore anymore. And she made it work, even if she didn't know it.

Billy knew that dating Shelby would be a very big deal for a lot of reasons. For one, Billy almost never dated. A year ago, a sophomore named Rachel had asked him out and they went to a movie and that was the end of it. She had tried to kiss him, but he quickly backed off. There were many girls he'd wanted to ask out, but there was a language barrier with Billy and girls. Secondly, Shelby was a senior and a year older. That might be big news in gossip circles, and he hated the idea of that.

"The coolest thing is that she's a senior, dude," Kenny said, as if reading his mind.

"You think?"

"Hell yes! You'll be the man."

"I don't know. People might think I'm over-stepping my bounds."

Kenny pulled into a parking spot outside the Cue and Cushion and cut the ignition. "Are you nuts?"

"Why?"

"Give yourself some credit, Wirth. You're a football star."

"No, I'm not!" Billy said emphatically. "I play tight end. Nobody cares."

"How many touchdowns do you have this year?" Kenny's voice was increasing in pitch. Billy knew that meant he was getting annoyed.

"I don't know, Kenny."

"You don't know? You *are* nuts. It's at least five, right?"

"I guess. I really don't count them."

Kenny bit his lip and looked away. "Billy, there are people who would *love* to have five touchdowns this year, no matter what position they play. Would you please put your status as a football star to some use? You *deserve* to be dating a senior, especially one who looks like Shelby Cooper, now get a hold of yourself!" Kenny opened his door loudly and stormed out of the car.

"I didn't mean to upset you, Kenny. Chill out, will you?"

"Billy, I made six tackles yesterday. It was the best game I ever played. You think anybody cares? I broke up three passes. Are the senior hotties calling me? You better start appreciating what you have. Go out with Shelby and enjoy it. In fact, go out with anybody you want. They'll say yes. Trust me. And where's your stupid letterman's jacket?"

Billy decided to drop it. This was more trouble than he needed, and he was wishing more and more he was with Shelby Cooper right now. He got out of the car and the two began walking toward the entrance to the Cue and Cushion.

As usual, eight or nine teenagers were standing outside smoking cigarettes. Thanks to a controversial law passed in 2003, Delaware no longer allowed smoking indoors. There was, however, a longstanding law against children smoking cigarettes that went widely ignored. As they drew closer to the entrance, the figures began to take familiar shapes, and some of them were definitely students from Newark.

"Check it out," Kenny said pointing to one lone figure that was standing by himself near a far trashcan. Billy recognized the boy as Ryan Chambers' younger brother, a freshman. Kyle Chambers was not like his brother, and that was definitely on purpose. Kyle did practically everything he could to distinguish himself from his older brother. No football, no dances, no workouts, no cruising down Main Street. Kyle's social life consisted mainly of pool, cigarettes, and comic books. And he seemed to like it that way. However, nobody at school was sure how he was feeling lately, since he had no friends, at least none that anyone knew about.

"Poor kid," said Kenny. "It must be tough to lose a brother."

Kenny would know. He was the youngest of nine children; he had five brothers. All but one of them was no longer living at home. One was away at college in Baltimore, two were serving in the Army and had been stationed on opposite sides of the continent, and one was in jail for violating probation. The oldest was a Jesuit priest living in Philadelphia. Kenny had seen a lot of grown up things in his young life.

"He must be going through hell," said Kenny, a trace of emotion in his voice.

Billy had no brothers or sisters, but he sensed Kenny's pain. However, he was not prepared for what Kenny did next. Without warning, Kenny walked through the crowd of smokers toward Kyle. Billy was suddenly extremely uncomfortable, but knew he had to follow. He felt the blood rush to his head. Billy didn't know what someone was supposed to say to a kid who had just lost his big brother.

When the two reached Kyle, Kenny extended his hand and smoothly said, "I'm Kenny. I played ball with Ryan."

Kyle, clearly surprised by the gesture, shook hands and said, "I know who you are. Ryan always said you were a great linebacker."

Kenny felt a knot in his throat and smiled. "He never said that to me, but it sounds even better coming from you."

Kyle dragged on his cigarette. "Why?"

"I don't know. I guess it's just not something Ryan would have said."

Kyle chuckled. "You got that right. But he did say it. He always said, 'That Alvarez, he's tough.'"

Kenny shook his head and smiled. "Well, I'm not as half tough as you, Kyle. I can't imagine what it's like. I got some brothers myself."

Kyle looked down. "Yeah well...I guess I *have* to be tough now, don't I?"

Billy broke in, trying his best to do what seemed to come so naturally to Kenny. "He was a great guy, your brother. I'll miss him a lot."

Then Kenny put his hand on the back of Kyle's head and leaned very close to him. He whispered something in Kyle's ear. Kyle closed his eyes and nodded. Billy could see his lips say, "Thanks."

They said goodbye to Kyle and continued toward the entrance of the pool hall. Later, Billy would consider asking Kenny what he had whispered, but decided not to. It just wouldn't be proper, he concluded.

When they were inside, they went to the main desk to see about getting their own table. There was a long wait, but Kenny knew Billy wouldn't want to join in and play partners with anyone. Anyway, Kenny's hope was to set up shop and hopefully attract some ladies to their table. But before Kenny could give his name, a pony tailed attendant holding a waiting list held two fingers to Billy. "You guys need a table?"

Billy was confused. "Uh..."

"Right this way," the tattooed man said with a smile. "I got a special table I keep open for people who can't wait." Billy looked at Kenny in disbelief. Kenny looked with his eyes bulging almost out of his skull, as if to say, "Don't blow it. Just take the table."

Kenny reached for his wallet, but before he could the man said, "Great game last night guys. Your money's no good. Have a good time."

So they played, for free. Then the free sodas came from the snack bar, then the popcorn, then the girls. Kenny's face was a frozen smile, like a child discovering Candyland. This wasn't Billy's style at all, but for now he took it all in and tried his best to enjoy it. *Ryan would want it this way.*

Before they could get too wrapped up in the celebrity treatment, Billy heard the tattooed attendant yell, "Lively! Noah Lively!" Billy almost dropped his stick as he quickly scanned the room.

"Did he say Noah Lively?" But Kenny was too busy enjoying his new celebrity status to address the question. Billy kept looking in the direction of the front desk, waiting to see if his old trench-coated friend would answer the attendant's call. *What was he doing here?*

"He must have left," shouted an impatient girl who had spent more than an hour on the waiting list.

"Okay," said the attendant. "I guess it wasn't meant to be...who's next?"

The truth was at peace. Almost everything had come to fruition, just as he knew it would, and soon he could rest. He arranged the books on his shelves in alphabetical order, a job he had put off for a long time. But now there was time, time for all kinds of things. Finally he had heard the news he was waiting for, and he celebrated in private. No one else could ever know the truth. But he had been proven right, as he always had.

The newspaper said it was a "terrible coincidence." *What do they know?* But this notion of coincidence helped him greatly. Nobody would come looking for a coincidence. Those ignorant few would suspect, but would be too scared or too stupid to even try to find the truth. He had nothing left to fear. Best of all, he would get the respect he finally deserved.

He sipped his hot chocolate and looked out the window toward the cemetery. How he loved a rainy fall day!

seven

"Mr. King, if *I* can't see any dagger in front of me, how will the audience know what I'm looking at?"

Mr. King rubbed his head, slightly disheveling his thinning gray hair. "That's the point, Jerome. The dagger isn't really there. Macbeth only *thinks* it is. He's imagining it. He's thinking about killing the king so he can *become* king." Jerome was by far the best actor of this bunch, but certainly not the brightest.

"Wait, Mr. King, I have an idea!" It was Lisa Jenkins and Mr. King was cringing in preparation of hearing yet another asinine suggestion from her. "I saw this movie about Macbeth where they had kind of an image of a dagger floating in front of him. It was *so* cool. We could do it that way!"

"Thank you, Lisa, but the audience will use its imagination, exactly the way Shakespeare meant it. There were no digital images in the 1600s, people had to *listen* to know what to imagine. They couldn't rely on special affects to do the thinking for them. That's how we'll do it."

Lisa turned up her nose. "Well. This is the twenty-first century, Mr. King."

"Don't remind me." Mr. King turned his attention back to the stage and was about to give Jerome a pep talk when he was interrupted by Noah Lively.

"Jerome, if *you* know the dagger is there, then the audience will. It's called *willing suspension of disbelief.* They will believe you see a dagger because they *want* to."

Jerome gave his undivided attention to Noah. "How do I make them think I believe it, Noah?"

"Just believe it yourself. They'll do the rest."

Mr. King sighed and sat down in the front row of the auditorium and rubbed his head again. He was about to speak when, again, he was interrupted. This time it was the five o'clock bell, letting everyone in the building know that after school activities should be wrapping up for the day.

"Okay. Leads, memorize your lines," he shouted above the din. "Remember, they have a rhythm for a reason. Pick up the rhythm and you'll remember your lines. See you tomorrow. Noah, I need to speak to you for a moment."

Noah had a feeling this was coming. He picked up his bag and walked over to where Mr. King was sitting. The man never looked good, usually dog-tired. Lately, however, there had been a bit of a spark. His decision to perform *Macbeth* for the school was an unexpected surprise, though Noah didn't want much to do with it. He'd rather just sit and read Shakespeare. Unlike most people, he didn't need too see a performance to help him understand the material. It just came naturally to him.

Mr. King removed his glasses. He looked very different without them. "Noah, I've had a thought."

Noah waited, saying nothing.

"I know this play was my idea. I became so inspired with class last week that I wanted to put on a play. Now I'm worried that I'm in over my head."

Noah shrugged, a gesture that he hoped would affectively convey his unwillingness to participate. "What can I do, Mr. King?"

"Well, I'm realizing that I might be getting too old for this, too impatient. How would you like to direct this play, and just let me work behind the scenes?"

Noah did not expect this. He had thought Mr. King might try to convince him to take the lead role of Macbeth, but to direct the entire play? This was a shock, and Mr. King could see from Noah's expression that he was surprised.

"Take some time to decide, okay? Let me know tomorrow what you think. Either way it's okay. I just think you can bring to this thing what it really needs. You can bring that spark that I just seem to manifest anymore."

Noah had not said a word, and he wasn't sure what to say now. He finally said, "Thanks, Mr. King. I'm really flattered that you think I could do it. I just...I'm not sure. I'll let you know, okay?"

"May I ask you something else, Noah?"

"Of course."

"Why did you take my Shakespeare class? You requested it specifically, but you seem to already know all the Shakespeare you'll ever need."

Noah thought before he answered. He didn't like anyone, especially teachers, knowing his reasons for what he did.

"I had a friend who took the class last year and...she wanted me to take it."

"Oh? Who was that?"

"It was Samantha Selby. She talked about this class a lot."

Mr. King's expression turned to stone and he looked away. Then he broke into a chuckle that seemed almost manufactured. "I didn't think that poor girl cared for my class at all. That's a surprise and a half!"

"Well, she was full of surprises, Mr. King. She told me I needed to take this class. She said it was the only way I'd learn the truth."

The wrinkles on Mr. King's forehead became more defined. He was clearly puzzled. "What did she mean by that? *The truth.*"

Again, Noah carefully considered his response. "She liked this class a lot. She was always saying how it really opened her eyes, and she wanted that for me. I'm sure that's what she meant."

Mr. King smiled, almost to himself. "Well, that's very nice. It's a shame we can't thank people for the nice things that they say after they're gone. Isn't it, Noah?"

He felt a lump in his throat. "It sure is. I have to go now, Mr. King. Thanks again for the offer. I'll think about it."

"Please do, sir. Either way, I'll look forward to seeing you in class."

Noah gathered his things and left the auditorium and took a left turn toward the biology labs. Mr. King had caught him off guard. Noah didn't even like speaking to other students, much less *directing* them in a play. What a nightmare!

On the other hand, he was doing a lot of things lately that he normally wouldn't do. He had actually been to the pool hall Saturday night, but didn't stay long. All of this new activity was definitely keeping him busy, and he didn't think he could add directing a shortened version of *Macbeth* to the mix. He had serious work to do, work that nobody else was even aware of. He would have to tell Mr. King he was just too busy, but he wouldn't be able to tell him the truth.

The truth was that he was on a mission. Noah was going to find out the truth about the deaths of Ryan Chambers and Samantha Selby, and he was getting closer to the truth every day.

eight

"Billy, what are you wearing?" asked Goodwin Snow, the team's hugely overweight starting defensive tackle, as he grinned mischievously and ambled across the locker room floor.

Billy, who came so close to getting outside without being noticed, tried his best to look nonchalant. "What?"

Goodwin stepped closer, looking Billy over from head to toe. Billy had put on his newest pair of jeans and a navy blue sweater, his best color, according to his mother. He completed the outfit with a pair of hiking boots that he almost never wore. Goodwin was dressed only in his underwear and was himself a sight to behold, especially when he was nearly naked. "Man, I've never seen you walk out of practice in nothin' but old sweats and sneaks. What you up to, boy?"

"Nothing," Billy said dismissively. "I just have some place to go."

The massive player continued stepping toward Billy, his enormous midsection bouncing over his briefs. He began to wrinkle his nose in an exaggerated sniffing gesture. "What do I smell on you? You wearing perfume or something?" His voice was getting louder, deliberately drawing the attention of the crowded locker room.

"It's not perfume, Snow." Billy was sensing that he was suddenly on stage and was trying hard to get through this embarrassing situation with as little pain as possible.

Goodwin continued his investigation. "You got aftershave on, stud! And gel in your hair!" he announced with his belly gyrating in hysterics. He laid a massive hand on Billy's shoulder. "Ladies and gentleman, I believe the tight end has a date!"

The locker room erupted in noise, and Billy turned a stunning shade of red. Goodwin was in his glory. He put his enormous arms around Billy and lifted him off his feet. "Boy, I'm so proud of you! Make sure you give her a wet one for me!" The crowd kept laughing. Billy didn't try to break free; that would only add to the embarrassment. "What'cha think fellas? Maybe the coach'll let me run the ball just one time so I can get a date with a senior? All I need is one touchdown. Please, Coach, please!"

Again the entire room of half-dressed boys was laughing uncontrollably, even Mike Drummond. Billy looked in Alvarez's direction, but Kenny was avoiding eye contact. *Big mouth.* Billy finally managed to say, "I'll think of you the whole time, Snow." Goodwin let out a gigantic, gut-busting laugh, like only he was capable of. The rest of the locker room followed suit. Humiliated, but enjoying it in a way, Billy stepped sheepishly out of the locker room into the cool evening air, his bag slung snugly across his chest.

Shelby wasn't there yet. She would be picking him up in a few minutes. The scene inside the *Dragon's Lair* was actually a relief. There had been precious few light moments in there in a good while.

It had been four weeks since Samantha's accident, and five since

Ryan's. It seemed no one in town was unaffected by the tragedy. The school still seemed to move at a slower pace than usual, as if everyone was still at a funeral. There were almost no arguments in the hallway, and there had not been a single fistfight since the news about Ryan. Billy felt that four weeks of peace had to be a record at his school. Even after the Christiana game, there was no trash talk, no knocking of shoulders. Every game of the season had been that way. From every player on both teams, there was nothing but downright sportsmanship.

"Great game, guys."

"Sorry about your right tackle."

"He was an awesome player."

"Have a great rest of the season."

It was downright creepy. Billy's competitive spirit couldn't help but make him think maybe, *just maybe*, the other teams were taking it easy on them out of pity. No way. Sports was sports, and Billy knew he wouldn't ever do that himself.

Then there was the almost lunatic behavior of Mike Drummond - drinking two nights before a game, then that tirade at Iron Hill about how he *knew* they would win.

Mike's behavior was a problem, but Billy was trying to put things into perspective. On one hand, he knew that the deaths of Ryan and Sam had made him realize that there were things much more important than sports. On the other hand, he knew if the team was to continue to win and have success in the playoffs, Mike Drummond had to get his head on straight. Mike was going to have to figure out how best to deal with whatever was bothering him if that was possible. It would be the best thing, for his sake and the team's.

And Noah Lively. *What had gotten into him?* The kid had barely socialized with anyone in twelve years and now he was bordering on social butterfly. The float party, the pool hall. Billy had even heard a rumor that Noah might be directing a school play. What was going on? Of course Noah being Noah, there was no way to track him down to ask him these questions, especially since it was almost as if Noah was purposefully avoiding him. Billy wasn't even sure if Noah had a phone in his house, much less a cell phone. If he wanted to talk to Noah, he would have to get lucky, or unlucky, as was sometimes the case.

Billy didn't really have a reasonable theory that might explain Noah's strange behavior. Noah had mentioned that day in the cemetery that he had known Samantha well and that he would miss her. Was he living a private life that he had managed to hide from almost everyone? Then there were his appearances at recent social events, brief though they were. Was he trying to establish himself as something other than the strict antisocialist he had always been? Billy didn't have a clue, but right now he wasn't thinking about it. His mind was on the green Toyota Camry that was pulling through the parking lot. It was time to take a drive with Shelby Cooper.

When Shelby arrived, she quickly got out of her Toyota and ran to the curb to give Billy a big hug. Billy accepted the embrace, but cringed to himself, knowing that he was being watched from the locker room. "You drive, okay?" She was wearing jeans, and a white top. It was low cut enough to be daring, but high enough to be classy. Shelby was truly beautiful and didn't need to prove it to anyone. Billy hadn't seen her smile like this in so long, and he loved it.

Billy immediately got in the driver's seat and pulled away as quickly as possible, never once looking back at his teammates. "Sorry," Shelby said in a mischievous tone. "Did I embarrass you?"

"It's okay." It was. And it was even better to see Shelby smiling again. Billy had preferred being by himself for as long as he could remember, but the drives he would take after school with Ryan, Samantha and Shelby were always fulfilling in ways he could never achieve by himself. It was the only real time that Billy got to act like a teenager. His parents, who were already in their late fifties, expected him to act like an adult, no time for immaturity. Billy gratefully obliged, but he always looked forward to the rides after school.

Listening to loud music, venting about school, practice, and parents. The time was valuable to Billy even though he did the least talking of the group. When Friday and Saturday nights came, the other three would join their crowds, and Billy would retire to his home. At first Ryan would try to persuade Billy to join them, but after a while he stopped trying. Nowadays, Billy could vividly remember every time Ryan invited him. Ryan's disappointed expression tortured him every day. *I wish he could ask me one more time.*

Billy took the car onto the interstate and headed north toward Wilmington. It was one of the normal routes they had taken when Ryan and Sam were around. One year earlier, he had learned to drive a stick shift in this same car. Ryan was a good teacher, but a little bit impatient. The radio was on, an annoying afternoon radio shock jock. Shelby finally noticed and turned it off. "Thanks for asking me to come out, Shelby."

"The drive was your idea, Billy. It was a great idea."

"I always loved those drives we'd take," he said.

Shelby took a deep breath. "Well, let's enjoy this. I'm so sick of being sad, and around people who don't understand."

"Me too."

"And I don't know what to say to people, Billy," Shelby said, her frustration beginning to show. "If one more person asks me how I'm doing...," She paused, then said, "Thanks for not asking me how I'm doing, Billy."

Billy chuckled. "That's what friends are for, Shelby."

"But I did get one call, from that girl, Michelle Ramsey. You know her?"

Billy nodded. "I remember in first grade her dad died."

"Yeah. Were you in her class, or something?"

Billy nodded, keeping his eyes on the road. "I remember it like it was yesterday. We were in McVeigh Elementary. She was absent for a bunch of days and then our teacher told us one day she would be coming back tomorrow, but that we had to be really nice to her because her dad had died."

"Did she ever say how?"

Billy shook his head. "All she told us was that Michelle would be really sad for a while and we should be extra nice to her. I remember half the class started crying when she told us." He thought silently for a moment then said, "I remember I was playing with clay when she told us. I can still smell it."

"She's such a nice girl," Shelby said quietly. "I wish I could be that way. I wish I could call Sam's parents and be as comforting as she was to me. How come some people can be that way?"

"I wish I could, too," Billy agreed. "Saturday night at the Cue and Cushion, we ran into Ryan's little brother, and he looked *terrible*. I mean he just had bugs under his skin. I didn't even want to see him. But Kenny walked right up to him and shook hands and chatted like they'd been best friends for years. I wish I could be that way."

"I like the way you are." She took him by the hand, and he squeezed.

And they drove. When they reached Wilmington, Billy took the exit for Route 100. In his short driving career, this was easily his favorite road. It was a long, winding road that made its way through Brandywine Creek where some of Delaware's wealthiest families' chateaus can be seen lurking high in the tree line.

When they reached the park, Billy pulled into the small gravely parking lot. After exiting the car, they walked along the river, taking in the cool, clean autumn air, and enjoying each other's company. When they came to a small stream Billy took Shelby's hand and helped her balance. He didn't let go, and they held hands for the rest of their walk.

Billy had introduced this place to Sam, Ryan, and Shelby, remembering it from when he was a child. His parents would bring him here on weekends to fish for trout or have a picnic. He had always loved coming and could not remember why they ever stopped. He had discovered that one of the great freedoms that came with growing up was the freedom to re-visit his childhood on his terms, remembering all the good times and leaving the bad behind. This was a part of himself that he shared with Ryan, Samantha and Shelby, and they had all come to love the park almost as much as he did.

When they came to the horse farm, a beautiful stretch of land owned by the DuPont family, they stopped. Like most places in Wilmington that bore the name DuPont, this one was stunning. The DuPonts had long been the most wealthy and influential family in all of Delaware. Their reign as Delaware royalty began in the 18th century when one of their ancestors set up a gunpowder mill along the Brandywine River. Many American wars and many bullets had helped the family's fortune swell over the centuries until they became the most prestigious chemical company in the world. Several DuPonts still lived in Delaware on palatial estates that were barely visible to their fellow citizens. But this horse farm backed right up to the park, and it was the enjoyed by many pedestrians who happened to walk through.

It had always been their favorite place. Sometimes, the four teenagers would sit in a circle and tell jokes, or just talk about anything. Today, neither said a word, but soon enough Billy turned toward Shelby and looked deeply into her green eyes. They were happy eyes, but they betrayed a sadness, and he knew his eyes were the same. It was nice being here together, but they both longed to be with their friends again. Shelby smiled and leaned forward for a kiss, and Billy obliged.

If only Goodwin Snow could see me now.

When Billy got home it was after eight o'clock. He had missed dinner, but his mom had left it on the table for him - lemon chicken and brown rice, which Billy quickly put in the microwave. She and his dad were in the basement, probably watching an old movie. Billy noticed a message posted to the refrigerator: *Kenny called 3 times!*

He started the microwave and dialed Kenny's number. He answered on the first ring.

"Dude, you have to get a cell phone." There was panic in his voice. "I've been trying to get you all day!"

"What's wrong, Kenny?"

"You haven't heard?"

"Heard what? I've been out with Shelby all day."

"Man, forget that! Mike Drummond walked out. He's off the team!"

Billy couldn't respond.

"He quit. He told the coach right after you left today. You better loosen up your arm, dude. You're the quarterback."

The truth arrived at home and immediately ran to his bedroom and started his computer. Hands sweating, bladder ready to burst, he fidgeted impatiently as his computer warmed up. There wasn't a lot of time. He had work to do. At the prompt, he quickly hit the required "control-alt-delete" keys and logged in. While the computer continued to load, he ran to the bathroom.

His footsteps woke his mother.

"Is that you?" she cried. "I need to use the bathroom. Come help me."

"In a minute, Mom. I have some important work to do," he said as he unzipped.

"What work? I have to use the bathroom. You've been at school all day! Come help me you ungrateful lout."

"Okay, okay. I have to finish peeing *myself* before I can help you though."

"How dare you talk to me that way! Is that what they teach at that school? If I had my way I would..."

"Yeah, yeah. Just give me thirty seconds." After finishing in the bathroom, he ran by his mother's room and back into his own. The truth had work to do.

The computer was ready now, and he quickly went to task. He had saved almost every Internet chat room conversation he had joined over the past year. *Saved them for what?* But no more. He highlighted them all and hit the "delete" key. Then he emptied his recycle bin and let out a sigh of relief. *They'll find me eventually, but the truth is never easy to catch.*

"I'm coming, Mom," he said.

"You better be," she said with a trace of a sob. "And could you please bring some clean sheets?"

Newark to start Wirth at QB
Tight end has been a backup since last season

By Michael Talley

NEWARK-"It was an easy choice."

That was the only thing Newark Coach David Scott had to say Wednesday when asked about his decision to start junior Billy Wirth at quarterback when his team faces Brandywine this Saturday.

Until this week Wirth had been an outstanding tight end this season, hauling in twenty-one receptions including six touchdowns for the Yellow Jackets, who are unbeaten after seven games. The last time Wirth played quarterback was in November of last season when he saw action in the forth quarter of a lopsided victory against Middletown.

The decision came two days after the surprising news that senior quarterback and team captain Mike Drummond had walked off the team for unknown reasons. If Drummond does not return, Wirth will remain at quarterback for the remainder of the season and into the playoffs. With a 7-0 record, Newark will almost definitely see the post-season.

Drummond, who was honorable mention to the All-state team last season, had been having an excellent year, only struggling in last week's win against Christiana. He threw three interceptions in that game and the Dragons only narrowly escaped being handed their first loss.

Senior defensive tackle Goodwin Snow, who was named the team's new captain, said he was confident the team could keep winning with Wirth at quarterback. "That boy watches a lot of film, and we're always amazed at how much he knows about the other team's defense. We always thought he was crazy, but I guess it pays off for all of us now, don't it?"

Junior linebacker Kenny Alvarez, who will now be pulling a double shift at tight end in Wirth's place, was also confident in the team's chances. "Billy's been taking reps at QB since camp back in August. He knows the offense and he knows the defenses he plays against. We plan to keep winning."

The team and coaches continued to have no comment on the reason for the sudden departure of Mike Drummond. When asked about widespread speculation that Drummond's decision was related to the death of teammate Ryan Chambers, Scott answered, "Absolutely no comment on that."

Wirth declined to make a statement but when asked how he felt about being named the starting quarterback, he waved a videotape, presumably a game film. It seems he'll have plenty of work to do. With one of the toughest defenses in the Blue Hen Conference, Brandywine is 6-1. A win this week will put them into a tie for first place with the Yellow Jackets.

The phone on the desk rang and the clean-cut young man in uniform answered, spoke into it briefly, hung up and said, "The major will see you now, sir."

The young officer, who had been waiting patiently, stood. "Thank you, private," he said as he turned toward the battalion commander's office. He took a deep breath and opened the door. He snapped a salute when the major saw him.

"Major, Lieutenant Charles..."

"At ease, Charlie," the major interrupted. "I know who you are. Sit down."

"Yes, sir." He sat. The major was still sitting.

Major Henderson was in no mood for games. "What's this about, Charlie? And no bull, let's get right to it."

"I'm afraid I don't understand, sir."

Now the major stood. "Don't understand?" he barked. "Well, let me fill you in, Lieutenant." He began to pace behind the small space behind his desk, obscuring the huge American flag that hung on the wall. "Captain O'Neill, your company commander, says he tried to appoint you as his executive officer, yesterday. That would make you second in command of Bravo Company." He leaned down to look the young officer in his eyes. "Am I ringing any bells yet, Charlie?"

He shifted in his seat. "Yes, sir," he said.

"Good," the major said. "And Captain Waters tells me that you told him you'd rather not be in command of the company. He says you told him you were happy enough being a platoon leader, as if you had a choice in the matter. Am I still correct, Lieutenant?"

"Yes, sir."

The major sat. He let out a frustrated sigh. "Well, why the heck not, Charlie?" The rumor was that the major had taken to profanity so much since his return from the Middle East that his wife had forbade the practice entirely.

"Sir, it's just I don't see myself in charge of the company. I think there has to be a better man than me."

"A better man than you?" the major asked incredulously. "Your men would follow you anywhere, and smile while doing it. I've never seen

49

that much loyalty to a platoon leader. You're the best officer in the company. What's going on here?"

"Well, I sure appreciate your saying that, Major, but I..." He couldn't find the right words.

Major Henderson's eyes bore deep into Charlie's. He held the stare for several seconds. "We've played a lot of poker, haven't we, Charlie?"

The lieutenant smiled. "We have, sir."

The major chuckled. "Back in Saudi, it became a hobby for us all, didn't it?"

"Yes, sir. It was a good way to pass the time."

"Well, after all that poker, I know a couple of things," the major said. "I know that you can spot a tell from any officer in the battalion. You know when a man is holding something or bluffing."

"I know the same about you, sir."

The major smiled. "So what is it, Charlie? I spotted your tell as soon as you came in here, and I know there is something on your mind other than thinking there's a better officer than you in this company."

Charlie lowered his eyes. "There is, sir."

The major stood again and walked from around his desk. He was a small man for having so much authority and such a big voice, much smaller than the young man who sat in front of him. He rested on the edge of his desk and crossed his arms. He spoke in a much gentler voice. "Is it Sergeant Ramsey?"

Charlie held his eyes on the floor for a moment then looked at the major with troubled eyes. "Yes, sir," he said almost inaudibly.

The major shook his head at the memory. "That airfield," he said. "You grew up that day, son."

Charlie nodded.

"And you lost a good man."

"We all did, sir," Charlie said. "And yesterday was his little girl's birthday."

Henderson closed his eyes and paused. Charlie thought the major might be offering a prayer.

"That's the business we're in, Charlie," the major said in a sincerely sorrowful tone. "Good men have to die to defend a free country. It's always been that way."

"I know, sir. I just keep thinking of all the things I could have done differently that day." He paused, trying to collect his thoughts. "They haunt me, sir."

The major nodded and looked Charlie in the eyes, and both men knew they were each haunted by their own separate demons.

"You did everything right that day, son." He paused to let the words sink in. "It was just his time."

Charlie began recounting the details of Carlton's death, saying them as if he could somehow prove the major wrong. "The captain told me to take my platoon to the left, to secure the motor pool."

Henderson listened, even though he knew the story well. He understood that the best thing now was to let the young man talk this through.

"We went right in and secured - no sweat," he continued. "Then we started taking fire from a sniper in a shed about thirty yards to our right. So I sent Ramsey and his squad to take him out." He pinched the space between his eyes with his thumb and forefinger, closing his eyes tightly. "I could have sent any one of my squad leaders. I could have gone *myself.* I just sent him because he was closest to me. It could have been anyone of us."

He stopped and breathed deeply. He was fighting tears now. "Because of an order *I* gave, his daughter had a birthday yesterday without her dad."

The major knew the hell the lieutenant was going through; he had experienced it himself. He placed his hand on the back of Charlie's neck, noticing it was soaked with sweat. "It wasn't you, Charlie. It wasn't even that Iraqi kid that got off that lucky shot to take his life," he said as consolingly as possible.

"Then who was it, sir?"

"Charlie, I did my time in Vietnam. I was there with you in Iraq, and I did lots of things in between. I've seen a lot of young men die under my command. Ramsey was one of them. And if there is one thing I am sure of, it's that you can't stop the inevitable." He nudged himself off his desk and went back around to his seat, leaving some space for the troubled soldier.

"It was his time, Charlie," he continued. "I know it seems like it was all chance, but the one thing that's kept me sane all these years is the hope that when someone dies it's because the almighty was ready for him. Even if you hadn't ordered Ramsey to check that shed, he would have gotten it somehow. Call it God's will, fate, whatever."

Charlie looked at the major as if he was begging for help. "You really believe that, sir?"

"I have to, son," he said. "If I didn't, they'd have to lock me up in the loony bin. And, don't forget this either." He leaned forward. "Ramsey's squad got that sniper before he could get anymore of our guys. Probably saved a dozen lives." The major pointed to the medals on the young soldier's chest. "And then what you did after that was just ..."

Charlie raised a hand to interrupt the major, something he had never done before. "With respect, Major, I'd rather not get into that," he said evenly.

The major smiled. "I know, Charlie. You hate to be a hero. That's one of the things that makes you such a good officer."

There was a long pause and neither man said a word. Finally, Henderson said, "Now what about your new assignment, Charlie? You're a born leader and we're gong to need someone like you for the next go 'round."

The young man lowered his head. The major knew his answer, so he decided to let him off the hook.

"This is it for you, isn't it, son?"

Charlie said nothing.

"Well, by my count you still have two more months in this man's Army before you're up for discharge. What then?"

"I don't know, sir. I just have to get out."

The major nodded sadly. "I understand that, son. But do me one favor."

"Anything, sir."

He raised his voice again. "Keep your head up. No more staring at the floor. I had high hopes for you and you know that. I thought you'd make a career out of the Army like I did, but I'll get over it. You've done your duty for your country, more than most can say. So no matter what you decide after today, hold your head up high. You're still a Ranger!"

"Thank you, Major."

"Whatever you do after the Army is your choice, of course," he continued. "You'll be good at it, too." He rose from his seat again.

Charlie did the same. "But remember one thing, Lieutenant: there is nothing we can do to stop fate. That's a fact that will relieve you of a lot of pain if you accept it."

"I'll try, sir," Charlie said.

"You better, or it will eat at you forever. Dismissed."

"One more thing, sir. If you don't mind."

"What is it, Charlie?"

He grinned sheepishly. "You said you spotted my tell when I came in. What is it, sir?"

The major laughed. "I guess it's no harm now, is it? Our poker days are over anyway." He leaned close and said, "You scratch your head every time you've got something, son."

Charlie shook his head in defeat. "I'll try to remember that too, sir."

And he left Major Henderson's office for the last time, not knowing what career lie ahead of him, but knowing he would never get over the death of Sergeant Timothy L. Ramsey.

nine

Noah Lively sat on the hard wooden bench outside of Mr. Remsburg's office. It was the first time this year he had been called to see the vice principal, but during his freshman and sophomore years it was a common occurrence. Skipping class to smoke would land anyone in his office, and security guards frequently caught Noah as he tried to duck behind parked cars next to the football field. It wasn't until this year, his third, that he had managed to find more discreet ways of satisfying his nicotine fits. As it turned out, the best place to smoke was behind the wood shop. There was a fence there that obscured the view from the main rear exit, the favorite place of the selectively zealous security staff to watch.

Noah had seen Mr. Remsburg so many times during his first two years at Newark High that the two had become quite friendly and would often talk about things that Noah could not with anyone else. Noah had always had a hard time speaking with others his own age because of his maturity, and not many adults were willing to speak to him at a serious level because of his age.

But Mr. Remsburg was different. He seemed to take Noah seriously and was genuinely concerned with him. Sometimes, he would even call Noah to his office just to see how things were going. Noah told no one about these talks, but they meant a lot. Mr. Remsburg was a smart man who never got too caught up in details. His concern was always the wellbeing of his students, even though so many feared him as the enforcer of the discipline code.

But so far this year, the two had not spoken at all. Normally, Noah would have made it a point to stop in and say hello, but he had been too busy for that. Noah was sure he wasn't in trouble for anything this time, so he wasn't sure why he had been called. Maybe Mr. Remsburg just wanted to say hello.

Noah could hear the vice principal's deep, muffled voice through the thin wooden door. Having waited outside of Mr. Remsburg's office more times than he could count, he was used to the sound of one of his fellow delinquents being grilled about a minor or major infraction. Noah knew the truth that Remsburg cared very little about most of the things students came to see him about. Infractions were part of being a teenager. He was much more concerned with what he called "the big picture of beer." After such grilling sessions, Noah would often walk into Remsburg's office to hear him say, "I hope that kid *thinks* I'm upset, because I'm not." The two would laugh.

Noah tried not to smile as a red-faced boy emerged from Remsburg's office with an exaggerated smirk on his lips, his day ruined by a chewing out from the vice principal. As expected, Noah heard Remsburg's angry voice. "Lively, get in here!" Again, Noah tried not to smile.

As he entered the familiar room, Noah decided to quickly beat Mr. Remsburg to the punch. "I hope that kid thinks you're upset."

Remsburg laughed and shook his head. "Noah, how the hell are you? And where the hell have you been?"

"Just trying my best to stay out of trouble."

"I was starting to think you'd quit smoking or something."

"Not yet," Noah answered. "I'm just getting good at finding the right place to do it."

"Feed the cancer genes in private. Good thinking."

Mr. Remsburg almost never spoke of his past, but it was an interesting one. And it tended to creep out with phrases like "feed the cancer genes." Many students had heard from Mr. King that Remsburg was a war hero. According to the story, just after he had graduated from college, the country was gearing up to go to war with Iraq – the first time. Remsburg, being raised as a patriot, thought it was his duty to join up in the fight. So he put his degree on hold and enlisted in the Army. He was quickly sent to Officers Candidate School where he excelled and proved to be a natural leader. Within a year and a half he found himself in charge of a platoon of Army Rangers who were preparing to wage war deep inside of Saddam Hussein's Iraq. Only having been with his men for a few months, young Lieutenant Remsburg was counting heavily on his veteran platoon sergeant to competently lead his men into battle. However, just one day before the mission was to begin, the sergeant accidentally shot himself in the foot while cleaning his pistol. The sergeant would walk with a limp for the rest of his life, but would never see combat. That left twenty-two-year-old Lieutenant Charles Remsburg to lead his twenty-five men, many of whom were older than him, into battle.

Those were the facts according to Mr. King, Remsburg's closest friend on the faculty. Everything else was a closely hidden secret by Remsburg, and the U.S. government. Rangers are good at being tight-lipped, and Remsburg was no exception. His mission had been called *classified*, and it would stay that way forever. However, it was public knowledge that Mr. Remsburg left Iraq with a purple heart and a bronze star for valor. To most of the public, the war was sanitary and precise, a "walk in the park." But Remsburg had seen the demons of combat, and they stayed with him every day. The only references he ever made to his military service were his nearly unconscious uses of phrases like "feed the cancer genes." Sometimes he would announce to coworkers that he had to excuse himself to "hit the head." Other than that, he preferred not to talk about his past at all.

"Well, Noah," Mr. Remsburg said, looking deep into him. "Where have you been?"

Noah shrugged. "Same old thing…making the rounds."

The vice principal smiled mischievously. "That's not what I hear, son. And you know that I hear *everything*."

Noah shifted in his seat. "So what have you heard?"

Remsburg scratched his dark brown hair, a gesture that Noah recognized that always meant Remsburg knew more than he was letting on.

"You know me better than that, Noah. You tell me."

The truth was that Noah was up to so many new things lately that he wasn't sure what Remsburg knew. He sat silently, as did Mr. Remsburg.

Finally realizing that Noah would not be sharing, Mr. Remsburg decided to break the ice a little bit. "I haven't seen you since the funerals."

This surprised Noah. He didn't think *anyone* saw him at the funerals of Ryan and Samantha. Noah did not go to the viewings or the church services, but he did pay his respects at the cemetery. He stood many yards away from the crowd of mourners, half hidden behind trees and sunglasses where he hoped he would not be recognized. He should have known that almost nothing got by the vice principal, especially this one.

Noah sighed, knowing that once again Mr. Remsburg had him, and he would have to talk, at least a little bit. Remsburg had taken the initiative away, and Noah had no idea what Remsburg knew and didn't know. Seeing how uncomfortable the last comment made Noah, Remsburg decided to make it easier. "My friend Mr. King tells me he wanted you to direct his play, but you turned him down."

Noah was relieved, but not completely. "I have a lot to do. I don't think I could give that project the time it deserves. And if he's your friend, why do you always refer to him as Mr. King?""

Remsburg ignored the question, and focused squarely on the first part of Noah's answer. "Well, that's really what I wanted to talk about, Noah. What has been keeping you so busy lately?"

The tension returned and Noah shifted in his seat. *Could he know that he, the trench-coated chain-smoker, had been investigating the strange circumstances of Ryan and Sam's deaths?* He felt his palms getting sweaty. "Junior year is the toughest. You told me that last spring. I just have too much going on to take something like that on."

"I see," the vice principal said, removing his thin designer eyeglasses. "Have you considered that the experience could build character?"

"What do you mean?"

Remsburg leaned back, the lines of thought forming on his forehead. He scratched his chin and finally said, "Well, when someone takes on new responsibility, he can either flounder, or rise to the occasion and get the job done, and that makes him a more complete person. It helps to realize potential. I know you're a fairly responsible person, but a job like this could really change you forever. And frankly, Noah, I think you're up to it." His words, as always, were flat and even, never letting on that he took any of it personally.

Noah thought carefully about his next words, knowing he *should* tread lightly, but decided not to. "Is that what happened to you in Iraq?"

The question hung thick in the air. In his more than two years of meeting with the vice principal regularly, this was the first time Noah broached the subject. During the long pause, Noah's mind was simultaneously glad and terrified that he had asked the question.

Remsburg never flinched.

Noah was the first to break eye contact, and after he did Mr. Remsburg deftly twirled his freshly sharpened pencil in his right hand. Again, he leaned back in his chair slightly and finally said, "Something like that."

"Sorry, Mr. Remsburg. It's none of my business."

Remsburg smiled. "No, it's not. But it's a fair question." And it was, for a teenager. Remsburg knew there had been stories and rumors of his service in the Gulf War, and it was only natural for someone like Noah to want to get to the bottom of it, or at least break the surface. Remsburg himself never spoke about his service to students, and only on rare occasions to his friends. He understood full well how the presence of a former Special Forces soldier who had been in combat could be fascinating to teenagers, but that was not why he was here. It wasn't his job to impress his students and colleagues with the past. He decided to change the subject. "From what I hear, Noah, you've become quite social - float parties, pool halls, Internet chat rooms. Why the sudden openness?"

Noah shrugged. "You really *do* hear everything. Do you have spies or something?"

"Not important."

"Why is *any* of this important?"

"I think it's important, Noah, because for two years now you've been telling me how much you hate social gatherings and how you'd like to be a loner your whole life. I'm interested to know why the sudden change."

Noah was clearly getting flustered. "What does it matter?"

"I think it matters because it might be a good sign, that you might be opening up to the idea of positive interactions with people your own age."

"For the record, Mr. Remsburg, I've only discovered that I was right all along. Most people my age *are* shallow, self-important, and generally think the world owes them."

"All very common in teenagers. But who are the exceptions?"

Noah looked puzzled. "Excuse me?"

"You said *most* adolescents are all those things. Who are the exceptions? I'm sure you've made a list."

"I said most *teenagers* are that way. There are a few who aren't"

Remsburg persisted. "Like who?"

"I don't know!" Now Noah was broken; Remsburg had done it again. "Why are you asking about all this anyway?"

"Because I think we're getting to something here. I think you're looking hard for something or someone, and I might be able to help you."

Noah laughed to himself, and smiled on the outside. If only Remsburg knew who he was looking for. "I doubt that." He swallowed hard. "But I appreciate your concern."

"Okay, Noah." Mr. Remsburg's voice had not changed in the slightest degree. The discussion had sent Noah on an emotional roller coaster and he was totally flustered. This was often the case in Remsburg's office. The vice principal was breathing normally, while the adolescent was fighting tears. But Noah knew Remsburg had only the best intentions. At least he hoped he did.

"Can I go?"

"Sure. It was nice seeing you again. You know I'm always here."

Noah nodded and stood, so did Remsburg. Remsburg's chiseled physique always astonished Noah, especially after having not seen him for a few months. The two shook hands.

Noah turned to leave. He reached for the doorknob and just before he turned it he paused. "Why don't you ever talk about Iraq?"

Again, Remsburg stood stone-like, paused and said. "I'm more interested in your future than in my past, Noah. I know you're taking a lot of interest in examining the past, but sometimes it's best to leave things alone." He raised his eyebrows. "Do you understand, Noah?"

Noah nodded slightly and finished his exit, completely bewildered.

Somehow Mr. Remsburg knew that Noah was chasing after the truth.

ten

Charlie Remsburg was in a hurry. He rushed out of the double doors of the main rear exit of Newark High School, turned and walked at a fast pace toward the faculty parking lot, barely noticing the crowd of young smokers who quickly dropped their cigarettes or ducked behind cars, or both. He hurried into his red Chevy and started the ignition, dropped into gear and pealed away.

The shopping center was just a few blocks from school. There was no chance of seeing any truant students there since it lacked a fast-food restaurant or a pool hall. He found an isolated corner of the parking lot in front of an office supply store. Once safely out of sight, he fumbled for the pack of cigarettes that he had confiscated from a guilty student. He struck a match and lit up, his first in months.

He had become very good at showing no emotion when dealing with the kids, but it always took a toll, and today was especially tough. Remsburg thought that if for the rest of his life, no one ever asked him about Iraq, he might just be happy. Or maybe he needed to tell everything. There was a lot to tell.

Eight years earlier, Nate King had pressed him for details about his service. It was an after school happy hour, and the beer tasted particularly good that day. He told his friend the details he was allowed to talk about, but nothing else. Of course he mentioned that there *were* more details that he was simply not allowed to tell anyone. That sparked King's curiosity all the more, which might have been his intention all along. Remsburg had been a young English teacher, new to the school and looking for a little bit of attention, especially from an established figure like Nate King, anything to earn the respect of his mentor. But that was a long time ago, and he'd grown up a lot since then. At least he hoped he had.

Inevitably King passed along the news he had heard in small bits and pieces. He'd probably encountered a student who claimed to hate the tough-grading literature teacher who seemed to have a chip on his shoulder. In his friend's defense, Nate probably informed the young delinquent that he was talking about a Special Forces officer who won a bronze star and a purple heart. It was natural for a teacher to defend another, especially a friend.

Remsburg inhaled deeply and blew a cloud of smoke out the crack in the window. *I had to open my big mouth.*

Once the rumors made their way back to him, Charlie decided that was the end of happy hours with faculty, and war stories. His past was his past. But Charlie and Nate remained close friends, even after he was promoted to vice principal in charge of discipline. Many more experienced teachers who had wanted that job shunned him, and swore to themselves to always challenge the new administrator. Two even quit their jobs and went to teach elsewhere. Nate King was a faithful friend, and one of the few on the faculty whom Remsburg really trusted, even if he did have a problem with "loose lips."

The former Ranger liked being in charge of discipline, and in a high school of over fifteen hundred students, he kept very busy. Mr. Remsburg quickly developed a fair, no-nonsense reputation that he backed with consistency and respect for students and teachers alike. His goal as disciplinarian was not to punish, but to correct behavior that needed addressing. Unfortunately, a lot of students never corrected bad behavior *until* they were punished. It was the same in the Army, even with the best of the best. That's probably why Remsburg was so good at it.

And he *was good* at it. The vast majority of students whom he dealt with were freshmen, not yet used to the rigid expectations of high school. Of course there were a few hardheaded sophomores who didn't want to change, or liked the attention of getting into trouble. As for juniors and seniors, Remsburg almost never saw them, and he liked it that way. Noah was no exception. He hadn't been in any trouble all year, but Charlie had been anxious to catch up with him, and encourage him to direct King's play. That's what led to their meeting that morning, and to Charlie's resuming of his dirty habit.

He finished his cigarette and flicked the butt out the window, a maneuver he had learned as a bored soldier waiting in the desert. His first cigarette was in the terribly hot desert of Saudi Arabia, offered to him by his platoon sergeant. Sergeant Taylor had been a good man, and Remsburg looked to him as an example of being a good soldier, a man of positive energy in a situation that should have been gravely stressful. All of that positive energy quickly evaporated when Sergeant Taylor put a bullet in his own foot. Remsburg's smoking habit increased exponentially from that day on. He quit the day he gloriously returned to the States, but struggled with making it permanent ever since. When the stress hit, so did the nicotine fits. And for some reason, Noah had caused him a lot of stress today, more so than he ever did when he got into trouble.

He would have to talk with Noah again soon, get some facts straight. Remsburg's mission was to get Noah to succeed. And if he knew how to do anything, he knew how to accomplish a mission.

Wirth passes first test as Yellow Jackets top Brandywine
Yellow Jackets remain unbeaten after 8 games

By Michael Talley

NEWARK-A heroic defensive effort and an impressive performance by quarterback Billy Wirth helped undefeated Newark, 8-0, keep Brandywine, 6-2, from gaining ground in the Blue Hen Conference Friday night at Newark.

The Yellow Jacket's defense kept Brandywine running back Sean Money in check throughout the game and maintained a near constant pass rush. Junior linebacker Kenny Alvarez sacked Brandywine quarterback Tyler Wallace twice and intercepted a pass late in the forth quarter that all but sealed the victory for Newark. Newark won the game 14-7.

Money scored Brandywine's only touchdown after an impressive 22 yard run in the third quarter.

Billy Wirth, who made his first start after replacing All-State quarterback Mike Drummond, completed twelve of nineteen passes and ran for 38 yards. "I'm just glad there were no turnovers," Wirth said. "I didn't want any mistakes to cost us this game."

The victory is a huge step for the Jackets. They appeared headed for the playoffs until the announcement that Mike Drummond had left the team for unknown reasons. With this win, those hopes seem more intact than ever.

Newark coach Dave Scott said he was optimistic about the Dragon's post-season prospects, but wanted to focus on what's left of the regular season. "We have two more games to play, and we want to win both of them," he said. "As far as the playoffs, if it's meant to be, it's meant to be."

eleven

Wilmington's Brandywine Creek has a majestic beauty that Billy always had a hard time describing. He fondly remembered the trips he and his parents would take to the park when he was a child. Iron Hill was close and provided a quick escape. But Brandywine Creek was twice as big, and the thirty-minute drive always built his anticipation.

As Billy grew into adolescence and began to take a keen interest in local history, he discovered that the Brandywine Creek was where the first Swedish settlement took place in 1638. It happened right in what is now downtown Wilmington, where the Brandywine meets the Christina River. Year later it was the same waters of the Brandywine that powered the textile and gunpowder mills, creating jobs for thousands, and a flourishing culture for generations.

The trips with his parents had produced some of his greatest memories. They were not the kind of memories that family vacations often brought, in which he could recall specific events, but he could vividly remember the time spent with his parents at Brandywine. They were times of peace and happiness and today Billy longed for them.

The trout fishing, kayaking, and aimless hikes with his parents were a security blanket that he held onto when he was insecure. He had led Ryan, Samantha, and Shelby on many hikes through the park, and recently he and Shelby had taken a few long walks themselves. But there were still certain areas of the park he was always sure to steer clear from, except for when he was by himself.

The spot where he sat today might have been his favorite place in the world. It was a tranquil spot far from any trail, where water from a stream subsidiary poured over huge gray rocks, creating a small waterfall. The first time he came to this spot was when he was nine. He and his father were fishing for trout. Billy, having no luck, wandered up the offshoot, hoping to find a hidden treasure, and he did. Only there were no fish there, just peace. His father found him almost two hours later. Panicked at first, his father was struck to see his son sitting so pensively by the stream. He sat with his son and put his arm around him. "Peaceful here, isn't it?"

It was. In the years to come, it became a place where Billy could go where his parents never argued, where he could strip off his shirt and jump in the shallow water without embarrassment, and where he could simply enjoy being alone. His parents had not brought Billy up to believe in any God, but if there was one, Billy was sure he lived here. And sometimes he would talk to him. And he knew God was listening. He knew some day he would bring someone else to this special place, but not for a long time.

The anxiety that had brought him here today had stemmed from so many things. They burdened him in ways he had never known. He nearly cried thinking about the days when he came to this place to escape his parents' arguing over something as silly as which type of bait to use. He would have loved to have *those* problems again.

His new list of burdens was a long one: First, he was now fully established as the quarterback for the Newark Yellow Jackets after spending an entire off-season perfecting his game at tight end; he was terrified and excited at the possibility of starting a serious relationship with Shelby Cooper; he had no idea what had become of Mike Drummond after he seemed to loose his mind at Iron Hill; Noah, whom he still considered a close acquaintance, was getting stranger and stranger. Worst of all, he was still deeply saddened by the loss of his friend Ryan Chambers, and his girlfriend Samantha.

Friend. Billy considered the word carefully. Before Ryan died, he was sure he never had one.

Billy thought of what it had been like after a big victory, celebrating with Ryan In the locker room, then later on the drive home. He ached at the memories, wishing he could feel them again and be glad about it, instead of sad. The feeling after this last victory was so different from what he had felt before. As quarterback, he felt more like he had gotten an important job done, than won a game. There was no rush of excitement, just a warm, steady satisfaction, then thoughts of next week. These new experiences reminded him why he hadn't wanted to be a quarterback in the first place. Football wasn't fun anymore.

Billy picked up a flat rock and skipped it downstream. He had gotten very good at that over the years, and his arm had certainly been busy lately. After the victory over Brandywine, the coach was so glad that he gave the team a day off from practice on Monday. It wasn't totally unexpected; this was the time of year when injuries began to mount and a Monday off did a lot for team morale.

Billy knew immediately what he would do after school Monday with the free time. The field hockey team still had practice, so he would not be with Shelby. So here he was, by himself in his favorite place. He loved being here, but his work ethic told him he should be watching film of Sussex Central High's defense. He skipped another rock and tried to put the thought out of his head.

No one had even seen Mike Drummond since his disappearing act last Tuesday. Kenny had taken it upon himself to call Mike's parents, who lived in Newark, but he never got an answer. When that failed, he drove his mom's car to Mike's house and banged on his door. Kenny sure had a way with people. Again, there was no answer. The All-state quarterback was missing in action, and no one knew why. The only clue Billy could think of was that day when Mike had spouted off about how he *knew* they would win that game. Maybe the loss of Ryan had just been too much for him. But he hadn't even been to school, and that worried Billy more than he wanted to think about.

Billy cringed as his cell phone rang. He had almost forgotten the gift his parents had given him in honor of his first win as the starting quarterback. He was grateful for it, but at this place it was just inappropriate. It broke the beautiful quiet that was his favorite place, the annoying jingle drowning out the running stream and the distant calls of birds.

It was Kenny, of course. "Dude, what are you doing?"

"Enjoying my day off, getting used to my new phone."

"I'm *so* glad you finally got a phone."

"Yeah," Billy answered sarcastically. "Nothing like being in constant communication." In truth, Billy was very glad to have the cell phone, if for no other reason than he could call Shelby right after school was over. That was probably the reason his parents finally broke down and bought him a cell phone. They were both ecstatic that he was actually showing interest in someone of the opposite sex.

"Sucks they didn't give the field hockey team off too, huh?"

"They never do, Kenny. The only reason coach gave us off is because of all the injuries."

"Where are you, Billy?"

"Brandywine Creek. My dad let me take his car."

"Man, why do you always go up there? We should be at the pool hall soaking up the celebrity again. You're the quarterback now. You'll never pay to shoot another game of pool in your life."

"Or until I have a bad game. You know how it works for quarterbacks, Kenny. They love you when you win; when you lose, you're the problem."

"Drummond never said that."

"That's because he never *had* a bad game. Even when we lost in the playoffs, he had the best game of anybody on the field. We lost because of defense."

Billy regretted his last words as soon as he said them. Kenny had been beaten for a touchdown early in the forth quarter of their only playoff game last year. He slipped when the receiver he was assigned to cover made a cut. The field was muddy, and Kenny just lost his footing. *Why couldn't I have though of that two seconds ago?*

There was a long pause, and Billy heard Kenny take a deep breath. "Well, you just get us back there, Billy, and there won't be any cheap touchdowns."

"I didn't mean to say that, Kenny." Billy was trying his best to apologize. "You had a great game. We never would have even been close if you hadn't been on the field in the first half...all those plays you made." Billy bit his lip. *How could I be so stupid!*

"It's okay, Billy," Kenny finally said. "Just get us back there."

Billy was desperate to change the subject. "What else is going on?"

"Well, I found out why Mike Drummond's not in school."

"Really?"

"Yeah. He left town, dude. Gone."

"What? Where'd he go?"

"Nobody knows. He just left town. Took his dad's car."

Billy couldn't believe his ears. "He *stole* his dad's car."

"Not exactly," Kenny explained. "His dad's reserve unit was activated last month; he's overseas. Probably won't be back until next year."

"So where'd he go?"

"Like I said, nobody knows."

"What about his mom, does she know? I mean, I don't think a 17-year-old kid is allowed to disappear without telling somebody."

"I think she knows, but she won't tell anybody."

"Kenny, how do you know all this?"

"You know me, dude. I can talk to anybody, and I have connections."

Billy was pacing around the stream now. "Come on, tell me. How did you find out?"

"Alright, my aunt is friends with Ms. Downey, one of the secretaries at school. Apparently, his mom came into the school office and told her that he was going away for a while."

"Any word on when he'll be back?"

"Not yet, but I'm working on it. No time soon though, dude. Keep your arm loose."

"Don't worry." Billy found a big rock and sat carefully. Without even knowing it, he was loosening his shoulder by making small circles. "Kenny, what's going on here? Are you worried?"

"Are you kidding?" Kenny asked. "I'm petrified, dude."

twelve

"Crystal! You have to keep wiping at the blood spot!" The director was getting angry.

Crystal Madison, playing Lady Macbeth, was getting sick of the director. "There *is no* blood spot, Noah! Isn't that the point?"

"Your job is not to think about these things," answered Noah forcefully. "If you think too hard, this thing will be a disaster."

Crystal was furious. "Now you're *insulting* me?" she asked, mustering up as much indignation as she could manage. "Well, *Mr. Director,* maybe you should look for another girl to play Lady Macbeth!"

Noah took a deep breath and silently counted to five. It was true that he could not afford to lose Crystal. She was the best actress in the school, very loud and extremely beautiful. But did she have to be so stupid?

"Crystal, I'm sorry. That was uncalled for. But let me do the directing, okay? Just keep wiping the spot, because your character *thinks* there's a spot of blood on her dress."

The actress sighed as loudly as possible and shifted her hips. "Then shouldn't we put a spot there, so the audience knows?" She just didn't get it.

"The audience knows there is no spot! It's her guilty conscience! Just listen to me!"

Crystal's face lost all expression, then quickly turned into an evil stare, her beautiful eyes burning into Noah's. She turned and pranced offstage with her nose in the air. Marilyn Monroe would have been very impressed. Rehearsals were over.

"Okay everyone," announced the defeated director. "That's it for today."

Mr. King was shaking his head and smiling. He had seen it all before. As the cast filed backstage, he approached Noah carefully. "How's it going Spielberg?"

"I hate this," Noah said. "I can't believe I was talked into directing a Shakespeare play with *teenagers* playing all the parts. Never again."

"I think when you're old and gray, you'll be glad you did it. As for Ms. Madison, you can't get guilt out of someone who never feels any."

"What do you mean?" Noah was clearly annoyed by the unsolicited help.

"Crystal is not smart enough to feel guilt, Noah. It takes someone who can really *think* to portray guilt. She probably doesn't even know what it's like to have something gnawing at her conscience."

Noah dropped his clipboard on the table. "So what do you suggest I do to get guilt out of an idiot?"

"She's not an idiot, Noah. She's a great actor. You just need to find a way to draw it out of her."

"How?"

Mr. King smiled and scratched his thin grey hair with two fingers. "Give her something to feel guilty about."

Remsburg was halfway finished his second Bud Light when King finally showed up.

"Sorry I'm late, Charlie. I had to console my new director."

"Everything going to be okay?"

"He'll be fine," answered the aging English teacher. "That kid's a genius. Thanks for talking to him. I owe you."

"You sure do, Nate," Remsburg answered. "And I'm not one who sits for too long at a bar by myself. I've had a hard time fighting off the women."

They both laughed and shook hands.

Remsburg hated beating around the bush. "Now why don't you tell me why you've brought me here, Nate? We haven't come to this dive for drinks in a long time."

"I know. We used to come quite often, remember? We had some good times. Made me feel young again."

Remsburg grinned and gulped the last of his beer. "Yeah. Some good times, Nate."

King's face showed sudden remorse. "Then I had to go blabbing about your war record. That was the end of that," he said sadly.

Remsburg wasn't sure what to say. They had never discussed it, but both knew that was exactly the reason why the two of them hadn't been out for drinks after work in more than five years. Remsburg just nodded and said, "Well, you know me...nobody gets behind my curtain."

King nodded back. "I do now."

Remsburg signaled the bartender and the pretty brunette smiled as she promptly plopped two fresh draft beers on the bar in front of the men. King maneuvered onto an empty stool and leaned in for a big sip.

"Well," he said licking his lips, "I promise that anything that's said here today will stay here. No hard feelings, right?"

Remsburg shrugged. "Never, Nate. I just value my privacy, and there aren't a lot of people I can talk to."

"And you *thought* I was one of them."

"You were. I mean you *are*, I guess. I don't know. Why'd you invite me here, Nate? Just to catch up?"

"I guess so, Charlie. Yeah," King said, a little frustrated. "I don't have too many people I can talk to either, and I thought we could let off a little steam, like old times."

"Okay, okay. Don't get upset, Nate. It was just unexpected, considering everything that's been going on. And now with this play, I didn't think you'd have any time for drinks."

The two old friends awkwardly sipped at their beer glasses, neither sure what to say next. Strangely, there was so much to talk about, but neither seemed to have much to say.

Finally, Remsburg broke the silence. "How about those poor kids?"

King nodded slowly as he sipped. "Making your job tougher this year?"

"Not any easier. A lot of kids get in trouble, come to me, and say they're 'distraught' about what happened. Then I find out they didn't even know those kids. But who knows? Maybe they are distraught."

"I was pretty distraught over it myself, Charlie."

"*Was*? Don't tell me you're over it. I don't think I ever will be."

"That's not what I meant," said King. "It was just really tough to take at first."

Remsburg took another long pull of his beer and said, "Yes, it was."

"We've lost kids before. It's never easy." He looked in Remsburg's young eyes. "Were these your first, Charlie?"

Remsburg thought about his answer for a moment. "I've seen young people die before, Nate, and there is nothing as bad as that."

King understood. Remsburg was referring to his war experience.

"But these were the first *students* who I've known who died, yes," Remsburg said.

"Well, you never forget them. I think every teacher has those defining moments etched into their brains – the first student who you had that got pregnant, the first to get married…"

Remsburg smiled. "I had one buy me a drink a few weeks ago."

King laughed. "That was *years* ago for me," he said. "But the first to die. You'll never forget them"

Remsburg took a long drink. "I know I won't."

King leaned his weight onto the bar. "Well, I suppose it was their time, right?"

Remsburg put his glass down. "What do you mean?"

"If it was their time, it was their time. There was no avoiding it, right?"

The conversation was somehow familiar to Remsburg, and he still hated it. "What are you talking about, Nate? They were seventeen years old. Two freak accidents. How could it have been their time?"

King took off his glasses. "I'm not trying to say that it wasn't tragic, Charlie. Obviously it was. I'm just saying that all things happen when they're supposed to happen, and it just happened that they were supposed to go early in life. I'm not saying it…"

"Nate, what the hell are you talking about? Those kids should have lived into their nineties as far as I'm concerned. It was their time to be young and stupid, and learn about life, not to *die*." He signaled the brunette to bring more beer.

"All I'm trying to say here is that there are always bigger things at work, Charlie. All things happen for a reason. And when it's our time to go, there's nothing we can do about it. It doesn't always work out the way we like it. Sometimes bad people live long and happy lives, and the good die early. It just has to be that way sometimes."

"I don't think so," Remsburg shot back. "I know they went early, way too early. And it never should have happened."

The two sipped their drinks in awkward silence. They hadn't spoken at length in years, and were suddenly embroiled in a bitter argument that only seemed like it would get worse.

Finally, King said, "Charlie, can I ask you something personal?"

"Are you asking permission, or just prepping me?"

"Prepping you, I guess. I know how much you *love* personal questions."

"Go ahead."

"In the war, how'd you end up in charge of your company?"

"I was put in charge of a *platoon*, twenty-six men, not a company."

"Okay, but how did it happen?"

"I was a second lieutenant; that's what they do with officers in the Army. They put you in charge of people."

"But you were only twenty-three, right? How could they think you could lead people into a war at that age."

"Well, I had some help. I had two sergeants who had been around a couple years, and one sergeant who was a ten-year veteran, but..."

"But what?"

"The old man shot himself in the foot the night before we went into battle." It was the first time he'd said those words out loud in years.

"Was it a self-inflicted wound?"

"No way. He said he was cleaning his pistol. It was a mistake."

King was growing more interested. "So, one day before the ground war starts, you end up in charge of the platoon?"

Remsburg sipped his beer and nodded. "Something like that, yeah." He would never reveal that this particular mission took place long before the start of the "ground war" that King and the rest of the American public were familiar with.

"Is that why you won those medals?"

"You don't *win* them, Nate. It's not a competition."

"You know what I mean."

"I guess that had a lot to do with it. We had to go into battle without our best man. It was a challenge, but we were up to it. We got the job done." There was just a hint of pride in his voice.

"But it brought out the best in you, didn't it?"

The memories haunted him. *Can war bring out the best in anybody? Maybe the worst.* "That's what they said, Nate."

"Well, that's what I'm saying, Charlie." King had found his teachable moment and was relishing in it. "That's what was meant for you."

"What was meant for me?"

King rolled up the sleeves of his plaid sweater. "Have you ever heard of an Army Ranger wounding himself on purpose?"

"Hell no!" King was proud, and a little drunk.

"Okay. Did you ever hear of a Ranger screwing up like that the night before a battle?"

"What are you getting at, Nate?"

"You were *meant* to lead that platoon into combat. If you weren't in command, who knows what would have happened?"

"You don't even know what *did* happened."

"No, but it was obviously something pretty damn heroic to earn you those medals."

Remsburg tried to laugh. "One of them was for getting shot, not too heroic."

King grinned. "*You* say."

"I see your point, Nate. But I don't want to talk about that anymore. No sergeant was ever *meant* to shoot himself in the foot, no twenty-three year-old jackass was ever *meant* to go running across the desert with a rifle in his hands, and no teenager was ever *supposed* to go skidding off a road and into a tree in the middle of the night."

"I guess we just see it differently."

"I guess."

"But it is good to talk to you again, Charlie,"

"You too, Nate." They clinked their glasses and kept drinking.

thirteen

Shelby checked her hair one more time before she left the girls locker room. She was meeting Billy in fifteen minutes and wanted to look perfect, not that she didn't always. She grabbed her duffel and her purse and headed to the exit that led to the parking lot. "Bye, Shelby. Say hi to Bill for me," one of her teammates said. She practically sang the words. Shelby smiled, loving every bit of it.

The time she'd been spending with Billy was precious, and her demeanor had improved greatly since they began seeing each other. It was hard to believe it had only been a week. It wasn't the same as it had been before, when they would spend afternoons together with Ryan and Sam. This time it was somehow better. Billy was a great source of calm. She hadn't told him about what Sam had said to her the week before she died, and hadn't mentioned how the words haunted her. But it didn't seem like she had to; just being with Billy was helping her spirits. Maybe some day she would tell him about Sam.

She was fumbling through her purse for her keys and nearly jumped out of her skin when a voice from *beneath* her very calmly said, "Can I talk to you, Shelby?" The male voice was vaguely familiar, but the surprise was too much and Shelby let out a suppressed scream, which didn't seem to bother Noah Lively at all. He was sitting casually on the parking block in front of Shelby's car.

"Sorry to startle you. I'm Noah Lively. We met at the float party. Remember?"

Shelby was gathering herself and trying to catch her breath. *I'll bet I look great now.* "Yes, Noah. I remember you were waiting outside my car that day too. Do you ever just walk up to someone and say hello?"

Noah shrugged and looked at Shelby apologetically. "Social norms aren't my strong suit."

"I guess not!"

"I said I was sorry."

"What do you want to talk about, Noah?"

Noah looked at the ground between his legs and almost whispered, "Samantha."

Shelby's eyes filled with tears and she felt herself getting hot. "What about her."

"Well, I've been doing a lot of thinking about how she died, how *they* died."

"Everybody knows how they died."

Noah stood and looked across the parking lot to the empty football stadium. "I don't think they do, Shelby. I think there's a lot more to their deaths than a lot of people know."

Shelby was terribly nervous now. Did Sam say something to him too? She was fighting tears when, with as much sarcasm as possible, she said, "Really?"

"Yes, and I think you do, too."

Shelby looked away.

Noah walked in front of her. "I know that she was your best friend, and nobody likes to dig up old memories, Shelby. But I know there was more to it."

"How?" She was crying now.

He handed her a tissue from his pocket. "I can't tell you now, but I need something from you."

"What?"

"I need to know anything you know."

"Like what?"

"Like, is there anything Sam said or did in the last few days you saw her that were out of the ordinary?"

Shelby didn't know what to say. She just wiped at her eyes and kept looking away.

"Shelby, this is important."

"What are you a cop now? What business do you have conducting your own little investigation? This is crazy!"

"I'm not crazy, and this isn't crazy. The police want nothing to do with this. You heard them 'all some terrible coincidence.' I don't believe that and neither do you."

"It's not my business."

"It is if you know something, Shelby."

"And why should I trust you? I don't even know you, Noah."

Noah leaned against the car and put his hand on his chin. "You're right. You have no reason to."

Shelby sighed. "At least you're honest."

"I'm honest to a fault." He offered Shelby a cigarette. She smirked at him in rejection. He lit up and said, "I need to ask you one more thing. I understand if you don't want to answer."

Shelby barely shrugged her shoulders, a gesture that let him know she would allow a question, but didn't appreciate any of this.

"Do you chat much online?"

She was disgusted. "What? Now you want my screen name?"

He shook his head slowly, deliberately. "No. I want to know if you've ever heard of a screen name called *fatum*."

Her face filled with puzzlement. "*Fatum*? No. I've never heard of it."

He clearly doubted her sincerity. "Are you positive?"

She was getting impatient. "I think I'd remember a weird screen name like that. I don't even know what it means."

"It's Latin for fate, or destiny." Noah picked up his bag, which had been lying on the ground. He could see her frustration. "I'm sorry about all this, Shelby. I know this is terrible for you, for everybody...but all I can tell you is that I'm trying to do the right thing here. I'm the *only* one trying to do the right thing. And I'm afraid that if I don't, nobody will ever know."

"Ever know what?" Shelby asked, trying to keep herself together.
"The truth."

Billy could tell Shelby was flustered when she got out of her car. He
wanted to ask her right away what was wrong, but knowing Shelby, he
decided to wait until the time was right. They embraced and kissed each
other on the cheeks. She smelled wonderful, as always. "How was
practice?" Billy decided that was the best way to begin.
"It was fine. This time of year it always gets boring, but at least it's
a nice day."
"Yeah. The rain finally let up."
"Don't act like you're happy about it, William," she said with a sly
grin, cheering up a little bit. "I know how much you love the rain. You
probably miss it already."
"William?"
She held her smile. *Beautiful.* "And how did you spend your
precious afternoon off?"
"Brandywine Creek, of course."
"I see. Do you think you'll ever take me to your private place?"
"Would you like to see it?"
"Only if you want to take me there, William."
Why is she calling me William? Billy blushed, wondering what
business he had talking to a girl this gorgeous. "So anything new with you,
Ms. Cooper?"
She was serious again. "Well, since you asked..."
"What?" Billy held her by the elbows.
"That kid, again. Noah somebody?
"You were talking to Noah?
"He was talking to *me!*"
"Okay. Try to calm down. Did he upset you?"
She was breathing deeply, eyes closed. "Yes, but I'm not sure
why."
"What did he want, Shelby? Did he ask you out, or something?"
She laughed uneasily at the suggestion. "No. Nothing like that."
He hugged her, and held her tightly to his chest. She felt so good
against him.
She was starting to cry, but was able to keep it together. "I'll tell
you later," she said. "Let's take a drive."
"Good idea."
And they drove, holding hands and listening to music. Neither said
anything for most of the time. They stopped to eat at Friendlie's, burgers
and fries. They stuck to easy topics: school, jobs, college, football, field
hockey, never mentioning Noah. They agreed that the upcoming game
against Sussex Central would lack excitement, but that it should be a victory.
Sussex Central hadn't won a game in the past two seasons.

By the time they were almost to Billy's home, darkness had fallen and it was nearly eight o'clock. Before he could turn off the main parkway toward his house, Shelby took his hand and said, "I'm not ready for you to go home yet, okay?"

"Sure," he said, taking her hand. Feeling a sharp twinge of anticipation in his stomach, he steered the car into the parking lot of the elementary school at the end of his street and they parked. She climbed into his lap and rested her head against his chest. It was a long time before she said anything. "Billy," she finally whispered.

"I'm listening," he said quietly, taking in the aroma of her hair.

"Noah. He wants to know things."

He wasn't sure what to say. "Like what?"

She swallowed hard and adjusted her head to look into his eyes. "He wants to know about Sam. He thinks there's more to the accidents than everybody thinks. He said people need to know the truth."

Billy was bewildered, but calm. "What does he know?"

"I don't know, but he wanted me to tell him everything, everything I knew about Sam."

He rubbed her shoulders, feeling their tension. "You don't have to tell him anything, Shelby. Noah's just weird that way. I'll find him and tell him to leave you alone. You won't hear from him anymore, okay?"

She pushed her face into his chest and squeezed him tightly. "What do you know about Noah?"

"I've known him since second grade, and I know that he's a little bit crazy, but very smart. Sometimes he gets caught up in things a little too much. What could he possibly know about this whole thing that the police don't? What else *could* there be to know?"

She looked into his eyes again, a fresh tear trickling down her cheek. "Billy," she whispered softly. "There *is* more."

fourteen

"Listen up all you pansies!" Goodwin Snow announced to the locker room full of anxious faces. "We're in uniform 'c' today. So you all get a break from me. Otherwise, you'd all be chewin' dirt like usual!"

For such a small state, Delaware had a wide range of accents. The new captain had what was sometimes called a "below the canal" drawl. He had grown up in Middletown, and the accent there smacked of rural southern influence. This was in sharp contrast to the urban particulars of Wilmington, some of whom mimicked their neighbors to the north in Philadelphia, others sounded truly Delawarean, insisting that the *"wooder* tasted funny,"* or that "your street isn't as nice as *my-en.*"

Goodwin loved his Middletown accent, and loved even more that he no longer needed any excuse to open his big mouth to the boys in the locker room anymore. He was the captain. Mike Drummond usually went about making announcements in a much more subtle way, telling one or two seniors to spread the word. Goodwin, however, saw no need to be so reserved. If a player showed up in the wrong uniform, there was no way he could claim he never got the word. With Goodwin Snow in charge, *everybody* got the word whether he liked it or not.

It was Friday practice, the day before a game, and uniform 'c' was the usual outfit, no pads, just helmets and sweats, and cleats. Billy and Goodwin hated these practices, but they were probably the only ones. Goodwin hated to miss an opportunity to knock somebody off his feet and Billy knew that casual dress led to casual performance. He'd much rather dress in full gear and not be allowed to hit hard than go with no pads. But the coaches were always fearful of injuries, especially this time of year. So practice would be loose and informal, a simple run-through of all the plays they might use the next day.

"And I'll tell you sissies somethin' else," the captain continued. "The coach don't want to see none of you wearin' your own gear. Newark sweats only!" There was a collective moan. This infuriated Snow. "I don't want to hear it! The coach comes to me last weak and says we look more like the crowd at the Christiana Mall than a football squad. If you ain't got the right sweats then borrow some!"

"What do you know about the mall Snow?" one brave senior shouted. "You never shopped anywhere but Wal-Mart." The jibe was greeted by loud laughter and cheers.

"That's it!" shouted Snow, his massive mid-section gyrating. With that he launched himself across two sets of wooden benches toward his waiting target, wrestling his victim to the concrete floor in one motion. For a big man, he could move like a ballet dancer.

Billy was slightly amused but decided to duck away from the action, the complexities of Sussex Central's defense weighing heavy on his mind. Shelby's words were lingering, trying hard to get the forefront. But Billy wouldn't let them; there was work to be done, and for now football was his occupation, and his escape.

There was a lot to think about when it came to Shelby. On Monday night she told him there was more to Ryan and Sam's deaths than the public knew, but that's all she would say, except that she was sure what she knew didn't matter to anyone other than her. Billy hadn't wanted to press her, but he insisted that whatever she knew was important to him too. *What else could there be?* Sam was Shelby's best friend, so it could really be anything - maybe they had a conversation about death; that certainly happened a lot in high school. Maybe Sam had been so upset over Ryan's death that she told Shelby she was contemplating suicide. There were so many possibilities, but Ryan was sure there could be nothing for Noah Lively to be sticking his nose into. That night Shelby told Billy that she really trusted him, but that she wasn't ready to tell *anyone* what else she knew. Then they kissed and held each other for a long time, and nothing else seemed to matter.

Billy walked into the bathroom area of the locker room and had to smile when he saw the locked stall door. He remembered how that stall was *always* occupied by Mike Drummond before practice. Every day he would be jeered by any teammate who happened to come to use the facilities.

"What's taking so long, Mike?"

"What'd you have for lunch?"

"Whoa! I hope it smelled better on its way in!"

Everyone had a theory as to why Mike spent so much time behind the locked stall door before practice started, but Billy knew the truth: Mike had terrible nerves. He made the jobs of starting quarterback and captain look easy, but inside, it really took its toll. Whether he spent the time sitting or standing, the minutes before a game or a practice always wreaked havoc on his digestive system.

Billy laughed to himself, still hearing the roaring laughter from the locker room. It struck him that he suddenly felt like he no longer had two dead friends, but three. *Where was Mike and why did he leave?*

This sad thought was interrupted by a tall, skinny figure emerging from behind the stall door. "What's all the shoutin' about?" asked Corey Curtis, a fleet-footed senior wide receiver with a knack for gossip.

"Just Cobb. He's busy making enemies. Uniform 'c' today."

Corey looked in the mirror and fixed his hair, a peculiar habit shared by many high school football players: checking hair *before* putting on a helmet for two hours.

"Well, maybe we'll get everything right the first time we do it today, and Coach Scott will let us go early," Corey said.

Ever since Ryan's accident, Corey had tended to be anxious about practice ending early. It was his car that Ryan had been driving when he lost control. Corey had developed an understandable fear of driving at night.

"Maybe," Billy answered with an edge of apprehension. "I'm a little worried that we're getting winner's disease."

Corey shook his head and smirked. "Don't worry about us. We won't choke. Just keep throwin' that ball."

"Just keep getting open." They slapped hands and Corey slapped Billy on the back. It felt good to have the team's confidence, but Billy really was worried about the team being too confident. A perfect record after seven games meant that every team in the state was hoping they would lose, especially Sussex Central.

"Hey," said Corey, a hint of mischief in his voice, "how's that going with Shelby Cooper?"

Billy had spent enough time in a boy's locker room to know exactly where the question was going, so he did his best to avoid the inevitable question. "It's going fine, taking it slow. Know what I mean?" He hoped that would imply the obvious, but of course, Corey was not satisfied.

"*Slow,* huh? What's the hold up?"

Billy remained outwardly calm but was getting very uncomfortable. This was the kind of thing he *hated,* personal questions about very private matters.

"It means neither of us are in any hurry to do anything. And by the way, you're hair is perfect, Corey. Now go get your helmet on."

Corey got the hint and smiled to cover the slight tension that had developed. "Okay. Sorry, Billy. I'm just asking. She's hot man. You know that. And she's hot for *you.*"

"Thanks," Billy said with finality, trying to bring some closure, but it was to no avail. Corey continued his uninvited interrogation.

"So, you think this 'relationship' is gonna' advance into somethin' soon?"

Billy clenched his fists. "Something like what, Corey?"

"Somethin' like you 'getting some,' Billy! You're the quarterback now, buddy. You should be all over that!"

Billy's instinct was to reach out and grab the skinny receiver by the throat and stuff his head into the nearby toilet, but being quarterback for two weeks had thankfully given him an even greater level of calm than he already had. Instead, he stepped toward Corey, strong steps that had purpose, eyes that meant *serious* business. Corey retreated, walking backwards into the small space between the sink and wall. Billy was on fire.

"This is the last time I'll discuss this," he said trying hard not to shout. "What I do, or don't do, with my girlfriend, is not a subject of discussion unless *I* bring it up. Is that clear?"

Corey raised his open hands as if Billy was pointing a gun at him. "I'm sorry, Billy. You're right."

Billy was still intense. "And since you like to spread the word so much, spread this: I am not discussing my private life with anybody in or out of this locker room. Get it?"

"Chill out, Billy. I said I was sorry."

Billy could see the fear in Corey's face and decided to let him off the hook. He gave Corey a playful slap on the shoulder, which made the receiver flinch. "Go get ready for practice, Corey." And he was quickly out of Billy's sight.

Billy ran some cold water and splashed it on his face and closed his eyes. He told himself to remember these guys are teenagers, and this *is* a locker room, so things like this will happen. Hopefully, this would scare them off for at least a while.

He put his hands on the sink and leaned in close to the mirror. Things *had* gotten pretty heated on Monday after Shelby told him she knew more about Sam and Ryan than she had told anyone. At first it seemed like she kissed him more to keep him from asking questions than out of affection. Billy didn't argue, but it seemed to never end. And Billy didn't want it to end. After a while their hands started wandering and Billy's heart was beating like it never had before. Finally, Shelby whispered, "Maybe we should stop."

Billy bit his lip and agreed. He knew they weren't ready to take the relationship any further, especially after a very emotional exchange. She got off his lap and sat back in the passenger seat, still holding his hand. Billy collected himself, gave himself a few minutes to settle down, and drove the short distance back to his house.

It was the most he had ever done physically with a girl. Of course he had enjoyed it, but he was very unsure as to how much he could control himself in future situations like that. They would have to talk about it, and as of today, Friday, they had talked about a lot of things, but not that. That would have to change. Billy was supposed to meet Shelby right after practice. They were going to go eat at some pizza then see a movie. He would be in bed by eleven, plenty of sleep the night before a game. But he would have plenty of time to spend with Shelby, and his stomach tingled nicely at the thought.

For a guy who never knew the language of women, he was sure having an easy time communicating with Shelby, even if it was a horrible thing that had brought them so close together.

fifteen

The director was in his glory. The cast of *Macbeth* was coming together so well that Noah thought this production could rival that of any of the Royal Shakespeare Company's, at least in the director's mind.

The witches prophesized of Macbeth's ascension to the crown with all the wonder and doom of the book of Revelation, Macbeth thirsted for the crown like any power hungry corrupted politician, and Lady Macbeth, who had been the biggest obstacle on Noah's course to perfection, was about to experience a major lesson on guilt.

As Crystal Madison took center stage, Noah could see that his plan had worked perfectly. Crystal looked flustered and full of guilt. Mr. King, who was standing far off in a corner saw her and turned around so as not to be seen trying to hold his laughter. As she delivered her lines perfectly, she wiped at the nonexistent blood frantically and recited her lines in perfect rhythm. "Out damned spot!" The rest of the cast watched on in amazement as Crystal became the guilt-ridden Lady Macbeth of Scotland. Noah cracked a smile, and did his best to conceal his jubilation. He was playing Crystal like a violin, a delicate, beautifully complex violin.

As it turned out, Noah had "accidentally" left a note from his mother on a desk backstage near Crystal's dressing area. By coincidence, Crystal, who could positively never walk by a note without taking a peak, especially this one sitting so temptingly in plain view, decided to read it. In the note, Noah's mother apologized to him for giving away his beloved toy poodle, Rexy. His mother explained that the whole family adored Rexy and that it wasn't fair to such a sweet dog to have his schedule change so drastically. It seemed Noah's new schedule, which included staying after school to work on this play, was just too much for Rexy. In fact it seemed that Noah had told his mother there was one young lady in particular who was causing Noah too much distraction to be able to devote to Rexy the attention he needed. Therefore she hoped that Noah would understand that they had no choice but to send little Rexy to their Uncle Frank's home in Reading, Pennsylvania. There Rexy could receive the love and attention he was so used to.

That was enough to put Crystal over the edge. Not only had she snooped into someone else's private note, but she also found out that *she* was the reason Noah had to give away his dog. How terrible! After that, the guilt came naturally.

Noah reveled at his own genius, and he would have to relay the story to his Uncle Frank, who was making a decent living selling jewelry in Reading, but like Noah, was terribly allergic to dogs and could not have one in the house.

With exactly one week until the play was to be performed, the director had finally managed to summon the guilt he knew Crystal had inside her. Only now she was not acting. Noah decided to hide the truth about his unfortunate, but nonexistent, pet from her until after the final performance. He figured she would either thank him and fall in love with him or slap him across the face and wish to never see him again. Noah would have greatly enjoyed either outcome.

Further inspired by Lady Macbeth, the rest of the rehearsal was an absolute pleasure. Only missing a few very complicated lines, the cast was dazzling. They conjured up demons of Macbeth's past, fought to the death, and with the help of a stellar prop department, cowered in fear as all of Birnam Wood came to destroy the new King Macbeth.

Watching with the greatest pleasure was Mr. King. The experience almost made him weep with sadness and joy simultaneously. At once he was overcome with the feelings of exhilaration that a good rehearsal of Shakespeare once brought; at the same time he wished in his heart that he still had the energy and enthusiasm it took to bring it out of them. *Why must we get old?*

And he delighted in watching Noah, his young Shakespearean genius. Part of him felt that he was handing over the reigns to a much worthier successor. The boy who hated to speak in class had become a natural leader, innovator, motivator, and artist. He had known all along that Noah could be this strong, and Mr. King saw to it that it would happen this way.

Noah fumbled through the heavy ring of keys, looking almost frantically for the right one. Shortly after rehearsals had ended, Noah noticed how elated Mr. King was and decided now was his chance. He casually asked the smiling teacher for his keys, appealing to his good will, and saying that the student restroom simply didn't afford him the privacy he needed, especially after a stressful day like today. King got the message and, with a wink, handed over his set of master keys. Noah had hypothesized correctly that King had a complete set, having been at Newark High for so long and having spent so many late nights working on productions. It had to have simply been a matter of time before *someone* of authority decided to hand over the precious *grand-master* key. That was the key that would open any door in the building, with the exception of the closet in the principal's office.

And Noah found it. After turning the corner out of the auditorium, Noah quickly turned left and headed directly toward Mr. Remsburg's office. Having seen the vice principal leave for the day at three o'clock, Noah was fairly certain that the coast was clear. If not, he would have a hard time talking his way out of what he was about to do.

A strange feeling came over Noah as he took the chair behind Mr. Remsburg's desk. He looked across to the chair where he had sat so many times and was almost overwhelmed with simultaneous feelings of guilt, exhilaration, and duty. He was trespassing in so many ways, betraying the trust of a man who had been such a source of strength and calm. But this was important. He booted up Remsburg's computer, which seemed to take an eternity. When the prompt finally came up, Noah quickly typed the password he had seen Remsburg type so many times: jackswired. *It pays to get in trouble.* Remsburg must be a poker player.

Within a minute, Noah had found what he was looking for. The student database contained the name, address, and schedule of every student in the school. Noah hoped that the list included students who were recently deceased. It did.

He typed the names of Ryan Chambers and Samantha Selby, and hoped that the query would produce a list of classes the two had taken together last year. It did. By instinct, Noah nearly hit the "print" command. But realizing that Remsburg's printer was not turned on, he decided not to. There were too many variables anyway. What if his printer had been acting up and he set his p.c. to print to the computer lab, or the principal's office? *Mr. Remsburg, did you print this list of classes that those two dead kids shared? No? Then who did? The record says it was sent by your computer at 6:58 p.m. last night.* Noah knew what would hit the fan if that happened.

The list of classes they shared was short anyway, and Noah could remember it easily: *Marketing 2, Physical Science,* and *Shakespeare.*

Bobcats break loosing streak
Yellow Jackets suffer first defeat in stunning upset

By Michael Tally

GEORGETOWN-For the Newark Yellow Jackets, it was a setback to what has been an otherwise very successful season. To the Sussex Central Bobcats, it was the victory they've been waiting on for two long seasons.

The Bobcats pulled off a stunning upset over the Dragons Saturday at Sussex Central, handing the playoff bound team a 22-10 loss at Sussex Central.

Central's special teams play made all the difference as the Dragons consistently faced bad field position and were unable to contain Central's kick returner, Freddie Allen who scored a touchdown off a punt in the first quarter and ran back the opening kickoff of the second half to Newark's five yard line. The Bobcats scored two plays later.

Central Coach Larry Walker was jubilant, but reserved after the game. "I can't put into words what this means to these boys who have worked so hard this season. They deserve it," he said. "But the reality is that Newark is going to the playoffs, and that's where we'd like to be, instead of celebrating our first win in two seasons."

Even with the loss, the 8-1 Dragons qualified for the playoffs when Mt. Pleasant lost to William Penn Friday Night.

Newark quarterback Billy Wirth, who struggled early in the game throwing two interceptions in the first quarter, said the loss comes at a bad time for him and the team. "We found out Friday night we were in the playoffs, and I think that took our edge away. I don't think we were hungry anymore, and Central was. That's a bad place for a playoff team to be," he said. "Hopefully, we'll get over it fast."

Wirth replaced Allstate quarterback Mike Drummond two weeks ago after he unexpectedly quit the team. He has since withdrawn from school for unknown reasons. Newark Coach Dave Scott refused to speculate as to whether his team might have won with Drummond. But one player, who spoke anonymously, said he hoped Drummond might come back for the playoffs.

Next week Newark faces A.I Dupont at home and Sussex Central will travel to play Salesianum.

sixteen

Sudden changes in temperature are all-too-common in the state of Delaware and this autumn week was no different. Monday had been a fairly dreary, but mild day. The weather matched the mood of the football team, which had gathered formally for the first time since the embarrassing loss to lowly Sussex Central. The mood of the practice and of the locker room was such that an outsider could never have guessed that the team had just qualified for the state playoffs. They had been pretty sure for some time that they would make it to the post season, but they were hoping for that rare undefeated season that only a few teams in history had ever achieved. It was something that was never talked about, or even alluded to, but it was on everyone's mind. And now that the perfect season was out of reach, players discussed it openly and with great frustration.

Goodwin Snow did his best to keep his teammates focused and positive. "We got two more games, ladies," he'd say. "We win'em both and we can still get home field advantage. That's what we're playin' for now, you sissies!"

There was added tension caused by the anonymous comments made to a news reporter after the loss. At least one player held the opinion that had Mike Drummond been the quarterback, the team would have found a way to win. The loss could have in no way been blamed on Billy Wirth, but there was a sense among several players that Drummond could have managed a victory with some late game-magic. Billy sensed it, and tried his best to ignore it. He knew that would come sooner or later, and better now than in the playoffs. He brushed it off as best he could, but it was rather awkward walking into the locker room and listening to every player shut up at the same time. On Tuesday he'd decided to break the tension with some humor. Turning the corner on his way out of the shower, he found five players who immediately went silent, nervously looking at each other as they toweled off. They had obviously been discussing Billy's performance.

Billy surprised them all by saying, "Damn! I'm finally ready to discuss my sex life, and you all have nothing to say!" The five ripped into hysterics, much to Billy's satisfaction.

"Billy," Curtis Henry finally answered, "if it's *your* sex life, there *is* nothing to talk about."

Billy appreciated the jibe, and laughed his approval.

His expression turned slightly serious as he said, "Listen, guys. There's nobody on this team who wishes that Drummond were here more than me. I'd give anything to be playing tight end again, but this is just the way it happened. It was just meant to be this way and we all have to deal with it, okay?"

Corey Curtis was the first to speak up. "The guy sold us out, Billy." The others nodded. "He up and left, and you've done a heck of a job filling in. We're with you." The others voiced their approval, and Billy was somewhat convinced. He figured that would have to do.

By Wednesday the mild weather had turned to bitter cold. Even though the cars had been covered with a thin layer of frost in the morning, any resident of northern Delaware could still half expect to see a nice weekend. Autumns in Delaware are very unpredictable, and people usually try to stay keenly aware of the next day's forecast.

Practice had ended early and Billy and Kenny decided to retreat to the east gym for a little one-on-one basketball. Short practices always left Billy with energy to burn, and playing quarterback didn't help matters. Instead of spending two hours running pass routs and pushing the blocking sled, he was dropping back and passing. Only occasionally would he break into a run, which usually ended quickly when he'd be hugged by a defensive back. So today he decided the best way to get some excess sweat out of his system was to drag Kenny to the basketball court. As always, Kenny grudgingly agreed, even though his practice had been exhausting since he was now starting at linebacker and tight end.

In Kenny, Billy was beginning to realize that he had a good friend. He knew because Kenny never spoke out of turn when it came to Shelby, and *never* pressured him on the subject. It was strange how through his new relationship with Shelby, Billy's eyes were opening to Kenny's devotion. Kenny was always polite, asking how Shelby was, or if they had plans - he offered no locker room comments, and Billy always appreciated it.

They arrived at the east gym and began to take shots - very lazy ones. It was supposed to be warming up, but the fact was it was the end of the day and they had just finished a football practice. The gymnasium was busy with kids from various programs coming and going, and some just there to socialize. Through the thin, temporary wall of the east gym, the two could hear the sound of the field hockey team practicing. Kenny made eye contact with Billy and knew what he was thinking. Billy missed not being with Shelby every minute they were apart, and feeling that way made every moment they spent together all the better. These feelings were new and exciting, and they made every day better than the next.

Kenny was finding his touch with the basketball and Billy watched as more and more of his friend's outside shots began to hit the bottom of the net. Kenny smiled, letting Billy know he was ready.

"First to ten?"

"Take the ball first," Billy replied.

"*Right by you,*" Kenny said as he made a strong move to the hoop, laying in the first basket of the game. He whooped in triumph.

Billy couldn't help but feel sorry for Kenny who made no secret of the fact that he was constantly searching for female companionship, always unsuccessfully. He was the last single man in his family, except his oldest brother, who was a priest. True, Kenny was only seventeen, but he was constantly looking for the right girl, and Billy knew it irked him that, without trying, he had managed to land a beautiful and brilliant girlfriend. Billy knew all too well what Kenny was going through, and made it a point never to mention Shelby unless Kenny asked, which he always did.

At the top of the key, Billy bounced the ball twice and lunged forward. Kenny bought the fake and began to retreat, his expression quickly showing frustration. Billy stepped back and lined up for a jump shot, which fell gracefully through the bottom of the net.

"Damn!" Kenny shouted. "I fall for that once every game."

"I know. I figured I should use it early."

The game continued this way, two friends who knew each other way too well. Every move was anticipated, and there were absolutely no surprises. They had played more than a hundred games just like this, but somehow they were never boring. The competition and the trash talk made every game as exciting as a day at Iron Hill chasing each other up Duncan Slope. Sometimes the games became so physical that they would end in wrestling matches.

After the third game, the two decided to call it quits. They each won a game, and the third was stopped prematurely by the suggestive whistle of an impatient janitor. All the other teams had stopped practicing and the gym had been cleared of almost all stragglers. Realizing the time, they decided to call it quits and began to make their way back to the varsity locker room. Kenny asked, "Going out with Shelby tonight?"

Billy shook his head with disappointment. "She's hanging out with Jackie. Girls night out."

Kenny smiled devilishly. "I'd love to be a part of one of those."

"You're sick, Alvarez," Billy said, wiping his sweaty forehead.

"I know. Nothing I can do about it."

But Kenny wasn't sick. He was a teenaged boy, and he knew where to draw the line.

As they crossed one of the main hallways, Kenny pointed to a figure in the distance. "Isn't that your boy Noah?"

Billy looked up to see that Kenny was right. Noah Lively was emerging from the backstage door of the auditorium. Billy quickly stepped to the side so Noah couldn't catch a glimpse of them.

"Go on ahead, Kenny," Billy said. "I need to talk to Noah."

"Talk to *him*? About what?"

"I'll see you later. Give me a call tonight?"

Kenny got the message. "Okay. We'll watch some film." He smiled and added, "But now that I'm playing tight end, I'm calling Jackie O'Neill.

Billy waited around the corner of the darkened hallway for Noah. He had taken an alternate hallway hoping to take Noah by surprise, which he knew was almost impossible. But this time he had him.

Quiet feet.

Timing his jog perfectly, he slammed into Noah as he entered the main hallway, knocking the skinny director to the floor causing him to scatter his papers.

"Noah!" Billy shouted with mock confusion. "What are you

doing here?"

In shock, Noah began picking up papers. "I'm directing a play," he said from the floor. "What the hell are *you* doing here?"

Capitalizing on Noah's weakened state, Billy grabbed him under his armpits and, with his great strength, hoisted him off the floor in one motion. He planted his feet on the floor, and looked directly in Noah's dark green eyes. He smelled of cigarette smoke, as usual.

"Sorry about that, Noah. It's cold out, so I decided to jog through the hall."

Noah didn't buy that for a second; Billy loved the cold. Noah noticed Billy still had his hands tightly gripped around his shoulders, forcing him to remain with his back to the wall.

"I didn't mean to knock you down, Noah," the quarterback said. "How's the play going?"

Noah swallowed hard and answered. "It's going fine." Billy knew he had the advantage here. He had succeeded in intimidating Noah. Knowing Noah could talk his way out of anything as long as his head was clear, Billy decided to put some fear in him, physically. It worked.

"Shelby says you've been talking to her. What about?"

"How about you let go of me, Billy?"

Billy acted surprised. "Oh. Sorry, Noah. I wanted to help you up. What about Shelby?"

"Why don't you ask her?"

Billy moved in. "She's not here, so I'm asking *you*."

"Well, Billy, why don't you drop the meat-head act and go find her?" He started to wiggle away, but Billy quickly put out an arm and stopped him.

"I want you to leave her alone, Noah. Do you understand?" He spoke in a controlled, suppressed shout, much like the cadence of a quarterback, which Billy was becoming quite good at. "She's got a lot on her mind and all you're doing is freaking her out with this private-I act."

Noah was scared, but defiant. "I'm doing important work, Mr. Quarterback. I hate to distract you from your perfect season, but I need to speak to Shelby."

"I say you don't."

"What are you, her lawyer?"

"Sure," Billy shot back.

A stern voice interrupted them. *"Everything okay, gentlemen?"*

They both turned their heads to see the shadowy figure of Mr. Remsburg standing at the end of the hall. Billy knew better than to mess with the head of discipline.

"Everything is fine, sir," Billy said stepping away from Noah. "Just a chat among old friends."

Remsburg wasn't convinced. "Noah? Is that what's going on here?"

Noah didn't take his eyes off of Billy. "We're fine, Mr. Remsburg.

In fact I was just leaving." This time he did get away and, of course, Billy made no attempt to stop him. He had made his point anyway. Billy thought that it was probably good that Remsburg had come along. This way Noah had no way of knowing what Billy might have been prepared to do. Of course, Billy had no intention of becoming violent.

As Noah walked away, Billy turned toward Remsburg and said, "Have a good night, sir."

Remsburg smiled. "You football guys are too polite," he said. "Have a good game Friday. DuPont has a tough defense, from what I hear."

"They do," Billy said. "But we'll be ready."

Remsburg stepped very close to Billy and said in his quiet, trademark voice. "I hope so, Billy. You're a good kid and a great football player. I know you're nuts about preparation. But if you put your hands on Noah again, there's nothing you can do to prepare yourself for me. Understand?"

Now Billy swallowed hard. "Yes, sir."

The truth's hands were shaking. He nervously tapped at his I-pod, trying to find the song that would take his mind off the horrible developments that had consumed him. He hadn't slept in two days, and he knew it showed at school. All night he listened to his mother breathing, a thick diseased struggle that filled the house. She also knew he hadn't slept. Would she start wondering too?

How did it come to this? Everything was so *perfect*. Someone knew, and was getting close to the truth.

He yanked the loud plugs from his ears and threw the device at his pillow. He knew what had to happen.

The shaking stopped as he booted up his pc. He typed his password and logged on. An overwhelming feeling of relief came over him like a warm blanket.

The truth would have to kill again.

seventeen

Mike Drummond washed his hands for the third time. For some reason the water in the Pocono Mountains never seemed to get all the soap off his hands, a slippery feeling which he found terribly uncomfortable. He opened the creaky refrigerator and dug into the box of pizza left over from what he had ordered the night before. He also grabbed a can of Coke, popped it open and took a long drink.

Without a microwave oven, the pizza would have to be eaten cold. This was not a problem since there didn't seem to be any place in the area that could make pizza that was worth heating up. Cold pizza and soda for breakfast, he thought. This must be what it's like being a bachelor.

After eating two slices of pizza, the taste of which combined grotesquely with the stale taste from the night before, Mike decided go for a run. He pulled on his fleece and hat and headed for the lake.

The back door of the cabin opened onto a large wooden deck that overlooked Bear Creek Lake, a man-made fishing hole that was frequently packed with trout to please the tourists. But this time of year, there were very few people around. It was too late for swimming and too early for skiing, and hunting season was still a month away. Mike agreed with his mother, who told him that it was the closest thing to the perfect hiding place that they could find on such short notice. The cabin belonged to his mother's boss, and their family had been renting it once a year for as long as Mike could remember. But for the first time, he was *alone* in the cabin.

He was in total seclusion. The money had almost run out, but he knew his mother would be sending him more. Even though he usually loved the rustic surroundings of the cabin, he was quickly getting tired of being by himself all the time. Every other day he would drive his father's car into town to pick up some groceries and check his email at the coffee shop, an activity he found to be a necessary risk. Thankfully there were only fifteen days left to go, assuming he could make it that long.

As usual, he stayed away from the roads as he jogged - no need to have anyone stop and ask why he wasn't in school. He doubted anyone up here, including the rarely seen police officers, would care. But why risk it?

When he got back to the lake he took his shoes off and walked out over the short wooden peer, as he had done countless times since he was a child. The almost freezing cold wood felt good under his feet. He picked up a rock and skipped it across the lake. The motion of his arm summoned vague memories of a football career that seemed like a lifetime ago. His mother had sent him the clippings. The team was doing fine without him, and Billy had lit up the scoreboard against A.I. Dupont. His team had finished the season with nine wins and one loss. *Good for them.*

Unexpectedly, he broke into tears. He sat on the peer, put his head between his knees, and prayed to God that the truth would not kill again.

eighteen

"Captain Fahey," sang Charlene, the Chief of Newark Police's overly anxious and overly perfumed secretary, "Trooper Adam Graff is on line two."

The captain put down his coffee and sat up at his desk. "Thank you, Charlene," he said in a voice that sounded like he had just woken up. He ran a hand through his oily brown hair. "Do you know what he wants?"

"He didn't say. Just said he needed to talk to you."

State Police are a pain, he thought. *Why don't they do their own legwork?* He took a breath and picked up the phone. "Jim Fahey, Newark Police."

"Good afternoon, Captain," came the deep, official-sounding voice on the other end. "This is Adam Graff, State Police Troop Eight."

"Yes, Trooper, what can I do for you?"

"Well, Captain, I'm looking at a very strange anonymous letter we received this morning. I wanted to get your take on it."

Fahey sunk in his chair and sighed. "Let me guess," he said. "It's a list of strange coincidences between the deaths of the two kids at Newark High, right?"

"You received it too," the trooper said with affirmation. "What do you think, Captain?"

"Well, I would tell you, Trooper, but my mom told me never to curse at the state police."

"Exactly what is that supposed to mean?"

The captain's voice grew louder. "It means I think it's bull, Trooper Graff, as in bull – loney."

Graff's voice didn't change a bit. "Are any of these things true, Captain?"

"I guess some of them are. Just like all those stupid little coincidences between Lincoln and Kennedy." He was doing his best to let the other man know he was annoyed and had no time for this. "Lincoln's secretary's name was Kennedy, Kennedy's was Lincoln, and mine is Charlene. Who cares? That case is closed, Trooper. I don't have time for this kind of nonsense."

"I understand, Captain. Do you have any idea who may have sent the letter?"

"I don't know – how 'bout the Tooth Fairy?"

Graff was unfazed. "I'm sorry you think this is so funny, Captain."

"Well your guess is as good as mine, Trooper." He was getting louder. "I'd dust the thing for prints, but I already used it in the john when we ran out of toilet paper."

"Captain, I don't appreciate…"

"And if you think it was funny being on the scene when they pulled that poor girl out of that piece of twisted wreckage, you don't know me too well, *Trooper.*"

Graff refused to be flustered. "Listen, Captain. You're the one being flip here. I'm just trying to make sure there isn't someone out there who knows something about this case who hasn't come forward. And for your information, Captain, I was on the scene before any of your guys got there."

Fahey exploded out of his chair, his huge midsection colliding with the desk in front of him. "Listen Graff, this is *my* case. In fact, there *is no* case at all," Fahey shouted while jabbing a finger at the phone. "We have two *accidents* that involve two kids who just so happened to be lovebirds. If you want to turn it into a conspiracy, do it on your time! I have important work to do." He hung up.

Fahey really hated when the state police began to stick their noses into the affairs of his town. As far as he was concerned, they should stick to the highway and that's all. Give out as many speeding tickets as they want, but don't mess with the people of Newark. This was *his* town.

He picked up the envelope, which was sitting neatly in the center of his perfectly arranged oak desk. He began to open it for the second time, but thought better of it. He smirked at the envelope, which had no return address, shook his head, and tossed it into the small garbage can next to his desk. *That's what the old circular file is for.*

Putting the whole thing out of his mind, the chief of police returned to his computer screen, where he had just started a new game of solitaire.

The young man in the blue suit sat across the large oak desk of Edward G. Hayes, principal of Newark High School. He shifted in his seat as the principal read through his resume. After a few minutes of silence, Hayes removed his reading glasses and looked at Charlie Remsburg.

"Been out of the Army almost two years, I see."

"Yes sir."

The principal placed his reading glasses gently on his desk. "Charlie, you can call me Ed. We're pretty informal around here."

"Thank you, Ed."

The principal continued. "Pretty impressive resume you've got here, even though you have no experience in schools."

"Thank you, sir...Ed."

The principal smiled, his bushy grey eyebrows traveling nearly to his hairline.

"But, you spent five years teaching boys to be soldiers, so I guess I can't accuse you of not having experience with teenagers."

Remsburg smiled back. "I *do* have a degree in criminal justice and a minor in history."

The principal nodded his approval, then looked in Remsburg's eyes again.

"You're from Oregon?"

"Born and raised, Ed."

"May I ask what brought you to our beautiful state of Delaware?"

Charlie paused and scratched his head.

"I'm not really sure, sir. I knew a man in the Army who was from Delaware. It always sounded like a nice place, from what he said."

Hayes leaned back in his chair, clearly intrigued by what the young man had said.

"You up and moved to *Delaware* because a man you served with said it was a nice place?"

"Something like that, sir...Ed."

The principal looked curiously at the young man across from him, wondering what could have really compelled him to come to live and work in Newark, Delaware.

"Are you married?" the principal asked.

"No."

"No Kids?"

"No," Charlie repeated.

"Parents?"

"Back in Oregon."

Hayes knew he would not find the answer he was looking for, so he gave up trying.

Remsburg was one of hundreds of people Hayes had interviewed over the years. The old man had become so good at spotting a good candidate for a job that he had been asked on many occasions by other schools in the district to do their interviews as well. He had made an art of finding the right person for the job.

But this man was different. Hayes could sense that the man had a strong desire to teach, and would be a strong example to his students. He sensed a genuineness in him that had become too rare in recent years. He liked the man, a lot.

Yet there was still *something*. Charlie Remsburg was hiding something, and Hayes had no idea what it was.

"We start school in two weeks, Charlie. How'd you like to join us?"

"I would love to, sir."

"I'm glad to hear that," Hayes answered, smiling again. "I'm sad to say you won't hear too much from me in your time here at Newark. I'm nearing retirement, as you can see. I've discovered that the best way to do my job is to surround myself with competent people, and step in only when I need to."

"I understand."

"Good. Your supervisor is a great old guy by the name of Nate King," Hayes said, jotting down the information. "You'll find him in his classroom, top of the steps. He'll get you squared away." He handed Charlie the information.

"Thank you, sir."

They stood. Hayes extended a large hand to Charlie.

"Welcome aboard, Charlie. And for the last time, call me Ed."

Newark QB proves his Wirth
Newark's former tight has risen to the challenge

By Michael Talley

One week ago rumors were swirling that Billy Wirth had a mutiny on his hands.

It was the day after the Newark Yellow Jackets suffered a shocking loss to lowly Sussex Central High School and players and fans were starting to talk.

A few of those players, who remain anonymous, told reporters that they hoped Mike Drummond, Newark's All-State quarterback who left the team three weeks ago and has not been seen since, would return to lead the Jackets through the playoffs. One unnamed player even said he doubted Wirth could finish the season at quarterback even if Drummond did not return.

All that talk is over.

After Saturday night's routing of A.I. Dupont, which included a brilliant performance by Wirth, he has emerged as the unquestioned leader of the Jacket's offense.

The past few weeks have seen rapid changes, but for Billy Wirth, the junior quarterback who was playing tight end until Drummond's departure, nothing comes as a surprise anymore.

More importantly, he knew all along that becoming a strong quarterback wasn't going to happen overnight, and he knows there is plenty more work to do.

"Going from knowing what to do as a receiver to running the whole offense takes time," says the tall, sandy-haired Wirth as he scratches at an emerging crop of facial hair under his chin. "I've always known our offense well, but it's reacting to the other team's defense that's the challenge. Knowing what to do when they do something you weren't expecting. That's what's hardest."

It's a few minutes after a tough Monday practice and, as usual, Wirth is flipping through a lengthy playbook. Only it's not the playbook of the Newark Yellow Jackets. He's looking at a book that's been compiled over the years by coaches. The book outlines all of the defensive formations that Newark's next opponent, St. Mark's, has used in the past ten seasons. Wirth plans to be fully prepared for the team's first round playoff game on Saturday on their home field.

In case you're wondering how long it will take Wirth to memorize all of those formations, don't worry; he already has.

Wirth speaks slowly and seems to always be serious. "Once football is over I can go back to memorizing important things, like history and science. For now, I'm sad to say it's all football."

Preparation has been a key to Wirth's success as a player. As a receiver, he was sure to know everything there was to know about the players who would be defending him. As a quarterback, he knows the whole defense. And he does it every week.

"I was never worried about losing the confidence of my teammates," he explains. "That was an emotional loss (to Sussex Central), and players say those kinds of things after they lose tough games. But that's in the past. Everybody is on board now." One thing that definitely helped get everyone on board was Wirth's performance against A.I. Dupont last Saturday. In what was by far his best game as quarterback, Wirth passed for a whopping 363 yards and threw four touchdown passes. He ran for another 48 yards, picking up four first downs in the 49-0 rout.

The most important statistic to Wirth in that performance was the zero – zero interceptions.

"I don't want to make those mistakes that can cost us a game," he says. "If they break up every pass or stop every run, that's one thing. But we can't turn the ball over."

Turning the ball over is something that Newark has not been known for in the past few seasons. Neither Wirth nor Drummond has had a tendency to give it up. But when discussing Drummond, Wirth is guarded, and his body language screams of a desire to change the subject.

"All I have to say about Mike is that I hope he's doing alright, and that if he came back here, I'd give him a big hug and hand him the ball," Wirth says, his blue eyes filling with emotion. "This is his offense and I'm his tight end. But I don't think he'll be back for a while."

That subject is widely debated. School officials insist that Drummond's disappearing act is a private family matter, and that the absence is only temporary.

Newark Athletic Director Bill Conley says Drummond would be allowed back on the team if he returned before the end of the season, but the team will operate as if he will not be back at all. No coaches or school administrators admitted to having any idea where Mike Drummond is. Only one official, who asked to not to be named, said, "Mike and his family have decided for their own reasons that he should not be in school. The absence is indefinite but, for now, it is not permanent."

For a Newark football team that has been through very tough times this year with the death of teammate Ryan Chambers, and the absence of team captain Drummond, the presence of Wirth is extremely fortunate.

"I don't know what we'd do without him," says new team captain Goodwin Snow. "The way he's taken that job under his belt and led that group of guys on offense, it's almost like it was meant to be his job all along."

Maybe it was.

nineteen

Noah Lively left school shortly after 6:30 in the evening. With the first performance of *Macbeth* only one week away, he was putting in many late nights. But tonight was different. It was two days until his mother's birthday, and he a job to do. It was a job he had done on this same day every year since the death of his father, when Noah was in fifth grade.

"It's a big responsibility, Noah," his father had told him while he lay dieing in the downstairs guest bedroom. "I've written enough birthday cards to your mother for her to live to be a hundred, and I hope she does."

Noah had held back his tears while he listened to his helplessly ill father's instructions. He was to walk to the bank on North Chapel Street every year, two days before his mother's birthday. Once at the bank, he was to open his father's safety deposit box, which no one in the world knew existed besides Noah, his father, and the Newark Trust Bank. In the box were two piles of sealed greeting cards: one pile of birthday cards, the other Valentine's Day. Noah was to place one of the birthday cards in the mailbox on this day every year so the card would be sure to arrive at the house on his mother's birthday.

The Valentine's were to be sent similarly, his father explained, *unless* his dear wife happened to fall in love with someone else. She never did. Of course Noah felt it must be impossible to fall in love with someone when you keep receiving mail from your dead husband twice a year. But Noah had his instructions, and he promised his father he would follow them forever and he would *never* tell his mother the truth.

For her part, his mother never asked. She simply received her greeting cards from the afterlife and never said a word about them to Noah. As he matured, Noah decided his mother had probably assumed that her husband had made an arrangement with one of his many clients, or even left private instructions in his will for his law firm to send the cards every year. Or, just maybe, she believed her husband's love for her had in fact conquered death itself. Whatever the case, Noah never said a word to his mother about his twice-a-year trips to the bank on North Chapel, and she never asked.

Noah retrieved this year's birthday card from his father's safety deposit box. It was in a beautiful yellow envelope. He closed the lock box, thanked the attendant, left the bank, and headed for the post office on Main Street. It was his second trip to the post office this week. On Monday, he had sent three identical letters: one to the state police, another

97

to the Newark Police, and a third to the *News Journal*, though he wasn't sure what, if any, affect the anonymous letters would have.

He had been working hard for the past month conducting his own investigation into the deaths, which he considered murders, of Samantha Selby and Ryan Chambers. There were too many coincidences between the two tragedies to make them both accidents, and Noah knew that someone had to be behind them. He had uncovered countless compelling clues, but still had no idea whom the culprit could be.

His initial suspicion had come weeks before the sudden deaths had even taken place. Noah had known for quite some time that someone was out there pulling strings that were strangling an entire community.

He had known for a fact that there was an evil force who stalked his prey in chat rooms and private blogs, and Noah learned of him one very late night while he chatted online with the kindhearted but childishly naïve Samantha Selby. Noah had become worried that his friend and others like her were in great danger of something that was more evil than they could believe existed. But like the others, Noah did nothing and said nothing. He never contacted the police; he never told Mr. Remsburg. Even after Ryan's death, he accepted it as an accident. *What a terrible mistake.* The guilt sometimes paralyzed him, but there was not time to dwell on it.

Out of guilt, Noah had sworn to himself that he would find the truth, even if it meant he had to give his own life trying.

As he approached the blue public mailbox, Noah instinctively peered left and right before placing the yellow envelope in the box.

As he watched the yellow envelope fall, he realized his greatest worry.

If he died trying to find the truth, there would be no one to mail his mother's birthday cards.

twenty

Billy was jogging by himself through Iron Hill. Brandywine Creek was for pleasure and Iron Hill was for work. It was only Tuesday, and Billy had already surpassed ten miles on his feet for the week. No longer having to worry so much about keeping on the extra pounds a tight end was expected to carry, he ran for distance and stamina.

Practices were becoming too leisurely in his opinion, and Billy had energy to burn. Coaches were always sure to keep practices light this time of year, especially for teams headed to the playoffs. Do a little hitting, run a bunch of plays against the dummy squads, and run lots of drills. The end of the season was a good time for drills since many players were getting too comfortable with their techniques and relaxing on the fundamentals. "Re-learn the good stuff," Coach Scott always said.

But Billy left practice the past two days feeling he could use more, so he headed down the road to Iron Hill hoping to get a good jog in before the sun went down. The weather was nice by most people's standards and even though Billy loved the rain, jogging outside in dry weather was always much more pleasurable than trudging through mud. Kenny, who had now caught three touchdown passes, was happy to stay behind and wait for Jackie O'Neal to emerge from the girl's locker room after cheerleading practice. Jackie had undergone a change of heart since Kenny began putting points on the board. Somehow she was a little more willing to give Kenny some extra attention, and the rumor was that they had been speaking on the phone. This amused Billy somewhat, but he detested rumors, and was not about to start gossiping.

Since Sunday, when he was featured in *The First State News*, Billy had begun to remember why he liked being alone so much. Football was a team sport, and he had *always* been a team player, but there he was being heralded as a star in the local newspaper. He hated the attention, and was quick to leave practice before anyone else could congratulate him.

The experience was making him as upset at Mike Drummond as he was worried about him. No one had heard a word as to his whereabouts, except that the school administration said he was safe and doing his best to keep up on schoolwork. But where was he, and why did he disappear? Was he coming back? Not even Kenny, who seemed to have an uncanny ability to get the inside scoop on everything, was able to find out where Mike was. Besides, Kenny now had other things to keep him busy.

Billy was approaching Duncan Slope, but only quickened his pace slightly. He was no longer too concerned with exploding off the line of scrimmage with quiet feet. He was working on pure stamina now, so he took the hill fast and steady, like a quarterback running a two-minute drill. The burning in his legs felt good, but reminded him of the last time he had been to Iron Hill with Mike Drummond.

Billy could vividly remember the day that he had last seen Mike. He remembered the quarterback pounding his fist into the tree and reciting some strange words just before taking off up the slope at full speed. *What did he say?* He wasn't sure it even mattered.

Billy was sure that Mike's disappearance had something to do with that day, and with Mike's drinking, and his crazy talk about *knowing* they would win the Homecoming game. He wished he knew what was going on. More than anything, Billy hoped that Mike would come back, and tell everyone he was okay.

The ringing of his cell phone rudely broke his thoughts. He slowed his jog and fished through the zipped pocket of his warm-up pants. Hoping to see Shelby's name on the digital display, Billy winced when he saw Kenny's. *I slowed down for this?* He let it ring two more times before answering.

"This better be good, Alvarez. Day-time minutes are expensive."

Kenny was excited, as usual. "This is what they're for, dude. It's day -time!" he said. "What are you doing?"

"I'm at Iron Hill," Billy answered taking a seat on a familiar large rock. "I lost my pace because of you."

"You're at the Hill?" Kenny asked incredulously. "Man, you can't get enough!"

"You'll thank me when you catch another touchdown pass on Saturday."

Kenny's smile could be heard over the phone. "You got that right. I'll be open."

"You better be."

"So what are doing tonight, dude?"

Billy made his voice sound as sure as possible and said, "Studying: first chemistry, then game films." He knew Kenny would try to convince him otherwise. "I haven't even looked at their defense yet."

"There's *plenty* of time for that, man. Let's go to the pool hall."

"No way, Kenny. I've had enough people kiss my but this week already."

"Listen to *you*," Kenny said in his most annoyed tone. "Maybe you should try *enjoying* the attention for a change, like a normal person."

"Kenny, I don't want to discuss what's normal with you, okay? Besides, I think Shelby's coming over to study with me."

Kenny laughed hysterically. "Well, I know she doesn't take chemistry, and I'm pretty sure she's not an expert on St. Mark's defense. Anything else in mind for the night, *William?*"

Billy felt himself turn red. "Kenny, you call me William again and I swear the next pass you get from me will knock your teeth out."

Kenny knew not to push. "Okay, okay, have a good time *studying.*"

Billy chuckled and decided not to explain himself. "Thanks, Kenny. I'm sure you'll get the celebrity treatment without me."

"I get it every time, dude," he said. "They love me up there! They let me play for free last night."

"You went last night, and you're going again?" Billy asked with an edge to his voice. "Getting much work done, *dude?*"

"I'm enjoying it while it lasts, okay?"

"What's that supposed to mean? You think we'll lose on Saturday?"

"Whoa!" Kenny hated even the idea. "No way, dude. I'm just saying that all things come to an end, and I want to enjoy the spotlight while I have it."

Billy nodded into the phone. "I get it. I get it." He changed the subject. "Have you found out anything about Mike?"

There was a pause as Kenny seemed to consider his words carefully "I'm sure he's fine, Billy."

Billy wasn't going to let him off that easy. "Well, I'm glad to hear he's fine, but do you know where he is?"

"Kind of, okay? I have an idea, but I'm not positive."

"Well let's have it, Sherlock."

"Okay, I'll tell you," Kenny said. "But you have to promise…"

"Yeah, yeah," Billy said, cutting him off. "I won't say a word. Just tell me."

"Okay. Man, I shouldn't be telling you this."

"Come on, Kenny. Out with it!"

"Okay. Listen. My friend Devon works in the academics office, okay?"

"Yeah."

"Last week he mailed a package full of text books to an address in Pennsylvania and he noticed it was addressed to the initials 'MD.' No name, just the initials. That's why he noticed."

"That and you told him to be on the lookout for something like that."

"True," Kenny admitted.

"What else?"

"It was sent to a town called Jim Thorpe, PA."

"I know that town," Billy said. "It's in the Pocono's."

"Right," Kenny confirmed. "And I remember Mike always saying that he and his family go to the mountains for Thanksgiving and sometimes in the summer. They rent a cabin from his mom's boss."

Billy was smiling wide. Kenny had done it.

"And his mom works for that dentist in Wilmington that my aunt goes to, Dr. French. You know the one I mean?"

"Yes," Billy said.

"So I called up information in Jim Thorpe, PA and I asked for the phone number of a resident named French and…you get the rest."

"Way to go, Kenny. Did you talk to him?"

"Just for a minute," Kenny said. "Man, he was spooked. He said he was okay but that I better not tell *anybody* where he was or that I spoke to him." Then he added. "He doesn't want to talk, Billy, so don't even think about it, okay?"

Billy was full of relief, almost joy. "I get it, Kenny. I just wish I knew what he was afraid of."

"Who knows, dude? Who knows?"

Billy decided not to push Kenny into admitting that he had an address. It was enough to know that Mike was safe.

"Thanks, Kenny."

Kenny was eager to change the subject. "So what about tonight, Billy? You coming out?"

"Kenny, I need to be ready so we can win on Saturday, so we can all be happy. Then we go to the state championship. Understand? No playtime until then."

"I know. Sorry, man. It's just that the place was so hopping last night. He added, "Shelby was there."

Billy's jaw dropped as the happy news about Mike quickly went by the wayside. He had no idea Shelby went to the pool hall the night before.

"Really?" He was trying to sound like he didn't really care, but Kenny knew better.

"Yeah," Kenny answered. His voice suddenly turned cautious. "She was there with Noah Lively."

The words hit Billy like a left hook. "What do you mean? She was there *with* Noah, or you saw her talking to him."

"I didn't see any of her other friends there, Billy," Kenny answered.

Billy was standing again, pacing. "What the hell? Were they playing pool?"

"No, man. They were sitting off in a corner, just talking."

Billy was lost for words, feeling an anger he was not at all familiar with.

"I'm sure it was nothing, dude" Kenny said, trying his best to calm his friend. "You can't think…"

"Don't tell me what I can think, Kenny!"

"Okay, okay. Relax."

"I gotta' go," Billy said, ending the call. He stared at the phone, numb. *Why would Shelby not tell me she was meeting with Noah Lively? Why wouldn't she tell me she was going to the pool hall?*

The phone rang again, Shelby's name appearing. Seeing Shelby's number always filled Billy's stomach with butterflies, until now. Now, he felt a sharp twinge of pain. Standing in the same spot where he had stood with Kenny and Mike just a few weeks ago, he slammed his fist into the same tree that Mike had, only harder. Luckily, it wasn't his throwing hand.

Billy had finally met an opponent he could not prepare for by working out and watching tape. He was face-to-face with jealousy, and this new opponent was more dangerous than any he had faced before.

The appointed time had passed and the truth was growing impatient. This was rare since he was normally quite content to wait. He continued to click and click, exploring his favorite websites, though most of them had not changed since the last time he checked. For what seemed an endless amount of time, he read through courageous accounts of the US military's most recent Medal of Honor recipients: two poor souls whose families received the prestigious recognition after their deaths. The truth loved stories of courage, self-sacrifice, and rising to greatness, and many such tales could be found only a few clicks away from the U.S. Army's official website, one referred to him by one of the high school guidance councilors.

The stories passed the time, but there were steps that had to be taken, and the truth was getting agitated as valuable seconds passed. Finally, he heard the familiar electronic sound of a squeaky door opening and the truth knew who it was before even checking. *Yourinstrument has just signed on.*

The truth took a deep breath and began typing. Three minutes later it was done. In eleven days, the Fatum Club would be permanently dissolved, and none of its members would be alive to tell anyone about it.

twenty-one

"So, class," Mr. King proclaimed with satisfaction, "as you know, several of your friends and classmates have been working extra hard on our abbreviated production of *Macbeth*." There was an unusual excitement in his voice, a sound that would be recognized immediately by students from generations past. "Well, I am happy to announce that rehearsals are finished and their first performance will be tomorrow night at eight o'clock."

The class applauded respectfully, many confused glances were exchanged, but those who were in the production all took on an heir of pride. The director, of course, was unfazed. Noah sat with his nose buried in *Macbeth* as if he'd been told to count the apostrophes.

King was beaming. "And, even though I *know* he will be furious at me for again giving him the attention he deserves, I *must* congratulate, most of all, our director. Let's hear it for Noah Lively!"

Now the class erupted in applause, and Noah was forced to take note of the recognition. He nodded politely and when the cheering settle he said, "Mr. King, I wish you'd waited until we had at least one successful performance before you congratulated us."

"Not to worry, Noah!" the teacher said. "I've watched every one of your rehearsals, and the cast is brilliant, the crew is perfectly in place. It's a foregone conclusion: the performances will be one that would make even the Bard himself stand and applaud."

Noah smiled. "Well, I'm not one for foregone conclusions, Mr. King."

Lisa Jenkins couldn't resist. "Oooh! It's like in *Macbeth* when he's told he'll be king until Burnham Wood comes to Dunsanane Hill! That was a foregone conclusion and Macbeth refused to believe it!"

King thought this must be too good to be true. His class was putting on a Shakespearian play for the first time in eleven years, and Lisa Jenkins was actually using her mind analytically.

"Very good observation, Lisa!" he said almost unable to contain himself. "Macbeth accepted the premonitions that he would soon be king, but he refused to believe the news of his doom."

Mr. King could see that Lisa was thinking about what he had just said, probably much harder than she should be. She wore an expression of pain.

"But, Mr. King, does that make him a believer in fate or free will?" she asked. "I mean, he can't be *both*, can he."

King sat on the edge of his desk and raised his right hand as he spoke, karate-chopping the air in front of him. "Remember, Lisa, Shakespeare's characters are *human* more than anything else. Shakespeare knew human psychology better than anyone in his time. He had the ability to get in the head of *every* audience member. Royalty, commoners, anybody could relate to these characters," the teacher explained. "Macbeth just does something very human. He *changes his mind*. All of a sudden he doesn't want to believe that what the witches said would come true, even though he did what he had to do to fulfill the prophesy of becoming king."

Out of the corner of his eye, Mr. King saw another student who was visibly perturbed by what he was hearing. Kenny Alvarez wore a smirk that seemed to say, *"Are you kidding me?"* King was used to treading lightly with Kenny, who almost never added to a class discussion. Kenny mostly sat in his seat and waited to be called on and, unlike Noah, was almost never pressed for comment. Kenny had been in Mr. King's general English class as a freshman, a class that every ninth grader must take, and one that every English teacher must teach from time to time, though none of them liked it.

"Looks as if the quarterback is upset about something, eh Kenny?"

Kenny was clearly perturbed at the attention. "I'm not the quarterback, Mr. King," Kenny said with reserved disdain. "But I am upset."

"Well, please enlighten us," King said, enjoying himself even more. "What is it that has the uh…what position do you play?"

"Tight end."

"Yes, Mr. Alvarez! Prove to us that at least one member of our playoff-bound football team knows his Shakespeare. What part of *Macbeth* has upset the *tight end*?"

Kenny was taking his time. He played with his pencil, focused on the eraser. "*Macbeth* hasn't upset me at all," he finally said. "It's just all this talk. I don't believe any of it."

"Explain, please," demanded the teacher waiving a long finger at the student. "I need to know if I'm dealing with ignorance or genius!"

Kenny shrugged. The class watched and listened with patience, surprised by what could be Kenny's first real contribution since the class first met.

"There's no predicting the future. The witches didn't predict that Macbeth would be king. They *tempted* him," Kenny said with confidence. "All the other stuff is just a bunch of crazy coincidences that can *only* happen in fiction. All Shakespeare is trying to say is that a man will stop at nothing to get what he wants. Macbeth wants to be king, and Lady Macbeth wants to be a queen. That's all there is to it."

The finality in Kenny's voice was a surprise to say the least. The football jock who had barely said a word all year was angrily defending his conclusions in an honors Shakespeare class. Students exchanged awkward glances and Mr. King stared at the floor. The class waited for a response. When it came, King was angry, his complexion glowing in a deep red the class had not seen in their teacher before today.

"Is that what you *really* believe, Mr. Alvarez?" the teacher asked in a calm voice, though he was tempted to shout.

Kenny stood. "I *know* it."

King's face was pulsing, his eyes narrow. "And your recent success, Mr. Alvarez? In four weeks you go from just another football player to free pool and soda and a beautiful cheerleader on your tail. Was that fiction, coincidence, or just a man who would stop at nothing to get what he wanted?"

The class was stunned into silence. Most were trying hard to understand King's words. Most of them knew Kenny had become tight end when Mike Drummond quit and Billy Wirth had to play quarterback. *Was Mr. King implying that Kenny had something to do with Mike's disappearance? And why was Kenny acting this way all of a sudden?*

Kenny didn't flinch, but stared at King from across the room. His face was frozen in a twisted state of anger. After several seconds, he bent down to pick up his backpack. He walked directly at the elderly teacher and a few gasps were heard. Only a few inches from Mr. King, he said, "I've had enough of this class, King."

"Wrong again, Alvarez," growled the teacher. "This class has had enough of *you*."

Kenny turned and walked to the door. Again Mr. King looked to the floor and sighed. "Class is over," he finally announced. "Everyone out!"

Lisa Jenkins never knew when to shut up. "But, Mr. King," she said almost in a whisper, "there's twenty minutes of class left. If we're seen in the hall we'll get in trouble."

"Get out, Lisa!" he shouted. "If Remsburg gives you any crap, send him to me!"

twenty-two

Shelby was waiting for Billy on the porch of the East End Café, a townie-style restaurant that sat unassumingly at the end of Main Street. The East End was unique in Newark since it seemed to be the one bar in town that college kids from out of town didn't frequent. Plenty of Delaware natives, students and non-students, would go there to escape the nasal accents that characterized the other watering holes where Long Islanders and North Jersey natives would flock to wash away a day of boring lectures.

As a senior in high school, Shelby really had no business being there on this Wednesday afternoon. However, she wanted to be sure that she and Billy could meet without being observed by any of their nosey classmates. So she found a table on the enclosed porch, ordered a diet soda, and waited for Billy.

But where was he?

Since they had been together, Shelby had never had to wait for Billy. In fact, she could only ever remember him being early to meet her or pick her up. He was always so happy to see her, as if they hadn't seen each other in weeks. Today, she had been waiting for more than half an hour for him to show up.

"Are you sure you don't want to see a menu?" asked an obviously annoyed young woman whose apron identified her as a waitress.

"No, thanks," Shelby answered with just enough courtesy to annoy the waitress even more. "I'll just have another soda."

The waitress disappeared, but was not in a hurry.

Shelby had felt that her last few conversations with Billy were somewhat stressed. There were no harsh words, of course. But somehow the conversations seemed a little bit forced, and they were shorter than they had been.

Shelby knew there could be a thousand reasons for this. Billy was now preparing for a huge playoff game and the whole state would be watching. In the few weeks since he had taken over as quarterback, he had emerged as the team's leader, a job she knew he was uncomfortable with.

Shelby knew Billy was still worried about Mike Drummond, even though the school administration had made it clear that he was safe. She also knew he still missed his friend Ryan as much as she still missed Samantha.

What was so different lately was that, at first, they had found so much comfort in each other. They seemed to have brought each other back from their loneliness, and now she was beginning to feel lonelier than ever. She wondered to herself if she didn't look as good as she had in the past. Maybe she was putting weight?

When Billy finally showed up, he was wearing jeans, a Yellow Jacket Football sweatshirt, and sunglasses that Shelby had never seen him wear before. He walked casually to her table and smiled. "Sorry," he said leaning in to kiss her. "Practice went long."

He was not excited to see her.

"It's okay, Billy," she answered unsure of her mood. She smiled and said, "You know I don't mind waiting."

"Are you getting any food?"

"Maybe. Are you hungry?"

"I haven't eaten since breakfast," Billy answered. "I skipped lunch to watch game film in Coach Scott's room."

"That's not good for you, Billy."

"Thanks, Shelby. But I already know what's good for me."

Shelby looked at the table and took a deep breath. "What's that supposed to mean?"

"It just means you don't really understand. We've got a game in four days and I'm the only one on the team who's more concerned with playing St. Mark's than bragging about being in the playoffs."

"Sorry, Billy," I didn't mean to upset you. "But you really don't have to talk to me like that."

He shrugged.

"And what's with the sunglasses?" she asked. "What are you a rock star all of a sudden?"

"I forgot I was wearing them," he lied, with no inclination of removing them.

"Well can you take them off?"

"Why?"

"I don't know." Shelby was frustrated. "Maybe I want to look at your eyes?"

He removed his glasses with a grand gesture and placed them on the table. He glared at her. Seeing his, eyes, Shelby knew Billy had not slept in a long time.

"Billy, what is the problem?"

"I don't think I have one."

"Then what's with the attitude? You used to be so happy to see me."

He shrugged again. Shelby looked at Billy and knew he might break into tears, but didn't know why.

She took his hand. "Billy, what's wrong?" She waited and said, "We've told each other so much and helped each other through some really horrible things." Her voice began to break. "Let's not stop now."

He put his sunglasses back on and shook his head. "I'm just not sure of anything anymore," he said, on the verge of breaking down.

Shelby was patient, but the waitress was not. "Are you guys ordering anything?"

Shelby gave her a look that could have melted steel. "We'll have an order of Buffalo wings, hot," she said. "And a cheeseburger medium-well with mushrooms and bacon. And hurry. He's hungry."

"Anything to drink?" the waitress asked, obviously aware that she was no longer in charge.

"A large Coke and another Diet Sprite."

"Be right back." She disappeared.

Billy smiled "It didn't take you long to know my favorite meal, did it?"

She patted his hand with both of hers. "It's been more than a month, William. And you've ordered that at every place we've eaten except Pizza Hut."

He took off his sunglasses, revealing his tears. "I wish you didn't care so much, Shelby," he struggled to say. "There's so much going on right now that I don't know what to think or do."

Shelby was all compassion. "What are you talking about, Billy?"

"I have two dead friends, an entire town counting on me to win a stupid football game, and..."

"And me."

"Do I have you, Shelby?"

"Of course. You know that."

"I wish I did," he said.

"What do you mean by that, Billy?"

The wings arrived and Billy remembered that he was starving. "Let's eat first, okay?"

"Okay. I guess..."

Billy had known for a long time that he and Shelby needed to talk about many things. He had hoped to be having this conversation while walking through Brandywine Park, but with the autumn sun setting earlier every night, he knew that was not a possibility with their after school schedules. So they left the East-End Café and began walking up Main Street, the wind stiff in their faces.

Billy's nerves were killing him. Ever since Kenny had told him he had seen Shelby with Noah he was unsure what to think of his relationship with Shelby. He was sure he had been falling in love with her, but why would she keep something like this from him? His first inclination was to be angry. He still felt the pain in his right fist from hitting the tree, and his anger scared him. After a while the anger wore off as he considered how ridiculous the notion was that Shelby would be running around behind his back, and with Noah Lively of all people. *But why keep secrets?* He was still very upset, and he wanted answers.

So they walked along the busy street, looking in the windows and making idle chat about every unimportant thing that came to mind. They blended well with the busy, casually dressed college crowd. After every meaningless topic had been exhausted, Billy decided to get the ball rolling. "I heard you were hanging out with Noah Lively the other night."

Shelby curled her lips, which Billy recognized a telltale sign of nervousness. "I was. I have to talk to you about that, Billy."

"You do?" Billy asked, feigning disbelief. "Why didn't you have to talk to me about it before?"

"What are you talking about?" she asked.

"I'm talking about you going around with Noah Lively and me sitting home like an idiot with no idea where his girlfriend is or who she's with."

Shelby stopped walking and Billy did the same. "Is that what this mood is about, Billy? My talking to Noah Lively without your knowing about it?"

"I don't know. Maybe you should tell me how upset I should be."

Shelby was flabbergasted. "I don't see what any of that has to do with you, Billy. We had to talk about some important things and I was going to tell you about it. That's why I wanted to meet you here. I've never seen you like this."

Billy was trying hard not to lose his temper. "You've never seen me like this because I've never had to hear from a friend that you were out with someone else. You lied to me."

"I never lied to you Billy! There are things going on here that you don't know about."

"Well that makes me feel much better. Thanks a lot, Shelby!"

"No!" Shelby protested, beginning to cry. She looked around, hoping not be making a scene. "It's not what you think, Billy."

"Then what is it, Shelby? I need to know."

"And I *want* you to know. But I hate seeing you like this," she said desperately. "I've done nothing wrong, and this is ugly." She took a deep breath. *"You're* being ugly."

He was frustrated now, more at himself than her. "Look, Shelby, I know there is nothing going on between you two."

Shelby was startled even by the mention of such a notion, but Billy kept talking. "I just didn't like hearing about something like this from someone else. I mean, first you tell me how much the guy creeps you out because you think he's stalking you, then you go to the pool hall with him? What should I think?"

She sat on a bench and looked at the ground. She put her hands in her jacket pockets and squeezed herself tightly. Billy stood over her, waiting for her to speak. She took her time.

"It's Samantha, Billy," she finally said, gasping for air through her sobs. "Remember when I told you there was more to what happened than everybody thinks?"

He put his hand on the back of her head. "Yes," he said.

"Well, there is *a lot* more, and there is someone out there doing terrible things."

"What are you talking about?"

She reached up to grab his wrist, a gesture that begged him to hold her. "Billy," she gasped. "Samantha told me she was going to die!" The words escaped with such a force as if they had been fighting to get out for weeks. "She told me she was going to die! She knew!"

Billy finally sat next to her and held her close in his arms. He didn't know what to think, but he knew Shelby wasn't finished.

She continued. "She told me at the hospital that she would be dead in less than a week, and she was. And this kid, Noah, he knew too. Somehow they both knew."

She was simultaneously relieved and hysterical. It seemed that having finally said the words she kept inside of her for so long had released a terrible burden. "We have to talk to Noah, Billy, both of us. We have to find out who's doing this because the police don't care. Nobody cares."

She cried a cry that Billy had never heard before. He was ashamed of himself and confused about what Shelby was saying. He realized that his thoughts and actions had been despicable; he had abandoned Shelby when she needed him the most.

On the other hand, he couldn't begin to understand the news she had just given him. Had Noah really discovered something else about Ryan and Sam? Could there really be anything to what Shelby was saying?

For now, Billy just held Shelby and let her cry.

"I don't know what to do, Billy," she said. "What can *we* do?"

Billy thought about it. "I guess we need to talk to Noah Lively."

twenty-three

Ron Wade looked at the letter he had just opened and wondered if he should give it a second thought. It was possible that he was looking at the scoop of a lifetime, the kind of tip that propels a reporter's career into superstardom. The story he was looking at could turn his stagnant career around from an average city newspaper reporter in a small state, to a nationally recognized *journalist,* if it was true. It was also possible that he could be reading the nonsense that would sink his short career to embarrassingly low levels that even he had never known.

He bit his nails and looked at the clock. There were thirty-three minutes until the deadline and he simply did not have enough time to think too long about what to do with this letter. He already had some crime he needed to write about. In front of him were press releases describing two shootings and a case of breaking and entering. He had phone calls to make. A letter like this could not come at a worse time.

Like most of his work, none of these stories he was currently working on were front-page material, but all of them had to be in today's evening edition. Either he would decide to make a story out of this strange letter he had just opened, or he would file it in the back of his bottom desk drawer where he knew he would never see it again.

He bit his badly worn nails some more and read the typed-written letter again.

Dear Mr. Wade,

I think you and your colleagues at the News Journal should be aware of some strange but important coincidences in the untimely deaths of Samantha Selby and Ryan Chambers. It is my belief that these two teenagers were not the victims of accidents. I believe they were murdered.

I have no evidence besides what I have listed below, I can find no plausible motive, and I have not yet discovered any possible suspects. However, I do know that there is a killer who is stalking the youth of this town and that the police are unable and unwilling to stop him. Please take this seriously; I am anonymous, not crazy.

Obvious coincidences:

1. Both died between 10 and 11 p.m.
2. Ryan and Samantha were boyfriend and girlfriend.
3. Both apparently lost control of their cars.
4. They were both seniors at Newark High School.

5. Both were accomplished varsity athletes.

6. They were likely to be this year's *Prom King and Queen.*

Suspicious coincidences:

1. Ryan and Sam were both coming from work and had to leave unexpectedly, according to their co-workers.

2. Neither was wearing their seatbelts, though their friends and families say they always did.

3. Both were driving cars they had never driven before.

4. Ryan and Sam were in three of the same classes at Newark High last year.

5. Both left work to help friends whose cars had broken down.

In addition to this list, I happen to know that both of these murders were discussed in Internet chat rooms several weeks before they took place. Unfortunately, I cannot provide any further information on that matter, at least not yet.

I am seeking justice for the families of two children whose deaths have been dismissed by far too many adults as accidental, but I have neither the power nor the prestige to make a case. You do. Please help.

Sincerely,

A concerned citizen

"Wade!" shouted an annoyingly whiny voice. "You got a story there?"

"No, sir," the reporter answered, trying to collect his thoughts. "Just some junk mail."

"Well, deadline is half an hour away and we just got word of a robbery in Elsmere. You on that?"

"Yes, sir," he answered grabbing the telephone and tossing the letter into his bottom drawer."

As he dialed the phone number for the Elsmere Police from memory, Ron decided he might take just one more look at that letter. But it would have to wait.

The truth entered the narrow confessional and reverently took his place at the kneeler. "Bless me, father, for I have sinned," he said while making the Sign of the Cross.

The priest recognized the deep, even voice and kindly said, "It's been a long time since you last confessed."

"I know, Father. Thank you for seeing me."

"I can't *see* you at all," the priest replied. "You know, we usually do this face-to-face nowadays."

"It's better this way, Father. I don't want to be seen."

"Okay," answered the priest. "How are things at school?"

"Better, I guess."

"I'm glad to hear that."

The truth was struggling. "Father, I'm not sure you'll be so glad after you hear my sins."

The priest was patient. "I see. Just remember, God will forgive you for whatever you have done. Don't be afraid."

"Should I begin?"

"As soon as you're ready. But take your time; there's no one waiting."

"I don't even know where to start, Father."

"Why don't you start with what is bothering you most?"

There was a long pause. "Father, I need to hear you tell me that what I say will never be repeated to anyone."

"This is a confessional. You don't need *me* to tell you that."

"I'm sorry, Father. You're right." The truth took another long pause. "I'd like to begin my confession now."

"Go right ahead. God is listening, and he will forgive you."

"My envy, Father. It's turned to pride."

"I see," the priest answered.

The truth inhaled deeply. "Two people have had to die for it; and there will be more."

twenty-four

Remsburg had become very good at letting his words sink in. When disciplining a truant teenager, he had made an art of the dramatic pause. He would let words hang between himself and the recipient for seconds that seemed like hours. The poor offender would shift in his or her seat as the head of discipline looked on with eyes that begged a response that could not be found.

It was an art he had learned as a soldier. Even the most seasoned sergeant would be lost for words when the serious young officer would confront him with an observation that he took exception to.

"Barracks looked to be a little out of order, Sergeant," he'd say as casually as if he was commenting on the weather.

"I apologize for that, Sir," the sergeant would fumble in response. "Storm was coming quick, and I wanted to get the men out for P.T. ASAP."

And Lieutenant Remsburg would glare at the sergeant with those uneasy eyes. After what seemed like an eternity, the sergeant would finally say, "It won't happen again, sir. After all, we might need to go to war in the rain some day."

Then Remsburg would crack just the slightest hint of a smile and say, "Haven't you heard, Sarge? The next war is in the desert. But P.T. in the rain never hurts anyone."

"Yes, sir."

Conversation over.

Several years later, he was sitting at his desk staring at Ethan Boulden, a member of the junior class who had a penchant for graffiti. Not having been invited to sit down, Ethan shifted his weight from one foot to another as Remsburg glared at him, waiting for an answer that would not come.

Finally, the nervous student said, "I guess it won't come off. I'll have to pay for it to be painted."

Remsburg cracked his trademark smile and shook his head ever so slightly. Wrong answer. Now Ethan was sweating.

"I'll paint it myself?"

"Good idea, Ethan," the vice principal answered evenly. "You can start today after school." The glare continued.

"Was there anything else, Mr. Remsburg?"

"I think we're finished for now, Ethan. See you at three o'clock?"

"I'll be here."

117

Remsburg followed Ethan to the door. He could feel the student's relief. Like most students who ended up in Remsburg's office, he had been sure the punishment would be much worse, but Remsburg loved surprises. Ethan would be more surprised when he got home and learned that his father had already heard what had happened and that he and Mr. Remsburg had decided it would be best if Ethan's car was kept in the garage until after Christmas.

What Ethan saw when he emerged from Remsburg's office was an even bigger surprise. Standing next to the secretary's desk in an unmistakable, perfectly tailored blue uniform was a gigantic Delaware State Trooper with a polite smile on his face. Ethan stopped and turned to look back at Remsburg with desperation in his eyes.

"Is he here for me?" Ethan whimpered, on the verge of tears.

The vice principal, who was equally surprised, used the trooper's presence to his every advantage.

"Don't worry, Ethan," he said while patting him on the shoulder. "I'll tell the officer that the graffiti will be gone before dark."

Ethan gasped with relief. "It will!" he said to both of them. "I promise, right after school."

The young officer tried his best no to laugh. He found it amusing that he had unwittingly become instrumental in the discipline of a Newark High School student.

"Back to class, Boulden," Remsburg ordered. Ethan was gone and Remsburg finally couldn't contain himself.

"Trooper, I don't know what you're doing here," he said extending his hand. "But that boy's never going to deface public property again."

"Glad I could help," the officer answered shaking hands. "I'm Adam Graff, Delaware State Police."

"Charlie Remsburg. I guess you're not here to arrest graffiti artists, right?"

"No, I'm not," Graff said. "I have a few things I'd like to discuss with you, if you don't mind."

"Not at all. Come in the office."

The opened letter sat on Remsburg's desk as he shifted in his seat. Remsburg stared at the typed-written letter. Graff stared at Remsburg.

"Does Mr. Hayes, the principal, know about this?" Remsburg asked, getting the legal business out of the way.

Graff nodded. "He sent me to you."

Remsburg had expected to hear that. He looked back at the letter.

"I can confirm everything on the list that has to do with Newark High School," Remsburg stated after reading the mysterious letter more than a dozen times and double-checking the records kept on his computer. He tapped at the bottom of the letter. "Except this part about them both being 'accomplished varsity athletes.' That's a little subjective, I think."

"I know the Chambers boy was a hell of a football and baseball player, right?" Graff asked.

"He was," Remsburg said, his eyes narrowing as he leaned back in his chair. "But Samantha. She played field hockey and softball, I think. But I don't know how great she was. I think she was cut from softball her freshman year." He shook his head and waved the air in front of his face. "We're splitting hairs, aren't we? Either there's something to this list or there isn't. Like I said, that one could go either way. The rest is true."

Graff pursed his lips in thought. He had no need to look at the letter again. By now he had memorized it. "The thing is, Mr. Remsburg…"

"It's Charlie."

"The thing is, Charlie," Graff continued. "In a case like this we *have* to split hairs. We need to know exactly what the person who wrote this letter is getting at."

"You want to find out what the person who wrote this is trying to get across to us?" Remsburg asked.

"No," Graff answered insistently. "We know what the writer is trying to tell us. That's way too obvious. Whoever wrote this has no doubt that those kids were murdered and he wants someone to do something about it."

"So what is it you're trying to find out?"

The officer stood from his chair and walked to the large window next to Remsburg's college diploma. "I want to know exactly *who* wrote that letter, Charlie. That's the only way I can find out if there is any validity to this thing."

Remsburg stared at his computer screen. The officer continued. "I can't get anybody else at the station to even begin to take this thing seriously," he said with an edge of frustration. "No other officer even wants to hear about it, much less a detective.

"But I have a feeling that whoever wrote this thing knows something important, something that will make it clear whether or not I'm wasting my time."

He looked at Remsburg. "Do you think they were murdered, Charlie?"

119

Remsburg weighed his response carefully. "Trooper, I'm no conspiracy theorist, but…"

"Neither am I," Graff interrupted. The excitement in his voice betrayed his hope that Remsburg would help him.

"I always thought it was strange, coincidental, that these two were killed so close to each other in time and in the same way. But I trusted that the police had checked into everything. And…"

"And what?"

"And I still feel that way, Officer." Graff returned to his seat, his bulky frame crashing into the chair like a child who had been sent to the corner of a classroom.

"Dammit!" Graff shouted.

"What do you want me to say?"

"Help me figure out who wrote this thing, okay? I'll do the rest."

"How the hell do I know who wrote this thing?"

"I already spoke to your principal," Graff answered. "He says you know the kids of this school better than anybody, and he wants your full cooperation."

"He said *that*?"

"If those kids were murdered, he wants to know about it."

"But if he really believed they were murdered he wouldn't have sent you to me," Remsburg answered with just enough defiance. "He'd still be talking to you."

Graff shook his head. "He said *you* could help me."

Remsburg picked up a pencil and put it in his mouth, biting hard in frustration. As if surrendering, he said, "You think the kid who wrote this goes to school here?"

Graff nodded.

Remsburg scratched his chin. "Well, if I had to guess, I would say I think a boy wrote this. I taught for eight years and I know how boys write. Do you think a boy wrote it?"

Graff nodded again.

Remsburg sighed his frustration. "What do you want to know that I haven't told you?"

The trooper produced a small black notebook and began flipping through it. "Here's what I'm looking at. From what you said today, it sounds like a kid who doesn't play any sports, and probably doesn't go to any sporting events."

Remsburg smirked. "How do you figure that?"

Graff looked up from his notebook. "If he played, or went to games, he'd know the girl wasn't that good an athlete. He was probably pretty fond of this girl and is giving her more credit than she deserves."

Remsburg nodded his agreement. He was impressed. "That's another reason we're sure he's a boy. What else?"

"He doesn't have a girlfriend."

Remsburg grinned. "He'd never have time to do that kind of research."

"Right," Graff said, all business. "He's probably used to being somewhat introverted, the type who likes to observe people rather than get involved. Obviously smart."

"Okay," Remsburg said, thinking hard.

"But he knew all about the social lives of these kids: boyfriend, girlfriend, king and queen of the prom, same classes together, where they worked…"

"What's that mean?"

"It means he's been snooping, sticking his nose where a kid like him wouldn't usually be. This kid's been causing a stir and somebody had to notice."

A light appeared in Remsburg's eyes, and Graff saw it.

"What else?" Remsburg asked, as if in a trance.

"He's a good student with excellent grammar, and I think…" He was unsure of himself.

Remsburg was intense, his voice choked with urgency. He leaned on his desk and asked, "You think what, Trooper?"

"From reading this thing, it seems as though he has a flare for the dramatic."

Remsburg exhaled deeply and nodded his head slowly and deliberately. "Yes, he definitely does. He always has."

"You know him, don't you, Charlie?"

"I do."

Newark priest found dead in confessional
Beloved pastor of St. John's apparently suffered a heart attack

By Ron Wade

NEWARK-*The Rev. Thomas J. Nolan was found dead in a confessional booth at St. John's Parish in Newark yesterday evening while teenagers from the church's youth group had been cleaning the property. He was 68.*

Known by most as Father Tom, the very popular priest was believed to have been hearing confessions earlier in the day. Newark Police said they were fairly certain that he had a heart attack while waiting in the private booth and that his body was not discovered until several hours after he died.

"He was such a sweet man," said a tearful Michelle Ramsey, one of the youths who discovered Father Nolan's body. "I can't believe he's gone, but I think he died doing what he loved, being a priest and helping people."

It is not known if Father Nolan had heard any confessions yesterday. Parishioners said it was common for the priest to wait inside a confessional booth for a full hour without anyone going in. The youth group members had volunteered to help clean the church, beginning their work around 8 p.m. Father Campbell was found at about 9:15, four hours after confession hours had ended.

Rev. Dave Murphy, associate pastor of St. John's, had very little to say except that he was "devastated," and that he would be praying for Father Nolan and his family. "This is a terrible loss," said Murphy. "He seemed like he was in such good health."

twenty-five

It was three o'clock on Thursday afternoon and school had just been dismissed, but King wasn't going anywhere. This would be a special evening, and he could barely contain his excitement. At eight o'clock, the Newark High School community would be re-introduced to an art form that had been completely abandoned for more than fifteen years: the Shakespearean play. King kept telling himself that he had Noah Lively to thank for it, and he did. But there was more. In his heart, King knew that he had just as much to do with the resurgence as his young mentor. The wise old teacher had sparked Noah's creative flame and fanned it to grow into the inferno that would be unleashed on the audience tonight – *Macbeth*!

He could not wait to see the results. *What a great night this would be!* Everything had happened just as he knew it would.

At four, he would meet with the cast and crew in his classroom where dinner would be delivered – pizza, his treat. At that time he would deliver the speech he had waited fifteen years to deliver. It was the one in which he told them to make the Bard proud by conjuring up those glorious monsters and heroes that he had envisioned centuries ago. *Make Shakespeare live tonight!* He sat at his desk and felt the butterflies. It was bliss.

The bliss was interrupted by a familiar voice.

"Nate, I need you." King spun his chair to see Charlie Remsburg wearing a look of urgency he had not seen in the young man's eyes in a long time.

"What is it, Charlie? Sit down…"

Remsburg walked into the room and sat. "I have a real problem, Nate, and I need your advice."

King smiled, "Now, this really *is* like old times, isn't it?"

Remsburg didn't respond, just put his face between his hands and ran them through his through his thick brown hair.

King placed a wrinkled hand on Remsburg's shoulder. "What is it, Charlie?"

There was a long pause as Remsburg searched for what to say. He looked King in the eyes and told him his problem. "Nate, we might have a serious issue with a kid we both know well."

King removed his hand and leaned back in his chair. "Noah?"

Remsburg nodded. "I just got done talking to the police. They want to talk to him about Ryan and Sam."

He leaned forward. "Why?"

"They think he knows something," Remsburg said gravely. He shook his head. "I just hate to see this thing come back again, Nate."

"They think he knows something about what? Do they suspect some sort of foul play?"

Remsburg nodded. "At least one cop does, and he's digging hard."

King chuckled, seemingly amused by this turn of events. "Well, what could Noah have to do with any of that? He's not the kind of young man who could, or *would* cause two fatal automobile accidents."

"I know that, Nate. And the God's honest truth is that I don't think there is anything more to this case than two tragic, but coincidental accidents. But they do want to talk to him."

"Did they use the word 'case'? How seriously are they taking this?"

Now Remsburg chuckled. "There is one very young and ambitious cop who can't get anyone else to even listen to him. He says if his supervisor finds out he's wasting time on this he's liable to be working security at the Concord Mall by the end of the month."

King considered this. After a few moments he stood and walked to the dirty window that overlooked the parking lot and football field in the distance.

"Well this tells us a couple of things," he said, thinking out loud. "If there is only one officer who's out to save the world, there is almost definitely nothing to worry about in terms of *legal* trouble."

Remsburg nodded his agreement. "What else, Nate?"

"It seems we have to have a talk with young Noah. He's managed to get at least one police officer upset with him. Who knows what could be next? God forbid he starts talking to the children's' parents. He has a strange way of making people listen to him, even when it is nonsense."

"You're right about that, Nate," Remsburg said. The statement was more a sigh of relief than anything else. "Let's talk to him."

King stood still, looking out the window.

"You okay, Nate," Remsburg asked.

"I'm fine, Charlie. It's just funny how you mentioned God before."

"When did I mention God?"

"You said something about the 'God's honest truth,' remember?"

"Oh yeah, just an expression."

"Are you a man of God, Charlie?"

Remsburg thought about the question. "I guess I'm like most people. I tend to ask God for help when I need it, and keep him on the back burner the rest of the time."

King smiled. "Of course. You were a soldier once. I'll bet you had quite a dialogue with God in the days leading up to the…"

"Why do ask, Nate?" Remsburg interrupted.

King smiled. "I apologize. I forgot I'm not to mention your days as a hero. Did you know *I* used to be a man of God?"

"What do you mean?"

"I used to be a priest. Did you know that?"

Remsburg was taken aback. "How would I know that, Nate?"

"I guess you wouldn't. I just thought as an administrator, you might have come across my employment files and taken a look, maybe out of curiosity."

"That's not me. You know that," Remsburg said. "Besides, the boss has the personnel files locked up so tight you'd have an easier time getting an appointment with the president."

King smiled and raised his hands in defense. "No thanks!"

There was an awkward pause and neither man knew what to say. Finally Remsburg asked, "So, why did you leave the priesthood?"

"I left because I fell in love with a young lady. It never worked out with her, but the incident made me realize that being single forever wasn't for me. I also had some other family issues that needed my attention." He shook his head at the memory. "I was only 'in' for a few years, as it turned out. Sometimes I miss it."

Remsburg was still bewildered. "So what does any of this have to do with Noah?

He paused. "Nothing, I guess. It's just that I haven't spoken to God in so long, and I hope he has his hands on all of this."

Remsburg was silent.

"God has a strange way of making coincidences turn out to be part of a much bigger plan. I used to call it 'God's will.'"

"What do you call it now?" Remsburg asked.

King walked back to his desk and looked down at his copy of *Macbeth*. "I guess I call it fate."

He looked back up at Remsburg and his excited smile returned. "I'll talk to Noah tonight. We have a big show this evening. *Macbeth*. Have you heard?"

Remsburg smiled as he stood to leave. "How could I forget, Nate? I love Shakespeare, especially *Mac...*" He stopped himself, then said. "Especially the 'Scottish Play.' Break a leg."

In all his years as a bank manager Christian Aument had never heard a request like this. He scratched his head and looked across his desk at the polite young man who had come to see him. He wasn't sure what to say.

"So, Mr. Remsburg…"

"Call me Charlie."

"So, Charlie, you say you teach English at the high school?"

"Yes, sir."

"And you want to set up an account in which our bank draws three hundred dollars from your pay every month?"

"That's right," Remsburg answered.

"And you are *never* going to see this money?"

"It will all go to someone, but I'm not sure who yet."

The bank manager shook his head. He had set up plenty of accounts for people who wanted to put money away for their kids, or their retirement. But he had never set up an account for an *unknown* person.

"Charlie, you're not trying to hide any money you earned illegally or anything like that, are you?"

"Of course not, sir."

The manager considered this. "Well, how long can we expect you to have this account open?"

"About ten years, Mr. Aument. Maybe more"

"You'll have racked up a pretty good chunk of change by then, son."

"That's the idea, sir."

The bank manager smiled. "Well, I don't see why we can't do this for you. I appreciate your business."

"Thank you, sir."

They shook hands for the last time. They would never see each other again.

twenty-six

Noah shifted nervously in his chair. "Do you think these rooms are bugged?" he whispered.

Billy was still standing, leaning against the glass wall. He had not time for this nonsense. "Bugged, Noah? What are you talking about?"

"I'm talking about little microphones that pick up conversations. Do you think the University bugs these rooms for security purposes?"

Billy looked to the ceiling without moving his head. He held the suggestive pose long enough for Noah to notice. Choosing not to push the ridiculousness of Noah's paranoia, he finally said, "No. I doubt the University of Delaware is spying on its students for security reasons."

Noah stood and paced the small room, craning his neck to peer out the window. "Sorry," he said, realizing he was being overly cautious. "Why don't you pull that curtain closed?"

"Noah, if I pull the curtain closed, Shelby won't be able to find us."

"I know," Noah snapped. "Where is she?"

"I don't know," Billy replied. "This isn't the easiest place to find a parking space. Why did we have to meet here, anyway?"

"It was Shelby's idea," Noah answered, returning to his seat. "She didn't want to take the chance of anyone recognizing us. By the way, thanks for not wearing your letterman's jacket."

Billy ignored the compliment. "Well, she picked the right place."

The place was the library at the University of Delaware.

"Why are you so nervous, Noah?" asked Billy.

"Didn't Shelby tell you anything?"

Billy shrugged. "A little, and I don't believe any of it. Just a bunch of coincidences." Noah looked at the table and shook his head.

From his spot, Billy could see the elevator doors open. Shelby stepped out, looked left and right. He tapped the glass and waved until Shelby acknowledged him and she began to make her way toward them.

The enormous library at the University of Delaware was equipped with several private meeting rooms that students could use for group study. One wall was made of Plexiglas that could be covered by a thin curtain. The curtain was semi-translucent, preventing the undergrads from getting too creative during study breaks. Most importantly to Shelby, almost no high school students ever came to Morris library until term paper time, which would not be for another six months.

Billy and Shelby hugged briefly and Noah kept his seat. She smiled at Noah, who gestured for her to sit.

"I'm really sorry I'm so late," Shelby said. "Game went long and I couldn't find a spot out there."

"You guys win?" Billy asked.

She shook her head. The field hockey team had not won a contest all season, and losing Samantha Selby, who was a popular player if not a productive one, only served to destroy team moral. The team was just counting the days until their last game, while the football team was gearing up for a playoff run.

Shelby smiled and changed the subject. "Noah, I heard your play was amazing! My friend Michelle was there tonight and she couldn't believe it!"

The director attempted a smile. "Thanks," he said. "One more show tomorrow and then we're done. I'm glad it's over."

"You should be proud of yourself," Shelby said.

Noah shrugged off the praise. "Let's talk about why we're here, okay?"

"Good idea," Billy said as he pulled the curtain closed. "Should I barricade the door, too?"

Shelby and Noah looked at each other and frowned, half embarrassed, half scared. Shelby looked at Billy. "If you knew everything, I don't think you'd be so obtuse, William."

Billy smirked and sat down heavily. "Well, tell me everything. Then maybe I won't be so obtuse."

They both looked at Noah, who reached into his torn and tattered book bag and produced a thin manila folder. He placed it on the round, red table and opened it. "Okay," he said. "Here's everything. I only ask one thing from you, Billy."

"What's that?"

"Just hear and see everything before you call us both crazy."

Shelby took Billy's hand. "He will, Noah. Just tell him what you know."

It took Noah about twenty minutes to relate all of the information to Billy, with Shelby interrupting occasionally to add what she knew. Billy sat and listened, never once interrupting. This was not out of a lack of interest, but more out of distress. He was suddenly presented with fresh problems that were much more vital than a football game or a friend who was playing hide and seek. When Noah was finished, Billy sat silently, going over the details in his head. Finally, he decided to try to sum it up as best he could. He was careful not to sound condescending, even though he was still quite skeptical.

Billy took a deep breath and began his summation.

"Okay, so what happens is there is a club of five or six people that they call 'The Fatum Club.' You don't really join; you just receive an IM from a screen name called 'fatum.' When *fatum* IM's you, he or she or it gives you a prediction. And in almost every case, it comes true. Am I right so far?"

Noah nodded as if he was relieved that someone other than he finally knew. Billy continued.

"It starts off innocently. *Fatum* says that someone in the club will eat French fries for lunch, or someone will fail a quiz, and they come true, somehow. Later, it gets more interesting when this person begins predicting specific test scores, then results of sporting events." Billy paused and looked at the table. "He predicts football games."

Noah saw that this was especially troubling to Billy. "What about that? Do you know something, Billy?"

Billy felt he had to tell them what he knew. He could never have imagined that Mike's words could have been the re-telling of a mad man's prediction.

"Before Mike disappeared, one of the things he kept telling us was how he knew the outcome of the games before they happened."

Noah placed his nicotine-stained hands on the table with a thud, a gesture that seemed to say he was right all along."

Billy looked at Noah with affirmation, then he continued. "Then, *fatum* starts predicting big things, like when people will die." He found it hard to continue.

Shelby finished for him. "And they die," she said.

Billy repeated it. "And they die." He looked at Noah, then at Shelby. "You said Sam told you she knew she would die?"

Shelby nodded and said, "I thought she was just upset up from loosing Ryan. I had no idea..." She tried not to cry and Billy took her hand. Noah, always the gentleman, produced a small packet of tissues from his backpack and passed it across the table.

"She told me, too," Noah said in a whisper. "And Ryan. I think he told Mike. That's why Mike had to disappear. He couldn't take knowing."

Billy shook his head. "I don't get that. Why disappear? Why not tell somebody about it?"

"That's obvious, isn't it Billy?"

For a second, Billy wondered what he had missed. Then the realization hit him like a blitzing linebacker. "Mike was next," he said.

Noah nodded. "Mike *is* next."

Everyone now understood the ramifications of what was happening.

"Okay, now explain how the predictions came about. Would this *fatum* person just type them?" Billy asked.

"From what Sam said, they were poems, riddles," Noah said.

"When were you talking to Samantha Selby, Noah?" Billy still couldn't believe it.

"We chatted online. We weren't friends in school, but things were different online."

"I guess so," Shelby said. "I was best friends with Sam and she never mentioned you."

Noah swallowed hard and smiled at the memory. "Sam was very nice," he said. "On the computer, there was no social status, no cliques. We had a lot in common, as it turned out."

Billy was trying to stay on point. "Did she ever tell you the poem that predicted her death?"

Noah flipped through the folder and came up with a scribbled note. "I didn't want to print anything out. That always feels like invasion of privacy somehow," he explained. "But I wrote this down. Sam received this the day before Ryan was killed." He passed the paper across the table to Billy.

Billy felt icicles forming in his stomach as he read the lines. He still had trouble hearing that Ryan had been murdered.

The big man will be first
But I saved the next for worst
By weeks end, his little friend
Shall meet her untimely end.

He read the lines to himself over and over while Shelby and Noah waited. The realization that he was looking at evidence of murder was staggering. They had been sent to their graves as teenagers, with limitless futures ahead of them. Billy was lost for words. There was a heavy silence.

131

Finally, he managed to say, "The 'big man,' that was Ryan?" Billy asked Noah, though he knew the answer.

"It seems that way."

Billy was growing hot with anger at the thought of some evil being out there, preying on his friends' lives.

"Do you know who this is, Noah? Do you know who's doing this?"

"No."

"But you have an idea?"

Noah nodded slowly. "I have a short list."

Billy didn't ask. He wanted more facts first. He wanted to be prepared for what he heard. "So, that's what you've been doing all these weeks? Investigating?"

"That's right," Noah said. "Somebody had to."

"Noah, why didn't you tell the police these things?" Shelby asked.

"I did, Shelby. I sent all this stuff to the police *and* the newspapers. Nobody did anything about it."

"Did they even call you back?" Billy asked.

Noah looked at Billy with confusion. "Are you crazy, Billy? I sent it anonymously."

"Why?"

"Because whoever did this is still out there. Do you think I would expose a cold-blooded killer, who the cops have no interest in catching so he can come kill me?"

Shelby gasped when she remembered something. The other two looked at her.

"I saw a cop outside Remsburg's office today," she said. "Do you think...?"

"Oh no!" shouted Noah, panic stricken. "He knows it was me who sent the information! He'll find me!"

"Okay, Noah," Billy said, his hands extended in a comforting gesture. "Calm down."

Noah jumped out of his chair. "Calm down? Listen, *quarterback*, this is real. This isn't a game. This person wants to *kill* someone, and he will."

Billy glanced to Shelby, who was still choking back tears then back to Noah who was growing more and more panic-stricken. He realized that if there were to be a calming force to drive them toward a solution, it would have to be him. He stood and grabbed Noah by the arm. He tried to escape, but Billy's grip was too tight.

"Noah, listen to me," he said as calmly as he could. "We are all upset. *I* am upset. But we have to keep our heads about us. Whoever is doing this is keeping his. If we panic, we'll lose focus and we'll get nowhere. Okay?"

Noah took a deep breath, nodded and sat back down.

Billy continued. "I want to see everything you have. The three of us will come up with a plan to make the police understand what is going on here." He paused and looked at his two friends. "Or we'll find this person and take care of it ourselves."

Noah opened his folder and began examining the information he had collected. "You're right, Billy," he said as he sifted through papers. "Let's get to work"

Billy sat back down and the three students pulled their chairs close to the table and huddled over the materials. Billy put his hand on top of the pile of papers.

"Wait," he said. "It looks like we'll be here a while, so before we get started let's take care of a few things." He looked to Shelby. "Can you go down to the lobby and get us some sodas? We'll pay you back." Then he looked to Noah. "Noah, I think you should go down to the newspaper room and get all the clippings you can find from those accidents."

"I already have most of them, Billy," He answered. "But I'll see if I can find anymore. What are you going to do while we're doing this?"

Billy pulled his cell phone from his pocket. "I'm staying here. I have a phone call to make."

Noah and Shelby left in hurry.

Kenny was finally over being angry. A day ago, he had begun to suspect that his girlfriend, Jackie O'Neal, had only wanted him because of his recent success on the football field. Reading that play in English class and examining the overly ambitious Lady Macbeth had put all kinds of ideas in his head. Kenny had no desire to be anyone's trophy boyfriend. He had way too much self-respect for that.

To Jackie's credit, she was honest and forthright. When confronted with his suspicion, she explained to Kenny that *at first* she was attracted to him because of the prowess he was displaying on the field. But since then, she had truly begun to like him as a person. She went on to tell him that she believed she was falling in love with him.

That was enough for Kenny. He dropped the whole thing and immediately regretted making a fool of himself in Mr. King's class. They immediately planned a study date and decided to put the whole thing behind them.

The vibrating of Kenny's cell phone interrupted his deep stare into Jackie's bright blue eyes. The phone had been resting on the kitchen table, just inches away and, even though it was set to silent, it was loud enough to disrupt the moment. Making matters worse was that it was only an inch from the edge of the table and the vibration caused it to creep off the table and send the phone banging away on the hard wood floor.

"Sorry," said Kenny, his dark complexion turning red with embarrassment.

"It's okay. You should get it," said Jackie with a sympathetic smile.

Ordinarily, Kenny would not have considered picking up the phone in the middle of a "study session" with his girlfriend, but the tiny screen displayed Billy's phone number. Billy hardly ever called anyway, but to call on Thursday night, just two days before a huge playoff game was unheard of. It must be important.

"What's up, dude?" chimed Kenny.

"I need to know where Mike is, Kenny."

Kenny was taken aback. He attempted to cover his surprise by smiling at Jackie as he quickly got up to leave the room, frantically searching for privacy.

"What are you talking about, Billy? We all want to know where Kenny is."

Billy didn't want to hear it. "Knock it off, Kenny. I'm serious."

"I'm serious too, man." Kenny rushed into his bedroom and closed the door. "I spoke to Mike once for five minutes. I didn't ask him where he was."

"You didn't have to," Billy persisted. "You got his address from your friend Devon."

Kenny exhaled deeply. "You don't know what kind of trouble this could lead to, Billy. He's hidden for a reason and I say we let him stay hidden."

"This is important, Kenny. Mike is in trouble and I need to know where he is. Now."

Billy could feel Kenny struggling with what to do. He kept pushing.

"Give me the address, Kenny," he said. "Jackie wants to *study*. Don't keep her waiting."

Bard bodes well at Newark High

Talented teens conjure up Shakespeare's *Macbeth*

By Andrew Kwasnieski

NEWARK-*Ordinarily, the theater at Newark High School would never be mistaken for Shakespeare's Globe. The storied home of Shakespeare's masterpieces that rests across the Thames River outside of London bares no resemblance at all to the multi-purpose auditorium that sits just beyond the railroad tracks leading to Wilmington.*

That is, until last night.

Now the theater right here in Newark can claim at least one similarity to the one across the pond: talented actors who know their Shakespeare. The Newark High Drama Club's performance of Macbeth *proved that there are indeed worthy actors capable of performing one of the Bard's most complex and emotional dramas, and the audience reaction was proof of that.*

Upwards of fifteen hundred students, parents and other spectators turned out to see the performance, an abbreviated version Shakespeare's classic tragedy. As the final curtain dropped, the players took their bows to a thunderous ovation.

Nate King, faculty moderator of Newark's drama club, could not have been happier. "This was probably the best performance I've ever seen of Macbeth *by people this age. I am enormously proud of this achievement."*

King was also quick to point out that this was the first performance by the club that he had not directed himself. That credit goes to a junior named Noah Lively. "I am so proud of Noah," said King, who has been teaching English at Newark for 32 years. "He didn't want this responsibility at first, but he has created a masterpiece."

In addition to Lively, who made a speedy exit after the performance, Seniors Crystal Madison and Jerome Bond turned in stellar performances as Lady Macbeth and Macbeth respectively.

"I'm just glad we got through it without any

mistakes," said a highly charged and teary-eyed Madison. "We worked so hard and became almost like family over the past month."

Bond, who received the loudest cheers after the performance said he wished his director had taken a bow. "Noah disappeared so quickly after it was over," he said. "I think he deserves more credit than all of us.

He really pulled us together and showed us what this play is all about."

Then Bond smiled and said, "That's just Noah, though. That guy never wants attention for anything."

There will be one more performance of the tomorrow night at seven pm. All members of the public are welcome to attend.

The truth was running frantically from the building behind him. He practically slammed into his car as he tried to get the door open. Out of breath, he turned the ignition and sped off down the road toward home. He knew now that the police were on to him, and there were others who knew. He wanted to cry as he considered how foolish he had been. And he still had two more days until the third was dead!

He couldn't take it. He knew that the last death would lead everyone to him and he would found out. *Wasn't that what he had wanted all along?* But not like this. He eased off of the accelerator and settled into his seat.

He realized now that everything was out of his hands. He had created something that was growing beyond his control. All he could do now was sit back and watch.

And try his best to enjoy what he saw.

twenty-seven

"Take number nine, Mr. Remsburg," the girl behind the counter said with a sly smile. He thanked her with a nod and took his change. He could never get used to seeing students working behind counters. It didn't help that Remsburg was not good at remembering names outside of school and tonight at Vince's Batting Cages was no exception.

Being single, Remsburg ate out a lot. Being a high school administrator, he was very recognizable by those who worked part time jobs after school. He had learned quickly not to trust nametags. Most restaurant managers required their servers to wear them, but were not particular about what name was displayed. So when Remsburg tried to call a student by what the tag said, he was often embarrassed to reveal that he had no idea what the person's name was. The kids usually didn't take it personally, but Remsburg hated it anyway.

Tonight he didn't care about any of that.

He grabbed his usual bat, a huge black and yellow Easton and, ignoring the rack full of batting helmets, walked to the far end of the floor. The cages weren't busy tonight, and number nine sat between two other vacant cages. That was good. He felt like letting it all out and the last thing he wanted tonight was an audience.

He reached to set the pitching machine to "very fast" but stopped when he noticed it was already set to his speed of choice. Remsburg was a regular at the batting cages, having given up the actual game of baseball years ago. But it was still nice to get the hacks in. It was therapeutic, especially for someone who was still trying hard to give up nicotine for good.

The over-used baseballs started flying at him and he started grunting. He swung loudly at every pitch and watched as the spheres sailed over the far wall each time, occasionally banging thunderously against the huge Nathan's Hotdog advertisement that hung from the ceiling. Everyone at the cages except Remsburg himself knew that the louder the bang, the harder his day had been. And tonight the sign was taking a serious beating.

He felt the stress oozing out of him with every swing. As his arms began to loosen their motion became fluid, and he began to think. It was like this every time, the baseballs hypnotizing him into a focus that allowed him to concentrate on his life and his job without the accompanying stress that otherwise got in the way. He had recommended this type of therapy to more than a few of his students with temper problems. They reported varying degrees of success.

Tonight there were a few pressing matters at hand and he tried to maintain his focus on what mattered most at the time.

Noah Lively.

He had tried all day to get a hold of the outcast-turned-director, but to no avail. Every time he tried to pull him out of a classroom, he would be told that Noah had stepped out to use the bathroom. When he went looking for Noah in the cafeteria, he was told he might find him in the auditorium, shoring up some details for that night's performance. When he gave in and made a general intercom announcement, something Remsburg only used as a last resort, Noah was nowhere to be found. Then the conclusion became obvious: Noah Lively was purposefully avoiding him, something he had never done before. Right now, Remsburg knew Noah would be busy with the cast of *Macbeth,* going over their earlier performance. He had considered grabbing the director and pulling him aside during the performance, but thought better of it. He would wait until the performance was over. Remsburg knew just where he would find Noah Lively.

He kept swinging at the baseballs; every cut was now a line drive, and the sound of the controlled collisions continued to increase until it was a steady cacophony of aluminum against leather, and leather against plywood.

He kept focusing on the problem.

Remsburg had been elated when he heard Noah decided to direct the play. He had encouraged Noah so many times over the past two and a half years to come out of his shell and start contributing his brilliant intellect to the community, to do something productive. He recalled the countless conversations he and Noah's mother had over the years about how bright the kid was, how well-read he was, and how he had never gotten over the death of his father in fifth grade. Remsburg knew all too well how difficult it was to get over the death of someone close. He also knew it could not be done alone.

But, as he had suspected all along, Noah had had an ulterior motive. He wasn't directing the play as a way of dealing with difficulties, or out of his love for Shakespeare, not completely anyway. He was in it for something else. Noah wanted to *access.* He wanted to be able to stick his nose into things, to talk openly with the so-called popular kids. He wanted to find out why two of the most popular kids in school were dead, and why no adults in the community were doing anything about it.

Remsburg took an angry swing and the last of the first round of balls careened off the ceiling and hit the roof of the snack bar. The two teenaged girls working the counter barely noticed. He waited on edge for the next ball to come flying at him but, realizing his time was up, he eased out of his stance and wiped the sweat from his brow. Frustrated, he thrust his hand into his pocket, digging for more quarters. He was anxious to get back in rhythm. The conversation with Noah was looming, and Remsburg needed to rehearse it in his head. He would not be taking on the mind of Noah Lively without a plan, especially since the kid had nearly single-handedly kick-started his smoking habit a few weeks ago.

Remsburg knew Noah was a chess player, a master planner who could manipulate moves well in advance of his adversary. But even though Remsburg was not a chess player, he *was* a poker player. He knew all of Noah's tells, and he knew how to bluff, even when he was holding nothing.

Remsburg checked his watch and decided he had time for one more round. After feeding four quarters into the slot he took his stance at the near side of the red drawing of home plate that had been etched into the concrete floor. Then he had an impulse.

It had been more than two years since he had swung a bat left-handed and for some reason he had the desire to do it right now. He quickly tried to step across to the other side. Before he could plant his left foot, he realized he had made a big mistake.

The baseball came hurtling directly at his head, like a guided missile. He instinctively raised his right hand to shield his face, but it was no use. The ball struck the right side of his face between his temple and his eye. Remsburg grunted loudly and fell to the ground grasping the spot where the ball had hit.

In a daze, he could hear the concerned screams of adolescents clamoring to come to his aid. The balls continued to fly at him, slamming into the backstop making a sound that was entirely unfamiliar to him.

Someone shouted, "Turn off the damn machine!"

"Remsburg is down!"

"Jesus!"

He waved them off. "I'm fine. I'm fine," he said, scrambling to his feet. "Just bring me some ice." He shook his head and checked his hand for blood. He was furious with himself.

"Oh my God! What happened, Mr. Remsburg?" asked a petrified brunette with a nametag that read, "Sandy."

Remsburg just kept shaking his head. "I don't know. I guess I waited too long to make my move," he said. "I didn't see that ball coming until it was too late."

A heavy-set kid whom Remsburg didn't recognize fought his way through the small crowd. He wore a uniform golf shirt with a nametag that identified him as "Tim, Assistant Manager."

"I'll get you your money back right away, sir," he said with an official tone. "Your next round is on us."

Remsburg held up a hand and smiled. He was amused. "Thanks anyway, Tim," he said. "It's time for me to go."

"You know," Tim continued, "you really should wear a helmet."

"I'll keep that in mind, Tim," Remsburg replied weakly. "That *is* your name, right?"

twenty-eight

The three investigators were once again huddled around the table staring at the evidence provided by Noah. Currently, they were studying the poems that had been sent via Instant Messenger to Samantha. The three were each experiencing separate levels of uneasiness and grief.

Shelby, having been relieved of the burden of carrying her private truth, felt as though she were reading the final gasps for help from her lost friend. Sam had told Shelby that she knew she was going to die, and soon. Now she was learning that Sam had shared the same truth with Noah, whom Shelby did not even know until very recently. This left her feeling somewhat betrayed, but no less sad for her friend.

Noah shared a similar sense of relief, but his was mixed with vindication and urgency. He had been trying to get the police or the media to listen to him. So far, he had been completely unsuccessful in that regard. Now he was happy that he had help, help from two people who he knew were very smart.

Billy was all business. He was angry, focused, and anxious. He wanted to know who was responsible for the death of his friends. He wanted to take steps and execute.

They kept studying the poems. Billy slowly reached across the table and pulled one of the scraps of paper toward him. It bore Noah's distinct handwriting and conveyed one of the ominous predictions that had been sent by the anonymous stalker over cyberspace. Apparently, it had correctly predicted what the librarian, Mrs. Haney, would have for lunch, and that Tim Keefer, the best heavyweight wrestler in the district, would meet with an unfortunate fall when he left the cafeteria.

Billy read it aloud:

*"Watch the book keeper at noon and you will see
a plate of nachos, enough for three
Then the wrestler will head for the door
only to find himself sprawled on the floor."*

"This is a bunch of crap," Billy finally said.
"I thought it was, too," Noah retorted. "But they both happened."
Billy shook his head and smirked cynically. "Says who?"
"Say a lot of people, Billy." Noah looked to Shelby. "Do you remember this?"

Shelby nodded as if she was admitting a deep secret. "He tripped over a mop," she said weakly. "Everybody thought it was funny."

Billy wasn't convinced. "Everybody knows that Mrs. Haney eats those nachos. You can see her stuffing her face every time you go in the library."

"That's true," Noah conceded. "But Keefer falling on his face? You can't tell me *that* was a coincidence."

Billy leaned forward and raised both of his hands, dismissing Noah's statement. "That's not what I meant, anyway," he said. "I mean these *poems* are crap. They seem like they're written by a five-year-old." He looked through some more of them. "*I* could write better poems than this."

Shelby smiled. "You *do* write better poems than those, William."

Billy blushed. Noah tried not to laugh.

"So what, Billy?" Noah asked, ending the awkwardness.

Billy sat back and looked pensively at the opposite wall. He considered his words carefully and said, "So, we know this is not a student."

Noah and Shelby looked at each other. Each wore an expression of disappointment. They both wondered how Billy could have possibly come to that conclusion simply by discovering that the poems were poorly written.

Noah tried to break it to Billy gently. "Billy, we can't tell if this person is a student just by…"

"We can!" Billy interrupted. He stood and walked to the translucent curtain, peering out to the obscured rows of dusty bookshelves. He took a deep breath. "Any student smart enough to put this whole mess together would *never* write this kind of junk and try to pass it off as poetry." He shook his head and continued speaking to no one in particular.

"This person knows what he's doing. He's purposefully writing crappy poems, hoping the kids in this 'club' will think he's one of their own." He turned to face the other two. "It's a teacher at school, or an administrator. I know it."

Noah wasn't sold on Billy's logic. "Well, despite your thinking you're an expert on poetry all of a sudden, I'm inclined to agree with you," he said. "I don't think this is a student either." He looked back at the scrap of paper. "The bad poetry is just a coincidence."

But Billy was insistent. "It's not a coincidence, Noah. This guy, or *girl*, is trying to prove something, mostly that he is in control. He wants everyone to know he's *smart*. Any kid who was out to prove how smart he was wouldn't write bad poetry."

"And a teacher would?" Shelby asked.

Billy turned his attention to her. "Yes. If he thought it would make people think he was a kid. He'd deliberately write terrible poetry." He grabbed the poems and thrust them toward Shelby to emphasize his point. Shelby sighed loudly and turned her attention toward Noah, he shook his head in a dismissive manner.

"Okay, Billy," he said. "That doesn't really matter, does it? We both agree that this is not a kid, right?"

Billy returned to his seat and continued studying. The silence was heavy and it was clear that Billy wasn't satisfied with the agreement.

"I just think it's important," Billy said with a just a hint of desperation. "Why does he want us to think a *kid* is doing this? There are a million ways to hide your identity. Why take on the identity of a teenager who writes bad poetry?"

Noah returned to his seat and looked at Billy. He nodded as if to say he finally understood Billy's frustration.

"I'm not sure, Billy," he said. "I guess if I knew I could go work for the FBI in the criminal profiling department. We just have to go by what we have."

Billy understood. He looked to Shelby and winked, just to let her know he wasn't upset. She blushed. Billy turned back to Noah.

"What else do we have, Noah?"

Noah began rummaging through his bag again. He finally produced a small, unsealed white envelope, which he began to open. "There's one poem I haven't shown you."

Shelby inhaled deeply. "What does it say?"

Noah unfolded the paper and read it out loud:

It's been fun so far but soon it must end
I have time for one more little friend
In 21 days I'll make everyone flip
On a cold Monday, I'm taking the captain of the ship!

Billy spoke first, "Well, at least he's sticking to the bad poetry."

Shelby shook her head. "Noah, I don't understand. How did you get this?"

Noah shrugged. "The same way I got the others, from Sam."

"No you didn't," Shelby shot back. This was obviously written *after* Sam was dead. How did you get this?"

Noah knew he'd been caught in a lie. He searched for an explanation, but finally came clean. "I knew her password. I logged into the Fatum chat room with her name after she died. And I got this poem."

"Why did you do that?" Shelby asked incredulously. "Do you have a death wish or something?"

"No! I just wanted to tell the bastard off," Noah said in a voice that was way too loud for a library. "I wanted to tell whoever was doing this that he wouldn't get away with it." He stopped and took a breath. "Then he sent me this." He dropped the paper on the table.

Billy put his hand on Shelby in an attempt at comforting her. He asked Noah, "What does it mean? Is Mike the 'captain of the ship'?"

"He has to be," Noah answered.

"Twenty-one days. Is that this Monday?" Shelby asked.

"I got this seven days ago, so it would seem that way," Noah answered. "That's why he had to leave. He knew his life was in danger."

Billy knew Noah was right. Everything was beginning to make sense.

"I can't believe the police aren't doing anything about this," he said. "Do you think we can figure out who this is before Monday?"

Noah shook his head. "No way, Billy. This is Thursday. I have the last performance of the play tomorrow night. You have the game on Saturday and we're..."

"We're what?"

Noah was frustrated. "We're *kids*," he said. "Even if we figured out who this was, what are we going to do? The police won't listen to us. Are we really going to confront a crazed serial killer and ask him politely to stop?"

Billy and Shelby were silent. They had to agree with Noah.

"There's one thing we *can* do, Noah," Billy said.

"What?"

"We can go to Mike on Monday, and protect him."

"What are you talking about?" Shelby asked. "Nobody knows where he is."

Billy stood again, a look of fixed determination filling his eyes, a look that his teammates would be very used to. "I know where he is," he said.

Shelby and Noah were stunned.

"And I'm going there first thing Monday morning. And whoever this is will have to go through me to get to Mike."

Shelby and Noah were still speechless.

Billy looked at Noah and said, "Go back to that chat room, Noah. Tell *fatum* that I'll be waiting for him."

twenty-nine

It was dark and the wind was whistling down Main Street and through the chestnut trees as Noah took his usual shortcut through the graveyard. He had recently realized that this rout home was no shortcut at all and that going through the cemetery across from St. John's had been a conscious choice he had been making for quite some time.

As he tightened his black overcoat, he pondered his intrigue with the dead. He did this often, but could never quite figure the reason for his fascination. Of course, his father had died only a few years ago, but it had been months since he visited his father's grave, even though he could feel it every time he walked among the headstones. He often felt like a small child trying to avoid eye contact with his father, as he would go long out of his way to avoid the tomb. *But why?*

Like most sons of dead fathers, Noah harbored feelings of guilt that he knew would never go away - disappointments, insults, arguments. But Noah's relationship with his father had been a strong and loving one, and his father had left this world in a state of love, his son's and his wife's. It wasn't guilt that kept him away from his father's grave. He wasn't sure what it was.

Noah had decided once that it was more of a game of chase. He would wander the cemetery wondering whether his father was keeping track of him, taking of the graves he would visit. But tonight, he wasn't at all sure why he was here. *Maybe someday I'll get the answer,* he thought. He laughed to himself as he realized that maybe someday he would simply decide not to walk through the graveyard anymore.

He came to Samantha's grave, which still formed a small mound over the earth as it continued to settle. He felt the lump in his throat as he did the math on the newly-engraved headstone, again. Samantha was barely seventeen when she died. He lowered his head and thought of what might have been. He and Samantha had been close over the Internet, but nowhere else. They had both known they were too far apart socially that they could not be close friends in school. This infuriated Noah and he sometimes hated Samantha for being so wonderfully compassionate, and at the same time being such a slave to her clique. Noah knew it was only a matter of time before she would realize how silly she had been. Then they could be friends. He wiped a tear and tried to not think about what could have been.

Noah jumped when he heard the voice.

"Who do you think did it, Noah?"

147

It was calm and familiar, and had come from behind him. Instinctively he raised his clenched fists in a defensive posture as he frantically searched among the headstones for a face.

Remsburg emerged from the darkness with an expression of apology. Noah relaxed. Remsburg was wearing a brown overcoat and a knit hat, looking more like a character from a bad detective movie than a vice principal. He smiled and walked toward Noah, who seemed neither relieved nor disappointed to see his new company.

"What are you doing here?" Noah asked in almost accusatory tone.

Remsburg's smile disappeared. "You're not the only one who has friends here, Noah."

Noah wasn't convinced. "You're looking for me, aren't you?"

"I am," Remsburg said slowly. "I had a feeling you'd be here." He turned to look in the direction from which he had come. "But I really came here to visit an old friend. Today is his daughter's birthday."

"Then shouldn't you be visiting her instead?"

Remsburg frowned. "She doesn't even know me."

"Ever think of introducing yourself?"

Mr. Remsburg looked to Samantha's headstone and shook his head. "Where have you been, Noah?" he asked. "I've been looking for you all day."

"So I've heard."

"Why were you avoiding me?"

Noah shrugged. "I've been busy lately," he said. "I didn't think I had time for one of our little chats?"

The two looked at each other, knowing there was something of far greater importance going on. Remsburg decided to get to it.

He repeated his question. "Who do you think did it, Noah?"

"Are you saying you believe it?"

"Believe *what*, Noah?"

Noah's voice became tight with urgency as he stepped toward Mr. Remsburg. "Do you believe someone killed Ryan and Samantha?"

Remsburg looked away. "I don't know. But I want to know what you know."

"It doesn't work that way, Mr. Remsburg," Noah said, indignantly. "I need to know that someone in this town over the age of seventeen believes that those two were murdered."

"That's not how it works either, Noah."

"Why not?" he asked angrily. "Does something happen to your sense of logic once you reach adulthood? I've been breaking my back to figure out why these two are dead, and the only people I've been able to convince are a couple of teenagers. It seems like every adult in this town would rather see this murderer get away with it, or see me get killed trying to find him, rather than stick his neck out and tell me that I'm right." He paused to catch his breath, and then added, "There are too many coincidences."

Remsburg put a hand on Noah's shoulder. "I believe you, Noah," he said. "And I know at least one cop who's looking into it. He came to see me today."

"Did he show you my list?"

"He did," Remsburg said softly. "Why didn't you come to me with this, Noah?"

Out of habit, Noah reached into his pocket for a cigarette but stopped himself when he remembered who was standing in front of him. Remsburg was all-too-familiar with the movement.

"Have one, Noah."

Noah hesitated, then produced his pack. He offered one to Remsburg who refused. Noah lit up, then said, "I didn't know if I could trust you. That's why I didn't come to you."

Ever the poker player, Remsburg was stone-faced.

Noah continued. "I think whoever did this knew Ryan and Samantha pretty well. He knew their routines."

"What else?" Remsburg asked, still with no expression.

Noah studied him. "He had to know something about cars, I guess."

"Really?"

Noah inhaled again and nodded. "Samantha's brakes failed. Ryan's airbag didn't engage. He had to know how to do that."

Remsburg considered this. "So, you think there is someone behind those deaths, and he or she knew Ryan and Samantha well enough to know exactly where they would be, then arrange for them to leave their jobs unexpectedly, *then* tamper with cars that weren't even theirs?"

Noah nodded. "Then follow them to make sure the plan worked."

Remsburg took a few steps toward the stump of a tree. He leaned on it and said, "Sounds like a big job, complicated."

"Someone smart," Noah said.

Remsburg smiled. "So you've ruled me out?"

Noah chuckled and threw out his cigarette. "Something like that," he said. "Besides, if you were the killer, you probably would have killed me by now." He looked around. "We're all by ourselves out here. I've told you too much. You've got the perfect opportunity."

Remsburg dismissed the notion with a smirk. He changed the subject. "The police are on top of this now, Noah."

"*One cop?*"

"There will be more soon," Remsburg assured him. "That's why I was looking for you today."

Noah shook his head slowly. "Everything I know is in that note I sent." Noah removed his backpack and fished out the file he had taken to the meeting with Billy and Shelby. He handed it to Remsburg. "This will help you, if you decide I'm telling the truth. Open it after I leave."

Remsburg looked at the package, examining it curiously. Then he looked back to Noah. "Well, he wants to talk to you anyway. And you need to leave this to them."

"So noble," Noah said with as much sarcasm as he could muster. "I'm off acting like a social butterfly to try to find the truth and nobody cares for weeks. Now, the police want the children out of the way so they can do the *dangerous* work. I don't buy it."

"Life isn't fair, Noah. You of all people should know that. You have to let the police handle this from here on out."

Noah peered in the direction of his father's gravestone. He had felt it looking at him. He thought of what to say.

"I'm on a mission, Mr. Remsburg. I have been since Samantha died."

"What mission, Noah? You've done your job. Let the police do theirs."

"No. This is what I'm supposed to do," Noah said as if in a trance. "It's why I'm here."

Remsburg had had enough. "What are you talking about? Is Noah Lively getting philosophical on me now? There is no *purpose* here, Noah. You've got a bright future ahead of you. You're a great writer. You directed one hell of a play. You've just scratched the surface of what you can do with your life. It's what I've been waiting for you to do."

Noah laughed to himself. He looked back to Sam's grave. "Old Hamlet had it right, didn't he?"

"What are you talking about, Noah?"

The wind picked up and Noah had to raise his voice. "You know, how he went around acting crazy so people would open up and talk to him, figuring nobody would take him seriously?"

Remsburg saw where he was going. "Yeah."

"There's a lot to be said for that," Noah said. "When nobody takes you seriously, then you can't say anything wrong. And people will tell you *anything*."

"Is that what you've been doing all these weeks, Noah? Do you really think nobody took you seriously when you were directing that play, or speaking out in class?"

Noah smiled. "People thought I was crazy," he said. "And I used it to my advantage." He pulled the strings of his coat tighter, a gesture that let the vice principal know he was about to leave.

"Tell that cop to get to work, Mr. Remsburg."

"What about you, Noah?"

"I have my own work to do," he said. "And I'm sorry, but there won't be anymore plays. There won't be any time for that. My work has already been decided."

"What does that mean, Noah?"

Again, Noah peered at Samantha's grave. "Remember when you asked me who the exceptions were?" he asked.

Remsburg shook his head.

"I told you once that *most* teenagers were shallow and self-important. You wanted to now who the exceptions were."

"Yeah, Noah. I remember." It was from their conversation in his office a few weeks ago.

Noah choked up a little bit, paused, then said, "Samantha was an exception," He took one last look at her gravestone. "And she deserves much better than this."

Noah looked into the direction from which Remsburg had walked. "I'm sorry about your friend," he said sincerely. "I hope his daughter had a happy birthday. As happy as possible."

And Noah left the cemetery to complete the mission he had started two months ago.

Yellow Jackets advance to championship game
Newark rolls over St. Mark's, will face Cape Henlopen in finals

By Michael Talley

NEWARK-*One month ago, many members of the Newark High School football team were looking forward to basketball season.*

Today they are looking forward to playing in their first state championship game in twelve years.

With a 28-0 home field win over St. Mark's, the Yellow Jackets demonstrated the one thing they have been able to do consistently all season: win. The team that had overcome so many off-the-field obstacles, including the tragic death of offensive tackle Ryan Chambers and the mysterious disappearance of its all-state quarterback, dominated every aspect of the first round game.

Quarterback Billy Wirth threw three touchdown passes and ran for another. Despite having the top-ranked defense in the state, St. Mark's was unable to stop the Newark offense, which was able to drive down the field at will for most of the game.

Newark coach Dave Scott was elated with his whole team's performance. "Billy and the offense had a terrific game," he said. "But don't forget about the defense. They stopped one of the top running games in the state."

The Yellow Jackets blew the game open early in the third quarter when defensive tackle Goodwin Snow sacked St. Mark's quarterback Brian Diamond, forcing a fumble at their own twelve-yard-line. Wirth hooked up with wide receiver Corey Curtis in the end zone on the next play, giving Newark a 21–0 lead.

"I think that was what broke their back," Snow said. "After that, there just wasn't any fire in them."

As students and fans piled onto the field in celebration after the game, the chant "Sixty-five, sixty-five" could be heard above the roar, a tribute to Ryan Chambers who wore number 65 the past three seasons.

"We all miss him a lot," said Snow. "We're going to win one more for him. Just you watch!"

thirty

It was Sunday, one day after earning a trip to the state championship game and one day before Mike Drummond was supposed to die. The weather was brisk and damp and Billy and Shelby decided to take a walk through Brandywine Park. The walk was not meant so much to enjoy the beautiful autumn weather, as it was to escape, and to find a private place. No place seemed better than the park, where they had first opened up to each other, where they had first kissed. Now there was so much to talk about.

The elation they had felt the day before was now juxtaposed with the terror they felt about what lie ahead, tomorrow. Neither was sure what to say, but both seemed calm. The determination that had filled Billy three nights before was now turning to apprehension as he considered how to approach the next day. He was tough, but he was not a fighter. He could intimidate, but how does one intimidate a killer? Billy decided he would find out, and that he would win. One thing was for sure: even with the state championship game just a week away, the last thing on his mind was football.

"What time are we leaving?" Shelby asked him as they crossed over a small stream that crept from the river.

"What do you mean, 'we'?" Billy asked. He had assumed he would be making the trip by himself.

Shelby looked at him with fierce eyes. "You didn't think you were going alone, did you?"

Billy stammered a bit and said, "Yeah. I decided that the other night."

"And with whom did you make this decision?"

He was flustered. "I made it myself, I guess."

She stepped in front of him and the walking stopped. "Exactly when did you get this idea that *you* make the decisions around here?"

"I don't know, I…"

"Well, just because you run that offense doesn't mean you run this situation, get it?" she said, pointing to his chest. "You can be assertive when you need to be, William, and we needed that the other night. But that doesn't mean you get to run the whole show."

Billy took Shelby's arm. "It might be dangerous, Shelby."

She was unaffected. "Then why are you going?"

"Because my friend might be in danger."

"Don't forget I've lost friends, too, Billy. I'm going with you and that's it. Just maybe I'll keep you from doing something *really* stupid."

"Like what?"

"Like thinking you can take on a serial killer by yourself. Believe me, I'll be on the phone to the police at the first hint of trouble."

"I would do the same thing, Shelby. I'm not stupid."

She offered a smug smile. "Well, you won't have to, William. I'll do it for you. And maybe I'll let you drive my car, too."

He stepped to the side and continued down the trail. "Fine," he said. "I doubt anything will happen anyway."

"Why is that?"

Billy looked at her. "Whoever is doing this is smart, smarter than us. He knows we've figured this thing out and the last thing he wants is to get caught. *If* he goes up there looking for Mike, and he sees us there, he'll forget about it."

Shelby did not share his confidence. "You seem to know a lot about this person, Billy. Ever think about a career in criminal psychology?"

Billy shrugged off her sarcasm. "It's just a feeling, Shelby," he said. "I'm pretty good at feelings."

Shelby took his hand and led him to a small log where they could sit. It was situated by the edge of another stream that led deep into the woods, out of view. They sat and held hands and didn't look at each other. Shelby looked at the water and Billy looked up stream.

After a few minutes Shelby looked at him and noticed the intensity in his eyes, as if he were squinting to see something that wasn't there.

"What is it?" she asked.

He pointed with his chin, indicating the area up the steam.

"That place," he said.

"What is it, Billy?" She gently placed her right hand on his shoulder. She could tell the place was important.

"I used to go there when I was a little kid," he said. "When my parents started fighting, I'd sneak away to a place that only I knew about." He smiled at the memory. "After a while, I'd hear them calling for me. I'd give it a while before I came out, too. I didn't even care about getting in trouble."

Shelby was smiling, too. Moments when Billy opened himself up were very rare, so she was determined to sit and listen.

"I always saw it as my way to get back at them. *If you fight, I'll hide.* I loved the power it gave me. And it was the most calm and peaceful place in the world."

He didn't say anything for a long time, and finally Shelby said, "Let's go. I want to see it."

Billy stood and took her hand as they began to walk. Two steps into the trip, he stopped. "No," he said in a whisper.

She took his hand in both of hers. "Why, Billy?"

He looked into her eyes. "Because I don't *need* that place anymore, Shelby. You give me all the peace I need."

They kissed for a long time.

Remsburg was at his desk, putting in a rare Sunday at the office. But he wasn't doing schoolwork.

He had read over Noah's list of coincidences until he had it memorized. He had been through the chat room conversations and the bad poetry dozens of times. For the past forty-eight hours he had slept very little and had come to many conclusions, none of which seemed to stick. He had decided many times that the entire list was nothing more than coincidence. He had also decided an equal number of times that there was a crazed killer on the lose terrorizing his students. At one point he had decided that Noah was somehow involved, but discounted the idea. He was even convinced at one point that Mr. Hanagan, the auto shop teacher was in on it. But after considering the guy's five kids and two jobs, he would never have time to watch the news, much less conspire to kill two kids for no apparent reason.

He decided to put the project aside for a few minutes. He stood to stretch his legs and stepped across his small office to the mail slot that was fastened inside his door. He hadn't been keeping up on the disciplinary referrals he had received over the past few days and he decided now was as good a time as any to see if there were any major issues he should address personally. This was not urgent since he knew the real problems were not even given to him in the form of referral. The teacher would bring them directly to him. These small forms consisted mostly of what he called nuisance reports – chewing gum, coming to class late, checking text messages, etc.

He stopped flipping through them when he came to one that had been submitted by his friend, Nate King. Nate almost never submitted disciplinary referrals, so his curiosity was peaked.

The description at the bottom was perplexing, to say the least. He read it again.

Kenny Alvarez is guilty of being an unappreciative, ignorant, and argumentative ingrate! He should be barred from this weekend's football contest at the VERY LEAST!

Remsburg knew Alvarez, but had never had a discipline problem with him. *Had King lost his mind?* Remsburg knew it was too late to suspend Alvarez from playing in the game, which was played yesterday. But the note, which had been submitted Thursday, didn't even indicate what the boy had done to deserve *any* punishment. He decided he would have to talk to Nate personally about the situation before he called on Kenny. In the back of his mind, he was more concerned about King's mental health than the disciplinary problems of Kenny Alvarez.

He was about to file the referral slips when he had a disturbing thought. He put the slips back in his mail slot, returned to his seat and logged in to the computer. Working quickly he cross-referenced the classes of Ryan and Samantha. As he suspected, they had both taken King's Shakespeare class last spring. He took a deep breath. He then checked the results against Mike Drummond's schedule from the same semester. He got the same result; Mike was in the class, too.

He didn't need to check Noah Lively's schedule. Remsburg knew he was taking the Shakespeare class, as was Kenny. Remsburg felt a deep sinking in his stomach, and he hoped beyond hope that he had only discovered more coincidences.

He picked up his office phone and called the number on the business card he'd been given three nights before.

"Is this Trooper Graff?" he asked into the phone.

"What can I do for you, Charlie?"

"I think there's someone you need to talk to. Now."

"I'm on my way."

Billy held the door for Shelby as she climbed back into the Jetta. He carefully closed it and walked around to other side. Once inside, he leaned toward her for a kiss. "I need one more," he said.

She obliged and said, "You can have as many as you want."

He chuckled. "Well, there's what I want and there's what I *want.*"

She blushed. "We've talked about that, William. We're doing it the right way."

"I know," he agreed. He started the car and began the drive home.
"So, what time are we leaving tomorrow?"

Billy considered this. "You know, if we're *both* out of school tomorrow, people will be talking."

"Let them talk," she said. Billy loved her confidence.

"Well, I'd like to be there as early as possible," Billy said, back in planning mode. "I'd love to get there at midnight tonight. I do that in a minute would if I didn't know my parents would freak."

Shelby nodded her agreement. "So, let's leave at six in the morning," she offered.

"Sounds good," Billy replied. "That'll get us there by eight. Are you sure you want to come."

"Billy, we have been over this already," she answered. "Besides, a long drive together will be nice for us, won't it?" She reached across to rub the back of his neck.

He smiled at the thought of driving for a couple hours with just Shelby. He knew it would be nice.

"Okay. I just..." His phone rang. He paused as he looked at the number, which he didn't recognize. He decided to answer it.

"Billy?" He recognized the voice as Noah's. He had forgotten he had given him the number.

"Yeah, Noah. What's up?"

"What time are we leaving tomorrow?" Noah asked.

Billy looked at Shelby, but she already knew. The disappointment was all over her face.

The day had arrived and the truth was content. He had just finished getting dressed. He wore his best outfit. He had shaved carefully and even applied cologne from an inexpensive bottle his mother had given him last Christmas. He smiled at himself in the mirror.

"Today is the day," he said to his reflection. "No more mysteries. Today it *all* comes true."

His elation was interrupted by the voice from the next room. "Who are you talking to?" his mother demanded.

"It's the Grim Reader, Mother. He's here for you. Are you excited?"

"Do you think that's funny? Is that how you speak in school?"

He shook his head and ignored her anger. His smile returned to his face. He was happier than he had been in a long time. Today he would watch as all the pieces fell perfectly into place.

thirty-one

Mr. King pulled his Subaru Outback into his usual place. He was early, as usual. He rose every morning at five, sometimes earlier. His invalid mother required near constant attention and he was used to being exhausted. Once he finished getting her out of bed and ready for the day, he took care of himself, usually getting to school by six-thirty. He was always the first staff member there. But not today.

He could see Remsburg's Dodge parked in its usual spot. *Had it been there all weekend?* Remsburg was never early. He grabbed his bag, which was heavy with graded papers and a laptop computer, and slung it over his shoulder. As he walked toward the school, he could see from the parking lot that there was a light on in one of the classrooms. It was his. He took a deep breath and slowed his pace. He would have to think this through.

Remsburg had decided to wait in King's classroom. He knew well how valuable surprise was when facing an adversary, but he also knew how valuable it was to let an opponent out-think himself. Turning on the light and waiting would provide the perfect combination of both.

Remsburg felt the anticipation as he saw the headlights of King's car turn into the parking lot. There was no fear or nervousness. Remsburg was way too prepared for that. He had spent the night reading the Internet chat room conversations over and over again. More than once, he had felt sick from what he read. Could his friend Nate King really be the sick individual behind these twisted verses? Could he really be a killer? Remsburg was determined to find the truth, today.

King opened the door and entered his classroom without knocking. He looked at Remsburg who did not stand. Even though King smiled, he regarded the guest more as an unwelcome visitor than as a friend. Remsburg did the same.

"Good morning, Nate," Remsburg offered.

"Thank you, Charlie. It is a good morning, isn't it?" Remsburg fixed an uneasy stair at his friend.

King placed his bag behind his desk, near the window and sat in his chair. He rested his hands on his desk and did his best to get comfortable. "Is there a reason you are waiting for me in my room, Charlie?" He looked at his watch. "At six-thirty-one in the morning?"

"This room is *ours*, Nate," Remsburg said. "We just let you use it to teach."

King's eyes widened. "I beg your pardon, but this room has been *mine* since you were watching Saturday morning cartoons."

Remsburg said nothing.

"Why are you here, Charlie? What are doing in my...*this* room?"

Remsburg produced the small paper from his inner jacket pocket and placed it on the desk in front of him.

King recognized it. "Did you go out of your way to be here early so you could ask me about the incident last week with Kenny Alvarez?"

"Yes. You want to tell me about it, Nate?"

"That form says it all, I think."

Remsburg shook his head. "This doesn't say *anything*."

King's irritation was beginning to show. "It states clearly that the boy was argumentative. I will not allow a seventeen-year-old to argue with me! Is that clear enough? I want the boy *suspended*."

Remsburg looked at the form again. "You know what I see, Nate? I see a teacher who got upset because he had a kid who wasn't swallowing the nonsense that his teacher was trying to feed him."

King was furious as he raised a finger to address the younger man, but before he could, Remsburg continued.

"I see an old man who just doesn't have what it takes anymore, Nate. I see a man who's off his rocker."

"Off my rocker?" shouted the enraged teacher.

"You heard me, Nate. There was a time when you stood at the front of that room and every set of eyes was on you, amazed at what they heard. But now, well, they get better Shakespeare from Claire Danes and Leo DiCaprio."

King was fuming, but refused to allow himself to lose control. "How dare you, sir!" he managed.

Remsburg stood and approached King's desk. "Or was it deeper than that, Nate?"

King looked up at the vice principal, who was now standing over his desk. "What are you talking about, Remsburg?" he asked disdainfully.

"Was it that these teenagers care more about a kid who scores touchdowns than they do about your precious Shakespeare lessons?"

King tried to laugh dismissively. "Please, they are children after all. Of course they care more about..."

Remsburg could see he was getting to King. He persisted.

"You didn't like the idea of an *athlete* taking issue with you, did you? He actually argued with you, and you hated that."

King was sweating. "Charlie, I don't believe you would actually dispute me on this. I want that boy…"

"I remember when you could take a smart-alecky kid like this and eat him for lunch, Nate. Now you send him to *me*, to suspend him? There was a time when you could put a kid like this in his place all by yourself. What, can't you handle it anymore?"

King was losing his composure. "These kids have changed, Charlie. You know that. They have no respect for…"

"They haven't changed, Nate. *You* have," Remsburg shot back. "They're the same kids you were teaching thirty years ago. Too bad their teacher got old."

King jumped to his feet and thrust his finger into Remsburg's chest. "These children have no concept of what is important! It's up to me to teach them that. There are a few who want to learn, but I have to put everything aside to deal with a kid like Alvarez who wants to act like he knows more than me? I have to *argue* with him?" He stomped to the window and looked out at the parking lot toward the football stadium.

"Shakespeare is important! *Literature* is important! When did they forget that, Charlie?"

"They didn't."

"They *did*! I used to have students who cared. They would *listen*. They would want to know." Remsburg could see a tear emerging from King's right eye. "Now they listen to kids like Kenny Alvarez and Ryan Chambers and they treat a kid like Noah Lively as if he's a freak. Well, he's the smart one!"

Remsburg followed him to the window. "And Ryan, Samantha, Kenny, they were ignorant, right? They had no respect for you, did they? They had no respect for Shakespeare. You had to *prove* how important he was, didn't you? You lured those poor kids into a stupid mind game of fate and turned it into a sick and twisted way to get rid of them. You were jealous, weren't you?"

King spun around and looked Remsburg in the eye. The teacher's eyes were like stone - cold and unmoving. Both now knew the truth.

"And what about Drummond, Nate? Was he supposed to be next? Is he the 'Captain of the ship'? Is that why he disappeared?"

King slowly smiled, a grin that revealed nothing but evil and hatred. "You know *nothing* about me, Mr. Vice Principal. I'm the smart one here. I've proven it. You think you're so wonderful because you get so much respect form *teenagers*. You look down on me because my time has passed. Well, you'll be in my place someday, Charlie, and wait until you are! You'll wish you were as smart as me!"

"What about Drummond, Nate?"

"You're just like the rest - you and Ryan and Samantha and Drummond. It's so great to be popular and loved, isn't it? But who's got the upper hand now?"

"I give up, Nate. Who?"

"That smart ones, that's who! Billy Wirth, Noah Lively, and *me!*" he said with the satisfaction of someone who had just answered the million-dollar question. "We've proven that it's really us, the outcasts, the *losers*. We have the power!"

"What about Mike Drummond, you sick son of a..."

King began laughing uncontrollably, a deep disturbing laughter that echoed through the empty classroom.

Trooper Adam Graff appeared in the doorway. "Why don't you answer the question, Mr. King? I want to know what you planned to do to Mike Drummond."

King stopped laughing but was still smiling wildly. He looked from Remsburg to Graff. "You set me up, Charlie. I should have known not to trust a disciplinarian."

King raised his hands in mock surrender. "You've got me, Officer," he said. "But don't worry about the 'captain.' This is his last day on earth, no matter what you do to me."

"No way," Graff said stepping toward the teacher. "You're coming with me."

King was laughing again. "It doesn't matter. His fate is sealed and everything is falling into place. He is awaiting death right now. Don't you see? It's not up to me! It's fate!"

He looked at the confused expressions of his two adversaries. "We all have our destinies, don't we Charlie? We can't change that. You of all people know that."

Remsburg stepped close to King and leaned in to the point that he could smell the man's cheap cologne. "We make our own destiny, Nate. And you just made yours."

King smiled his evil grin once again and said, "What are you waiting for, Officer? Take me away!"

thirty-two

Mike awakened to the extraordinary realization that this was the last day of his life. It was an odd feeling – anxiety, anticipation, even a settling sense of relief. He was surprised at his calm demeanor as he rolled over to see the sun had risen over the lake just outside the small window near the bed where he slept. He knew it was about seven o'clock.

He was surprised to feel hunger pangs, and to be thirsty. Was this supposed to be how it feels? He recalled a special on Court TV showing how death row inmates either ate nothing on their last day, or ate like kings. Mike was hungry, but felt nothing like a king.

The familiar fear came over him like a flood. His sleep had helped him escape it, but now it was all coming back and the only thing that surprised him now was that he had been able to sleep at all.

His mother had grudgingly sent pills to help him sleep and he could now remember taking three, two more than what the label had recommended. *Should I take the rest now?* The pain he had become accustomed to returned to his stomach, first sharp, then dull, then quickly sinking. He raced to the bathroom, grabbing *Sports Illustrated* before sitting down. This too had become ritual. He hoped the end would come quickly.

The prediction he had seen just a few days ago had been clear enough.

"On a cold Monday, I'm taking the captain of the ship!"

He thought the morbid line left very little room for interpretation, and agonizing over it all this time had changed nothing. Today was the twenty-first day. It was Monday. His time was up.

The person with the *fatum* screen name had graciously called him 'captain of the ship,' and he wondered now if he even deserved that title. He was called the team captain every time his name was mentioned in the newspaper, but captains were supposed to stay with the ship, not run away to Jim Thorpe, Pennsylvania.

Who will be coming for me today? He thought about Ryan and Samantha. No one had come for them. They died because they didn't stay put. If neither of them had gotten into those cars, they would still be alive today, wouldn't they? *What could happen to me here?* He looked out the window again and saw the beautiful lake. It had frozen overnight and was just beginning to thaw.

If I jumped in now, I'd end it quickly, on my terms, and the prediction would come true. He dismissed the thought. He would stay

163

where he was. If this were to be his last day, someone would have to come and get him. And he would put up a fight, a *vicious* fight.

But who would it be?

Billy was pushing Shelby's Honda close to eighty miles per hour as it roared up the interstate toward Jim Thorpe, Pennsylvania. Shelby was next to him and Noah sat in the small backseat, constantly poking his head between the front seats to hear the conversation and offer directions, not that Billy needed them.

He had made the trip to the small town in the Pocono's countless times since he was a child. Once the site of a major mining operation, the town was now mostly known for its whitewater rafting, the excellent paintball facilities, and its unusual name. Originally called *Mauch Chunk*, the town was persuaded in 1953 to take the name of the recently-deceased, and wildly famous, Native American athlete who had won an Olympic gold medal in the decathlon and had been a superstar in the early days of professional football.

In exchange for his name, the town agreed to give him a proper burial place. The town leadership at the time was sure that having the name of a football Hall of Famer would attract tourists. The immediate results were mixed. However, the recent surge in interest in the sport of paintball had made the town a required destination for every camouflage-clad weekend warrior within a hundred miles.

This, combined with the nearby ski slopes, hunting cabins, and a charming downtown area, had made Jim Thorpe into a bona fide tourist town. It was in one of those rustic cabins tucked on the outskirts of town where Billy knew his friend Mike was hiding.

The conversation in the car was infrequent and Billy was enjoying the quiet drive. Despite all of the madness of the past few days, and indeed the past few months, Billy was managing to enjoy the ride. The highway was open, and devoid of heavy traffic, as would be expected on a Monday in mid-morning. It took about two hours to drive from Delaware, up the Pennsylvania Turnpike and into Jim Thorp. Along the way, the scenery alternated between picturesque, where Billy enjoyed the view of young mountains, rivers, and bridges, and dreary, when Billy would collect his thoughts and consider the course of action once they reached the cabin.

They stopped once at a rest stop along the Pennsylvania Turnpike for gas. They all chipped in ten dollars and Billy went to the pump. Shelby went into the small convenience store for snacks. Noah, fearful that the trio would be questioned if spotted by police for skipping school, stayed in the backseat with his head between his knees, covering himself with his jacket. Billy tried to explain how ridiculous the notion was, but Noah was unfazed.

"It's too risky," he said. "We need to get to Mike today. I'm not taking any chances." Billy finished pumping gas, deciding to save the conversation for when they were all back in the car.

Once they were, Billy opened a cold bottle of water, took a long pull and asked Noah, "So, what do we do when we get there?"

Noah had recovered from his hiding position and was ready to make a plan. He tried to find Billy's eyes in the rearview mirror, but decided to look at Shelby, who was turned around in the front passenger seat, instead.

"We find Mike and make sure he is safe," Noah said. "There shouldn't be too much to it." He said this with confidence but waited for the reaction of the two in the front seat.

Billy craned his neck to see Noah's face. "And why is that? If whoever did this was able to get Ryan and Sam, why not Mike?"

Noah was ready for that. "Only a few people know he's there, and by now Remsburg has read through everything and figured out who it is. He's called the cops and they're watching him. We just have to go there and be with him until midnight, make him understand nothing will happen to him today."

Shelby shook her head. "We should have just told the police, or told Mr. Remsburg where Mike was."

"No way," Noah shot back. "That would freak him out even more. We want him to see people he knows, who he knows won't hurt him. Besides, why would the police go there? You think they would listen to us?"

"Well, Remsburg listened to you, didn't he?" asked Billy.

"He didn't listen to me until I practically found the killer," Noah said sarcastically.

"What do you mean you *found* the killer, Noah?" Billy asked.

Noah leaned back in his seat. "It was all in those chat room conversations and in those coincidences. I know who it is, and I'm sure Remsburg does by now."

Billy turned the radio completely off and looked at Noah in the mirror. "Well, would you mind telling us, Noah?"

Noah looked out the window toward the mountains in the distance. "The Shakespeare teacher, Mr. King," Noah said. "He's the killer."

Billy and Shelby were silent, waiting for an explanation.

Noah continued. "He was the only adult they all have in common. I'm in his class now and I'm telling you the guy is not right in the head. He has this weird thing about getting his point across. I'm sure he was a good teacher once, but now he's just trying way too hard to convince his classes that he knows what he's talking about."

"How sure are you of this, Noah?" Shelby asked.

"As sure as can be," he replied. "Sam said the same thing. When they were reading *Macbeth* last year, she said he almost exploded in class when he was trying to make them understand fate and free will, but he could never provide any good examples."

"So? How does that make him a killer?" Billy asked.

"Can you think of a better example of fate for a teenager than a chat room that tells you when you are going to die?"

They were all quiet for more than a mile. Finally Billy asked, "So how does he go about making Sam and Ryan crash their cars in freak accidents like that?"

"They didn't crash *their* cars, Billy. They crashed their friends' cars. And their friends were both taking auto shop at the time. One of the projects they do in that class is to take certain parts of their own cars apart and examine them."

Billy was now having trouble concentrating on the road. He shook his head and kept listening. It was all making too much sense.

Noah kept talking. "It wouldn't take much for someone to sneak in, tamper with the brakes, or the power steering, disconnect the seatbelts."

Shelby's voice was quivering. "But wouldn't the cars have crashed on their way home from school that day? And how would he know Sam and Ryan would end up driving those cars?"

"He's a smart guy, Shelby," Noah said. "It would take some planning, but he could do it."

Billy was frustrated now. "So then would you please tell me why we are cutting school to go to the mountains? If we're not saving Mike from this killer, who are we saving him from?"

Noah leaned forward again. "We're saving him from himself, Billy." He let his words sink in. "Mike was so scared that he left town. He is convinced that today is the day he dies. He is his own worst enemy now. What kind of fear could he have that would make him go to the extremes he's already gone to? We need to watch him, and help him see that it's not his destiny to die today."

Billy and Shelby exchanged uneasy glances. Billy took another drink of water.

"It's hard to take, I know," Noah said in an almost consoling way. "But we have to stop this. This is how it has to be. Besides…"

"Besides what, Noah?" Shelby asked, sounding afraid to hear the answer.

"Well, you were right about something."

"What's that?" she asked.

Noah spoke as if there were hidden microphones in the car. He leaned in close to the two in the front and said, "The plan had to have been really complicated, and maybe he *did* have someone help him, someone who knew Ryan and Samantha really well. That is what really scares me right now."

Billy stepped on the gas.

Mike walked in from the porch and hung up his knit hat. He hadn't worn a jacket for his walk, just the sweatshirt he had worn every day since he had come to the cabin. He thought about starting a fire, then thought better of it. *What if nobody ever puts it out?* He hated the idea of the cabin burning down just because he was a little chilly.

He made himself some toast and peanut butter but wasn't able to eat it. He just sat inside beside the huge window and looked out over the lake and the sky. It was a beautiful day to make his last.

He looked at his watch and saw that it was almost eight o'clock in the morning. He thought of Ryan and Samantha and how their deaths seemed like they were meant to be from the very start. He knew his time was coming soon and the thought of how it might come was torturing him. He looked to the lake again, and saw the thinning ice. He figured it would take him less than five minutes to freeze to death at that temperature.

No. I'm going to fight death, in whatever form I face it.

As if on cue, there was a knock on the door. It was the first knock he had heard since he had been there. He anxiously considered what he should do, and how much time he had.

Billy was having trouble understanding the directions on the printout he had obtained from his computer. His bickering companions were of very little help.

"It has to be the other way," Noah said assuredly. "The way we were coming from."

"Noah, I know the house is on a lake," Billy responded. "He talks about the lake a lot."

Shelby chimed in. "But the numbers are going *up* when we get near the lake. We need to go in the other direction."

Billy was growing increasingly impatient. "Maybe there's a new numbering system," he said. "Some of these signs look older than dirt."

"Wait!" Noah shouted. "We just passed a sign for Lakeshore Drive. Wasn't that it?"

"Yes!" Billy said with relief. He turned the car around and headed in the direction of the sign. "Now we're going the right way."

Mike held the large knife tightly at his waist. Every muscle in his body was tight as he inched toward the front door. Since the cabin was unoccupied most of the time, there were no windows near the door that would allow someone to see who was knocking. This was supposed to make the house harder to break in to.

He cocked his chin and was about to ask who was there, but decided against it. He felt he should open the door quickly and be prepared to stab, hoping he could surprise the attacker. *Maybe I should just drop the knife and get it over with*, he thought.

He took a deep breath and quietly unlatched the deadbolt. He jumped as the visitor knocked again, even more loudly. He quickly collected himself and swung the door open. He raised the knife and stood ready to defend himself, ready to *kill*.

"Look out, dude!" Kenny Alvarez shouted, raising his hands in defense. "It's only me!"

"Kenny?" Mike said, flabbergasted, trying to catch his breath. "Is it *you*?"

"Of course it is, dude? Are you surprised?"

Mike returned the knife to his waist and exhaled deeply. "Get in here, Kenny."

thirty-three

Mike slowly led his guest into the small kitchen area of the cabin. He continuously looked back at Kenny, unsure if he should feel terrible anxiety or terrible relief. They had already embraced heartily, which made Mike believe Kenny had not brought a weapon with him.

"This place is great, Mike," Kenny said. "Is this where you come every year?"

"Yeah," Mike said, trying his best to sound calm. "I like it, but it gets boring after a few weeks."

"I'm sure. What's with the knife?" Kenny asked. "Is there a crime wave going on up here or something?"

"Something like that," Mike answered. "How did you find me, Kenny?"

Kenny chuckled as he made his way around the kitchen table to the large window to get a view of the lake. "You know me, Mike. I'm the one who finds things out."

Mike just nodded. "Is anyone else looking for me?"

"The whole *town* is looking for, you, Mike," Kenny answered. "Anybody who reads newspapers or watches high school football wants to know where you are."

Mike went to the refrigerator and took out two cans of Coke and walked them to the counter. He noticed that his hands were shaking. "You didn't tell anyone else where I was, did you?" he asked.

"Of course not," Kenny lied. "I just wanted to come up and see how you were. Your secret is safe with me."

"Thanks, Kenny." Mike poured the two sodas into large plastic cups with ice and handed one to Kenny. "It's good to see you."

"Good to see you, dude. It seems like years, doesn't it?"

Mike nodded, smiled and put a hand on Kenny's shoulder. "Thanks for coming up here. Call next time, okay?"

Kenny smiled. "That would ruin the surprise, wouldn't it?" They held each other's stare for a few seconds. "Why don't you show me around, Mike?"

"I never thought it would be you, Kenny," Mike said with a hint of indignation in his voice.

Kenny looked confused. "What are you talking about, Mike?"

Mike looked out the window to the lake, which had thawed to the point that it was now covered by large patches of thinning ice. "I never thought you'd be the one who would come up here and find me. I knew someone would, eventually, but not you."

Kenny put a hand on Mike's shoulder. "I'm only here to make sure you're okay, Mike. If you want me to go, I will."

Mike's eyes were fixed out the window. "Let me show you the lake," he said almost in a trance.

Kenny took a sip of his soda. "Okay."

"Bring your drink."

Kenny followed Mike past the wood-burning stove and through the back door. As they walked across the large porch they felt a strong gust of wind coming off the lake.

"I can't believe how much colder it gets up here," Kenny said in a pitched voice.

"Yeah," Mike agreed. "It's amazing what a little elevation does."

They made it out to the small dock that extended about eight feet over the water. The horizon across the lake was dotted with small cabins and docks for fishing boats. It was an awe-inspiring sight and Kenny shook his head in disbelief that a place this beautiful could be so close to home. "Now I know why you come up here every year, dude. It's *amazing*."

"It's a great place to relax."

"Well, you don't seem relaxed at all, Mike."

"What do you mean?"

"You've been all tense since I got here. Hell, you almost *stabbed* me when I came in."

Mike tried to smile. "Sorry about that, Kenny. I've been a little nervous lately."

Kenny nodded. "I guess so. There has to be a pretty big reason for you to up and disappear like that."

"Kenny, I didn't ..."

Kenny raised a hand to stop him. "It's okay," he said. "I'm not judging, and I don't need to know why you came up here. I'm just glad you're okay." He took a long pull of his soda, as did Mike.

Kenny continued. "So, are you going to be okay? I mean, did you do what you came up here for? Everybody misses having you around."

Mike smiled his appreciation. "Yeah. I've had some good down time. I'm going home soon."

Kenny finished his soda and stuffed the plastic cup in the pocket of his letterman's jacket. He was glad to free up his hand so he could put both in his pants pockets, protecting them from the bitter wind. "Good," he said.

"In fact, my mom has been sending me these sleeping pills," Mike continued. "They're very helpful."

"Good," Kenny said, his speech beginning to slur. "You're not taking too many, are you?"

Mike shook his head and watched Kenny's eyes closely. "No," he said. "I've only taken them once or twice, actually."

"Oh," Kenny said putting his hand to his forehead, his eyes beginning to glaze over. "I guess you haven't really needed them."

"Not until now, *dude*."

Kenny felt a rush of panic as he reached for the cup in his jacket pocket. He wasn't able to find it. He looked at Mike who was just standing there, watching him closely, an expression of disdain taking over his face.

"Mike," he said, gasping for air. "What did you do?"

"I knew those pills would came in handy eventually."

Kenny was beginning to lose his balance. He reached for Mike, hoping his friend would grab hold of him and walk him back into the cabin.

But Mike had other plans. He grabbed Kenny's hand and quickly pulled him closer. He spun Kenny's weakened body around and put his mouth to Kenny's ear. In Kenny's last moments of consciousness, he heard Mike whisper, but could not understand what he meant.

"Fatum should have sent someone else, buddy. You're too easy."

And Mike sent Kenny's limp body careening off the dock headfirst into the icy lake.

thirty-four

A large metal table separated Nate King and Trooper Adam Graff. Next to Graff, on his right, sat Detective Sue Curtis, who had recently been assigned to the case of the murders of Ryan Chambers and Samantha Selby. She was not in uniform, but wore a badge on the lapel of her grey wool jacket.

The room was brightly lit, with a large one-way mirror covering almost the entire side of one wall. King wondered how many blue suits were on the other side, listening to every word and examining every bit of body language. He intended to say very little, but worried he would not be able to control his elation. He shifted in his metal chair.

"Are you ready to answer our questions, Mr. King?" Curtis asked, sounding much nicer than expected.

"Sure," the teacher answered. "Do I get a lawyer or something?"

"We can arrange that, if you want one," the detective answered. She motioned toward Graff with her left hand. "I'm sure Trooper Graff made you aware of that when he placed you under arrest."

King smiled and nodded his head emphatically. "He did. Everything was done by the book."

Curtis was all business. "And you are prepared to answer our questions without a lawyer? All I have to do is make a phone call and..."

"No need for that, Detective. What would you like to know?"

Curtis smiled her appreciation. "First of all, Trooper Graff tells me you said there was still one more person...I believe you said, 'awaiting his death right now.' I'd like to know what you meant by that."

King grinned smartly. "Yes, the *captain*. He'll be dead soon, if not already. But don't worry. I will have nothing to do with it. You'll have to catch someone else."

Curtis leafed through the large pile of papers in front of her. Graff was showing signs of urgency, which she ignored. "You provided Trooper Graff with all of these documents voluntarily. Is that correct?"

"Of course," King answered.

"And I assume you are referring to this poem in which it is predicted that the 'captain' has 21 days to live.'"

"That's right," King said. "And this is day 21."

"I see," she answered patiently. "And exactly who were you referring to when you wrote that, Mr. King?"

King flashed a clever smile. He ran a thin hand through his gray hair and said, "I didn't mean anyone in particular. Actually, I had a few people in mind. We'll just have to wait and see." He thought for a moment. "I just hope it's not Noah. He's such a smart boy. But, like I said, it's out of my hands."

Graff had heard enough. He jumped to his feet and shouted, "Dammit, King! You said you would *cooperate*! Who is this? Who are you talking about?"

Curtis did her best to remain calm. "Trooper Graff, would you please step into the next room?"

Graff looked down at her. "We're wasting time here. Somebody's life could be in danger and we're sitting here..."

"Graff," the detective said in a firm voice. "Take yourself into the next room and get some coffee."

Graff was seething with anger, his eyes never breaking with King's. He exhaled and said, "Yes, Ma'am," then stormed out of the room.

King watched Graff slam the door closed then looked at Curtis and said, "You let the *bad* cop go. Will he be back?"

Curtis just shook her head. "We're not playing any games here, Mr. King. I need to know now if anyone is in danger and where I can find those people."

King was having fun. "I just told you that, Detective," he said. "But there's nothing you or I can do about it." He looked around the room. "We're in here. They're out there."

Curtis leaned forward. "Is it Mike Drummond?" she asked, a hint of urgency creeping into her voice. "Is that who is in danger?"

"Your guess is as good as mine," King said with a laugh.

"Is someone helping you? Is someone going to try to kill him?"

King tried to look as helpless as possible. "Detective, there is no stopping fate. I've been trying to teach these kids that for decades. And now they're finding it out for themselves. They're *doing* it themselves. All I did was put the idea into their heads. They did the rest."

She stood and walked around the table and leaned into his face. "*Who*? Who is doing this? Who is helping you?"

The door opened. This time it was someone else, a man whom King did not recognize. He wore a gray suit with a badge hanging from a chain around his neck.

"Detective Curtis," the man said. "May we have a word?"

Curtis straightened up and followed the suited man into the next room. Graff was there talking into his cell phone. He made eye contact

173

with Curtis, who closed the door loudly behind her. Graff was urgently finishing a conversation. "Okay, Charlie. Call if you hear anything else."

"What is it?" Curtis asked.

"That was Remsburg," Graff answered. "They've taken attendance at school. Noah Lively is absent. He's the kid who wrote the letters."

Curtis nodded and knew there was more.

Graff continued. "And Kenny Alvarez is also absent, he's the one who got in the argument with King in class last week."

"Anyone else?" she asked.

"Yeah. Billy Wirth, the kid who took over..."

"I know who he is. Who else?"

"His girlfriend. None of them showed up to school today."

Curtis looked from Graff to the other man. "What do you think, Chief?" she asked.

"Do we know where Mike Drummond is?"

Graff nodded. "Remsburg says he's in a cabin up in the Poconos. His mom sent him there for a few weeks."

The older man was taken aback. "He's living by himself?"

"The kid is eighteen. His mom had to keep working. He was upset about losing his friends. His mom thought it would be okay."

The chief stepped to the glass and looked in at King, who was whistling the tune of MASH. "Well, she probably didn't know this lunatic was after him."

"Probably not, Chief," Graff said. "So what should we do?"

"Does Remsburg have any idea why all those kids are out of school today?"

Graff took a deep breath, knowing his answer would draw some reaction. "He thinks Noah has figured out where Mike is and that they are all driving up there."

The other two faces dropped. Curtis looked at the chief. "They're on a mission," she said, hot urgency in her eyes. "They're either going to save him or kill him."

The chief pointed a finger at Graff. "Do we have an address on the Drummond boy?"

"Yes sir," Graff said.

The chief grabbed Graff's arm at the elbow and quickly led the taller man toward the exit. "Get me the Pennsylvania State Police on the phone. God only knows how much time we have."

thirty-five

Billy slowly pulled the Honda into the long driveway. The wheels spun slightly when they hit the rocks and gravel. He stretched his neck trying to see the cabin through the trees and around the curve. "Are you sure this is it?"

"Pretty sure," Shelby said. "That last house was twelve, so this must be ten."

Billy continued toward the cabin and found a grey Subaru Outback parked in front of the cabin's front door. "That's Mike's dad's car," he said.

"Good," Noah said from the backseat. Let's go say hi."

Billy turned his head. "Noah, have you ever even *met* Mike?"

"No, why?"

"Well, he's going to be pretty surprised to see us, don't you think? He'll be even more surprised to see you. Maybe you should wait out here for now."

"No way," Noah said with determination. "I'm in this all the way."

Billy looked at Shelby then back to Noah. "We're still pretty sure nothing is going to happen in here, right?"

"I'm starting to have second thoughts," Noah said. "I've got a weird feeling about this."

Shelby turned and looked at Noah. "Is there anything you haven't told us, Noah?" she asked.

Noah shook his head. "Let's go inside."

The three exited the car, Billy slipping slightly on the ice as he planted his left foot.

"Watch out," Shelby chided. "You've got a lot of people counting on you Saturday. Don't hurt yourself."

Billy gathered himself and stepped carefully toward the door. "That reminds me," he said. "I haven't been doing my football homework, lately. I've had slightly more important things on my mind."

"I guess this is what it takes to get your mind off of football, right?"

Billy knew this was sad but true.

As Shelby continued toward the cabin door, Noah, who was in the rear of the group gently took Billy by the elbow and drew him close. Somewhat confused, Billy leaned in to hear what Noah had to say.

Noah spoke in a tone that was certain, almost rehearsed. "Billy, I'm not sure what is about to happen, but I need you to know something," he said in a whisper.

Billy was unsure what to say, so he just listened.

"There is an envelope with your name on it," he said. "It's in the back of Shelby's car. Make sure you open it by yourself, okay?"

"Noah, I don't..."

"Just do it, okay?" Noah pleaded as quietly as possible.

Billy was about to say something but was interrupted by Shelby.

"Should I knock?" she asked, standing in front of the door. "I can't see anybody inside but there's a light on." Neither boy answered her.

She knocked and there was no response. She knocked louder. Nothing.

Billy stepped in front of her and slowly turned the doorknob. He poked his head inside and heard nothing. "Mike?" he called. "Are you in here?"

He looked back at Shelby, then at Noah. "Should we go in?"

"Of course," Shelby said. "We drove all the way up here to make sure he's okay, right? We *have* to go in."

Noah agreed. Billy opened the door all the way and stepped inside. Shelby continued calling Mike's name, hoping for an answer.

The three made their way into the kitchen and took note of the signs of life – soda cans, pizza boxes, newspapers.

"The stove is burning," Noah said pointing to the large wood-burning stove in the center of the living area.

Billy leaned on the kitchen table. "Maybe he's out."

"Wouldn't he have locked the door?" Shelby asked.

Noah walked to the large window in the kitchen. "Maybe not, there can't be much crime up here."

Then he saw it. His gasp was audible and Billy and Shelby rushed to the window to see what he saw.

"He's in the lake!" Shelby cried out as if to verify what they were all thinking.

They hurried frantically toward the back door. Noah was the first one outside.

thirty-six

Kenny was fully asleep by the time he hit the ice, his body striking with a thud that sent cracks outward away from where his body had impacted. The ice was giving way quickly and soon he would be immersed in freezing water.

Mike looked at what he had done and felt tremendously relieved. *It's all over. Maybe I'll survive after all.* He had thrown Kenny's body as far from the dock as possible, and the momentum had carried him a good fifteen feet. Mike had hoped that Kenny would fall right through the ice and never be seen again, but this was good enough. He knew Kenny would not be able to reach the dock even if he woke before the ice thawed. He had mixed enough sleeping pills into Mike's soda that there was no way he would have the strength to survive.

The only thing that Mike was concerned about was the potential for a witness. He scanned the lifeless horizon and realized he should not be worried. The few houses on the lake appeared to be completely unoccupied. Now he wondered if he should stay and watch Mike break through the ice or go inside, just in case a potential witness showed up.

Before he could decide, he heard the sound of a car approaching. *Is there a car in the driveway?* He heard three doors open then close, and the quiet chatter of the car's occupants. He had to get out of here.

He looked around and saw the small rowboat that was tucked under the porch. He decided that would take too long. He looked to his left into the dense woods. It was his only choice.

He dropped what was left of his soda and ran as fast as he could, disappearing into the trees.

thirty-seven

"Mike!" Billy screamed as he ran toward the lake. All he could see was the motionless body lying facedown on the cracked ice. He had outpaced the much slower Noah and was the first to reach the edge of the frigid lake.

"Is he alive?" Shelby shouted.

"I don't know," Billy said through labored breath. He frantically looked around for something that might be able to reach the body. The dark blue letterman's jacket was easily recognizable, but Billy could see that the person seemed to be smaller than the way he remembered Mike. Looking closer, he saw that the person on the ice had thick dark brown hair, as opposed Mike's close-cropped blonde hair. *Is he wearing a wig?* Billy was too panicked to put it all together.

Shelby noticed the same thing, but was thinking more clearly. "Who is that?" she asked.

"What do you mean?" asked Noah.

"It's not Mike," Billy finally concluded. "It looks like Kenny."

"Kenny *who*?"

"Kenny Alvarez," Shelby said.

Noah leaned out over the lake trying to get a good view. He remembered Kenny Alvarez from his Shakespeare class. "Kenny has nothing to do with any of this!" he shouted.

Billy ignored the observation and went to work, considering his options for saving Kenny from freezing to death. He put one foot gently onto the ice and it immediately began to give way. "It's too thin at the edge," he said. "He's gonna' fall right through. We have to get him out of there now."

Shelby ran to the end of the dock, sat down on the edge and placed both feet on the thin sheet of ice. Bill ran to assist her. But as soon as she put any weight on her feet, the ice began to break. She sat back down. "What do we do now?"

"He's falling through!" shouted Noah.

He was right. Billy could now see the water creeping up Kenny's body, starting at his feet. The ice was giving way to his weight and he would be submerged within seconds. Billy threw his jacket off, and prepared to jump through the ice. He had decided to take his chances to save his friend.

But he was too late. Noah was already in the water.

Billy and Shelby watched as Noah crashed his way through the thin ice toward Kenny. He had walked about eight feet until the bottom gave way and he had to swim. He swam a few feet until he reached the thin sheet of ice that separated him from Kenny. He was moving slowly now as the freezing water began to take its toll. He placed both his hands on the ice in front of him and leaned all of his weight until it broke, plunging Kenny's body into the lake. Noah wrapped his arms around him immediately and began to tread backwards toward the dock.

"You're really close, Noah!" Billy shouted, stunned by Noah's bravery. "Just a few more feet!" He looked over his shoulder to see Shelby who was shouting into her cell phone. He was glad someone had thought to call 911.

Noah was only a few feet from the dock now, but was going very slowly. He was struggling not only to keep Kenny from going under, but was now having a hard time keeping his own head above water.

Billy was on his stomach with his arms outstretched as far out over the lake as possible. "Come on, Noah," Billy encouraged. "You're right here."

Noah turned himself around so that Kenny was closest to Billy. Billy grabbed Kenny by his jacket and used all of his strength to pull Kenny's body from the lake. Shelby was finished the call by the time Billy had Kenny on the dock.

"Did you get through?" Billy asked.

"Yes," she answered. "The operator said the police are already on their way. How's that possible?"

Billy had no time to consider the question as he turned his attention back to Noah, who was treading water just out of his reach. "Good job, Noah," Billy said. "Come on, I'll get you in."

But Noah had had enough. He had almost no energy left. Unable to swim any farther, his head began to drop beneath the surface of the water.

"No, Noah!" Shelby screamed. "The ambulance is coming!"

"Don't give up, Noah," Billy said, trying to sound calm. "You're not that far away."

But his head dropped below the water. A few seconds later, his face broke the surface. Noah was struggling for breath, struggling for his life.

Shelby noticed the rowboat that sat about fifteen feet away. She rushed over to it and grabbed one of the oars. She ran back to the dock.

Billy was on his feet again, preparing to jump in, but Shelby grabbed his left shoulder.

"No!" she screamed. "Use this." She handed him the oar and Billy went to work.

He dropped to his belly again and extended the long piece of wood toward Noah.

"Grab it!" he commanded.

But Noah could barely raise his arms. He was looking directly into Billy's eyes when he his head dropped beneath the surface.

"I'm going in!" Billy said, jumping to his feet and throwing the oar.

"No!" Shelby said. "Even if you get to him, I'll never be able to pull both of you in. You'll both die."

"So what do we do?" Billy asked, showing his first real signs of panic.

Shelby was crying now. "I don't know, Billy," she said. She looked at Kenny. "We better get him inside."

At that moment they heard footsteps. It seemed like hundreds. They looked up to see at least a dozen uniformed police officers charging toward the lake. Billy wondered why he hadn't heard any sirens, then he realized he had not seen another car on the road for miles. There was no need for sirens.

"What's going on, here?" shouted an officer wearing a thick brown uniform.

Billy pointed to the lake and began crying uncontrollably. He had just witnessed the death of Noah Lively.

thirty-eight

Remsburg entered the cabin with Graff and Detective Curtis. They had driven in Graff's patrol car, going ninety until they reached the Pennsylvania state line, at which time they fell in behind a Pennsylvania State Police cruiser and followed it to Jim Thorpe at breakneck speed. The trip took less than an hour.

Remsburg followed Curtis into the living area and found Billy and Shelby sitting on the floor, huddled under a blanket in front of a wood-burning stove. They were both shaken up, and looked as if they had cried their eyes dry. Remsburg stepped around Curtis and dropped into a crouching position so he could embrace the two teenagers. The crying started again.

"It'll be okay," he said firmly. "We'll get through all of this." Billy and Shelby would normally have been surprised at Remsburg's display of compassion. But under these circumstances, there was no such thing as a surprise.

"Did you hear about Noah?" Billy asked.

Remsburg just nodded his head, which was still braced tightly against the cheeks of the two kids. "I'm sorry," he said softly. "I know it wasn't your fault." He pulled his head away and looked into their eyes, one by one. "We'll get to the bottom of all of this, okay?"

Remsburg looked around the room for Detective Curtis, but saw that she had stepped onto the back porch to talk to the investigators on the scene. She was busily writing all the details into her notebook. Graff was standing a few feet behind her, looking out over the lake. Several officers from various departments flanked him, pointing fingers at the lake, and talking loudly over the wind.

Remsburg looked back to Billy and Shelby. "Your parents are on their way," he said. "They'll be here soon."

The two nodded their heads. There was little that could be said or done to ease the terrible pain they were now feeling, and Remsburg knew this. Noah Lively was not the first young man whose death had affected him personally, but Remsburg prayed he would be the last.

"I'm going outside to talk to Detective Curtis. She's investigating this case," he said as if speaking to small children. "It is a murder case. It involves Ryan and Samantha." He squeezed his hands on the back of their necks. "She's going to want to know everything you know, okay?"

Again they nodded. Shelby said, "We already told the police everything."

"I know," he said. "You'll probably have to tell her, too. Okay?"

"Okay," Shelby answered.

Remsburg went outside and joined the conversation with Curtis.

Shelby started crying again, and Billy held her tightly. "I can't believe all of this happened!" she said.

"I can't either, Shelby."

"Where do you think Mike is?"

"I don't know. He must have run away," Billy said. "But he won't get far up here."

"Why would he run? Do you think Kenny came up here to kill him?"

Billy shook his head and exhaled deeply. "I don't know. I can't imagine why else he would throw Kenny into that lake. He had to have feared for his life."

"Poor Noah," Shelby said between sobs.

Billy was in tears again. "I can't believe how brave he was. He jumped right into that freezing lake. It was like he knew…"

Billy suddenly remembered the last thing Noah had told him before entering the cabin, and his thoughts went right to the envelope in the back of Shelby's car. He still had not opened it.

Shelby saw Billy's eyes, full of panic again. "What is it?" she asked.

But Billy's mind was in a million places. He was trying to add it all up. Did Noah know he was about to die, the same way that Samantha and Ryan had known? "My God," he whispered.

Shelby looked into his eyes eyes. "What, Billy? What's wrong?"

"I think Noah knew," he said.

"What?"

"He told me right before we came in the cabin."

Shelby's breath quickened. "We have to tell them…"

"No," Billy said. "Not yet."

"What are you talking about? You *have* to tell them."

Billy shook his head furiously. "I have to see something first, Shelby. Then I'll tell the police all about it."

Before she could protest any further, the porch door opened and Curtis, Graff and Remsburg shuffled back into the room and instinctively stepped toward the fire.

Curtis spoke first. "I'm Detective Sue Curtis. I investigate for the state of Delaware. I'll need to talk to both of you." She looked at her watch. "It's about lunchtime," she said. "We've got some sandwiches on the way."

"Thanks," Billy said.

"I was talking to Officer Forrester, the cop who took your statements," she continued. "He tells me it looks like Kenny Alvarez is going to be okay."

Billy wasn't sure how to feel.

"As for Noah," Curtis said removing her cap. "He didn't make it, but he most definitely saved Kenny's life."

"What about Mike Drummond?" Shelby asked. "Has anybody seen him?"

Curtis turned her attention to Shelby, who was still huddled on the floor. "Yes. He was picked up on the road about a half -mile from here. The ambulance that was carrying Kenny almost ran him off the road. He'll be fine, too."

Curtis looked at Billy. "Do you know why he was running away?"

Billy shifted out of the blanket and rose to his feet. "I think he was scared."

"Scared of what?" Graff asked, speaking to Billy for the first time.

Billy thought hard before he answered. "I'm not sure, but I think he was afraid that Kenny had come up here to kill him." Shelby nodded her agreement.

Curtis wrote the answer in her notepad. "What makes you think that, Billy?" she asked.

Billy didn't know where to begin. "Do you know about the Fatum Club?" he asked.

"I know all about it," Curtis answered quickly, surprising Billy.

Billy was relieved. "Well, I think Kenny was working with whoever was running that chat room," he said. "He came up here to make the last prediction come true."

"You think Mr. King sent him up here to kill the 'captain of the ship?'"

Again, Billy was surprised by how much the detective already knew.

"I do," he said.

Curtis looked at Shelby. "Is that what you think too, sweetie?"

Shelby nodded, thinking Detective Curtis must have a daughter.

"Okay," Curtis said stepping a bit closer to the fire. "Is that what Noah thought, too?"

Billy wasn't sure what to answer. Noah had known more than anyone else from the start. But if he believed Kenny had come to Jim Thorpe to kill Mike, why would he have jumped in the lake to save him?

"I don't know," Billy said.

Curtis asked the next question quickly. "Because if he did, I'm wondering why he jumped in the lake to save Kenny Alvarez. What do you think?"

Billy and Shelby looked and felt genuinely confused. Shelby finally said, "Maybe he just didn't think of it in all the chaos. Maybe he just wanted to save someone from dieing."

Curtis looked at Billy to see if he agreed with Shelby's assessment.

"That's what I think, too," Billy said. "Noah would have saved anybody from drowning."

Curtis studied their faces. "Sound good to me," she said. Then she added, "For now, that is."

Newark teen drowns after brave rescue
Police believe death related to prior murders

By Ron Wade

JIM THORPE, PA – Police swarmed a vacation cabin in Jim Thorpe, PA yesterday after a Newark High School student drowned while trying to save a classmate who had evidently been pushed into a lake and left to fall through the thinning ice.

Noah Lively, 17, of Newark was pulled from Bear Creek Lake at about nine a.m., shortly after police had responded to an emergency call from Delaware State Police. Authorities in Delaware had learned that Lively was traveling to the small Pocono town to investigate what he believed to be a series of murders that had been occurring since early September.

Police also said they were now treating the deaths of two other high school students, Ryan Chambers and Samantha Selby, as murders. A suspect was arrested yesterday and is being held without bail.

Delaware Police Chief Kevin Madigan issued the following statement: "We have arrested and detained Nathan King, a teacher at Newark High School. He is suspected of arranging the murders of the two teenagers in September and made them to look like accidental deaths. We believe that Noah Lively, acting on some inside information which he had obtained while conducting his own investigation of the deaths, went to Jim Thorp with the goal of rescuing who he believed would have been the third victim of Mr. King."

However, Madigan later stated that police did not believe that Kenneth Alvarez, 17, who Lively rescued from the lake, was intended to be the third victim.

Madigan went on to say that King was in police custody at the time of Lively's death, leading them to believe King had an accomplice.

According to police reports, Lively and two classmates had driven to Jim Thorpe to find Mike Drummond, the 18-year-old who left school last month for "personal reasons." Investigators believe that Drummond was the intended third victim and that he may have been responsible for pushing Alvarez into the freezing lake.

Madigan stopped short of naming Alvarez as a suspected accomplice of King's, but did say that the youth is recovering from his injuries and that his family has retained a lawyer to be present during police questioning.

"I won't speculate on anything right now," Madigan said toward the end of the press conference. "We are still investigating every aspect of this case and we plan to find out exactly who is responsible for all of these deaths, including Noah Lively." He then added, "Lively did an incredibly brave thing. He gave his own life to save another. As a police officer, I have always asked myself whether I would do the same, but I've never had to answer that question. Noah Lively is a hero."

Madigan would not comment on whether police had been following up on the suspicious circumstances of the deaths of Chambers and Selby, or if Lively had shared any of the information he had discovered with them. He did say that King and a few others were being questioned and that they believed they would find out the truth very soon.

thirty-nine

Detective Sue Curtis was back in the interrogation room with Mr. King. This time they were joined by two others. George Sabbath was the district attorney who would be prosecuting him for the murders of Samantha Selby and Ryan Chambers. He sat next to Curtis. Across the table from them was John Northrop, a veteran public defender. He sat next to the accused, furiously scribbling notes even before the meeting had started. King was in an orange jumpsuit and handcuffs.

Sabbath began. "Mr. King, this will be the last time we meet here in the police station," he said as a matter of introduction. "From here on out, we will be meeting at the Plumber House in Wilmington. Do you understand?"

King did not understand. He looked at Northrop, who was quick to explain. "They can't keep you here, Nate. There is only so much room at the station. They're going to move you to the county prison, where you'll await trial."

King frowned. "What about my mother?" he asked.

"Your mother is being taken care of," Sabbath answered. He looked through the papers in front of him. "The Division of Social Services contacted your brother, Ralph. He came to town last night and is staying with her."

He nodded his appreciation. "Does she know what has happened?"

Northrop fielded that question. "I spoke to your brother and explained the charges against you. He said he would speak to your mother about it."

King rolled his eyes. "I take care of her for fifteen years, by myself, and now he comes to save the day. Isn't that perfect?"

The others ignored the question.

"I'd like to talk to her soon, if possible."

Northrop patted him on the arm and nodded but was interrupted by the prosecutor.

"That's not what we're here to talk about, Mr. King," Sabbath said. "Mr. Northrop will help you attend to your private matters. I've asked to meet with you today to discuss the charges."

"What's do we need to discuss?" Northrop asked, indicating that all questions would go through him.

Sabbath understood. He looked back to the papers in front of him and said, "The evidence, combined with his earlier statements, have helped us build a strong case against your client, John.

"We have copies of all of the internet conversations your client participated in," he continued. "They indicate that he threatened Samantha Selby and Ryan Chambers by telling them they would die in the near future. We also have evidence that he used a student to help him carry out the murders of these two children."

"You have *circumstantial* evidence," Northrop interrupted.

"For now," Sabbath conceded. "But we will soon have a witness, who we believe will testify to the fact that he was coerced by your client to commit murder."

"Who do you have?" King blurted.

Northrop immediately grabbed the man's wrist and squeezed. "I understand you are interrogating a boy named…" Northrop looked at his notes, "…Kenneth Alvarez. Is that correct?"

"That's correct," Curtis said. "We believe he will soon corroborate the evidence against your client."

Again King couldn't keep quiet. "He'll do no such thing!"

Northrop put a hand on King's shoulder and glared at him, a stern warning to shut up. He looked at Sabbath. "My client has had no contact with this boy outside of class. He barely knows him," he said.

King couldn't help himself. "That boy couldn't commit *plagiarism*, much less murder," he said.

Sabbath was firm. "That's not what we think, Mr. King. We think he'll turn against you. And we think you're going to jail for a long time."

King laughed quietly. "For what? For two kids crashing their cars? Do you really believe I somehow made them *crash their cars*? It was their time! There is no avoiding our destiny! Don't you people understand?" Northrop was seething, trying to get control of his client.

But now it was Curtis' turn to be angry. She stood and pointed two fingers at the teacher. "And how did you know it was their time, King? Do you think your God, or something?"

King began laughing loudly.

"What is so funny Mr. King?" Sabbath demanded.

He caught his breath and wiped his mouth with his cuffed hands, the chains jingling as he did. "This child, *Detective* Curtis," he said. "She was the same way when she sat in my class. But back then she was little *Susie* Curtis." He looked to see the startled reactions of the two men. Curtis's face was red, not with embarrassment, but with anger.

"And she was just as jaded back then," he continued. His voice had taken a tone of complete satisfaction, and his eyes beamed with pride.

"She never believed anything I said about fate, about destiny. She never took me or anything I taught seriously. But who's right now, *Detective*? Everything I predicted came true. You and every single student who ever doubted me. You were all wrong!"

Sabbath stepped in. "Is that what this all about, Mr. King? Proving a bunch of high school students wrong?"

Northrop raised a hand. "George, you know my client has a right to..."

"Your client knows his rights, John," Sabbath shot back. "I think he wants to talk."

"Don't say anything else, Nate," Northrop warned.

"I don't need to," King said, feeling completely in control of the interrogation. "Everybody knows who was right. And I want it in all the newspapers," he said. "I want it printed just as big as one of those stupid football games. I want everyone to know I was right!"

The other three sat in silence, looking at each other, waiting for someone to speak.

Sabbath stood, signaling an end to the meeting. "We'll get back to you, as soon as we get a statement from Alvarez." He looked at King. "And we *will* get that statement, Mr. King. Don't you worry about that."

King just grinned. He had already won.

forty

Billy had always thought Remsburg's office would be bigger. He was sitting across from the vice principal and next to the State Trooper, Adam Graff. It occurred to Billy that the reason the room seemed small was possibly because its three occupants, especially Graff, were rather large.

They had been talking for about half an hour, Graff wanting to get as many details as possible in the wake of the death of Noah Lively. He told Billy and Remsburg that there was still a lot of investigating ahead of them, and that the police were holding Kenny for further questioning. He went on to say that the detectives thought the cars Ryan and Samantha were driving had both been tampered with. The brake fluid had likely been drained and their seatbelts had been disabled. Unfortunately, there was no longer a crime scene and both cars had been totaled and sent to the dump as wreckage.

Once he was sure he had everything he needed to make a full report to Detective Curtis, Graff closed his notebook, picked up his hat and stood to leave. Billy did the same, but Remsburg held up his index finger, signaling he wanted Billy to stay.

Remsburg thanked Graff and they shook hands. Billy also shook hands with Graff, his being swallowed up by the gigantic police officer's. When the door closed, Billy and Remsburg settled back into their seats. There was a long, heavy silence while Remsburg loosened his tie and undid his top button. He finally spoke. "I'm going to miss Noah, Billy."

Having no words, Billy simply nodded his head.

"He did a brave thing; so did you."

This time Billy offered no response at all.

The vice principal inhaled deeply. "Billy, I'm sure your head is in a million places right now, but I want you to know that as far as your game on Saturday..."

Billy's eyebrows arched. "What about it?"

"I know it's the state championship, but under the circumstances I don't think anybody in the world would blame you if you missed it," he said somberly. "Not even in this town," he added with a hint of sarcasm.

Billy was back to silence. He dismissed the suggestion by shaking his head.

The vice principal leaned back and studied the pencil he held in his right hand. "Well, I suppose playing in the game could be therapeutic anyway, at least something routine to get your mind off things."

"I don't know about that," Billy answered. "I just want to play it and get it over with."

The surprise registered on Remsburg's face. "Get it over with? This town will consider you a full-fledged hero for playing this game after what you've been through."

Billy's face reddened, not with anger or embarrassment, but with an emotion he could not identify. He shook his head and repeated the word Remsburg had used. "Hero."

The principal scratched his chin. "What? You don't like the word?"

"I don't mind the word at all," Billy said. "But not for me."

"Why not?"

"I used to think I could be a hero playing football. I've practiced and studied it all my life, but now it doesn't seem to matter."

"Go on."

Billy gathered his thoughts as best he could. "It's just that...I spent the whole fall trying to bring a football team together to win games because we lost Ryan and Mike. I never wanted any fame. I didn't want to be in the newspapers. I just thought it was important."

"It *was* important, Billy," Remsburg said, trying to reassure him. "Sports may be trivial in the grand scheme of things, but they have always been important *distractions*. They take peoples' minds off the realities of life."

Billy shrugged, and then continued. "While I was pretending to be Steve Young, Noah was solving the mystery of two murders. *That* was important, not what I'm doing. Then he gave his life for someone else, for the truth to come out." He shook his head in disgust. "Noah was right all along. I'm no hero. But if we win tomorrow, I'll hear it for the rest of my life. 'The quarterback who saved the football season for Newark – The *hero.*'" He was ashamed at the thought. "I wish the coach would just let Mike play instead."

Remsburg took everything in. "Mike isn't ready for that, Billy," he said. "But you're right about Noah. He was a special boy. And I understand how you feel. A lot of times it's the hero, himself, who feels the least heroic." The vice principal spoke the words slowly to let Billy know that he *really* understood. "Do you follow me?"

Billy looked in Remsburg's eyes. "You've been here too, haven't?" he asked quietly.

"I have."

Billy put his chin to his chest and looked at his lap. "I've heard the rumors about you," he said.

Remsburg barely chuckled and shook his head. "Old Nate King. He couldn't get enough of that story. He loved being friends with a war hero."

"He's a sick ..."

"Billy," he interrupted. "I know King is sick. He's lived a life devoid of any kind of excitement or happiness. He'd listen to these kids complain all day and then go home and work all night taking care of his sick mother like she was a baby. He had no time for anything else."

"You can't be trying to excuse what he did," Billy said, feeling a chill run down his spine.

"Of course not. What he did was terrible, inhuman. But what he was going through was terrible too. I'm not excusing his actions. I'm just...trying my best to explain them. He was once a good man, Billy."

"I'll take your word for it."

"I hope you do," he said. "As for the hero's guilt stuff, it will pass, son," he said. "It will always hurt, but it will pass."

There was a long pause. Finally Billy said, "Heroes are for big things, like saving lives, or risking your life in a war. Not football."

"Billy, what Noah did was heroic. I was trained for what I did. It was *expected* of me. Noah stuck his neck out like no kid I've ever seen, not even in war." Remsburg felt a surge of emotion in his voice and he stopped, waiting for the welling in his throat to subside. He changed the subject. "As far as football goes, it *can* be just for fun, Billy. You know that, right?"

Billy stood to leave. "Not for me. Not anymore."

"What are you saying, son?"

"Thanks for everything, Mr. Remsburg," he said. "I know Noah respected you. You made a big difference for him."

"We had a mutual respect. But right now I want to know what *you* plan to do."

"Well," Billy answered, "I have a game to win, and I will. After that, I don't think I'm too interested in football anymore."

Remsburg nodded. "I understand," he said. "But think about it before you decide anything, okay?"

"I think about *everything*," Billy answered. "But my mind is made up on this one."

"So what then? Just school? I want you to have a good senior year. You deserve it just as much as Noah, Ryan, or Samantha did."

Billy smiled and turned to leave. "Maybe I'll learn how to play chess," he said. "They say it's a real thinking man's game."

Remsburg smiled back. "I've heard that before. He was a smart kid, old Noah." Then he stood and said, "One more thing, Billy. There's something I wanted to ask you, but not in front of the cop."

"What's that?"

"This Fatum Club these kids were all involved in. There's still a few more things that don't sit right with me."

"*None* of it sits right with me," Billy answered.

"I know. I know," Remsburg said. "It's just that all this time, Noah never said anything about it."

"Why would Noah say anything about it?"

"Well, looking at all the evidence that was gathered, I think it's possible that Noah was in this thing, too."

Billy was puzzled. "You mean you think he was a member of the club?"

"Noah was in Remsburg's class," he continued. "He was nuts about the Shakespeare stuff. He always hung around that graveyard. It was like he *knew* he had it coming. Always smoking those cigarettes like there was no tomorrow. Maybe he *knew* there was no tomorrow. You know what I mean?"

Billy didn't answer.

"And on that day he saved Mike's life, he ended up dieing. Just like the prediction. Maybe *he* was the 'captain of the ship.' Maybe he was the one who was *supposed* to die up there."

Billy considered this. "You think the 'captain' referred to Noah, as director of the play?" Billy asked with just a hint of interest. "Do you believe that stuff?"

"No," Remsburg said emphatically. "I think we make our own fate. I'm just trying to get this straight." He was looking at Billy with a strange expression. There was just a hint of desperation in his eyes.

"So, what do you think happened, Mr. Remsburg?"

Remsburg looked at the large bookshelf next to his desk and seemed to study nothing in particular, the look of desperation had subsided. He spoke slowly. "I think Noah went up to that town expecting to die, and that's what he did."

Billy just stood there and turned his gaze to the aging brown carpet, unsure what to say. He thought of the ride to Jim Thorpe and what Noah told him just before they entered the cabin.

Remsburg wasn't finished. "The other thing is Noah never said a word of this to me, or his mom." There was a pause and Billy felt Remsburg's eyes burrowing into him, like a world-class poker player. "Did he ever tell you anything, Billy? Is there anything else you know that might make us understand this thing a little better?"

The vice principal was looking for a tell, something that would indicate a lie, and Billy gave him nothing.

"He never said anything to me about being in the Fatum Club," he answered with his eyes still fixed on the floor.

He looked up and saw that Remsburg was still staring. Billy remained stone-faced.

"Well, I guess it doesn't matter much anymore does it, Billy?" Remsburg asked, still trying to see Billy's hand.

"Thanks for everything, Mr. Remsburg," he said, trying to make an exit.

Unexpectedly, the vice principal grabbed Billy's elbow with both care and urgency. The desperation was back. "Bill, I need to know if Noah was in that club."

Billy was alarmed, and his face showed it. "He never said anything to me, Remsburg. I have to go."

But Remsburg persisted. "I just need to know if this was supposed to happen or if Noah *made* it happen. Was it fate or free will? Did he tell you?"

"I don't know what you're talking about," Billy said, yanking his arm away. I don't believe any of that crap about fate. I'm leaving."

Remsburg stepped back and collected himself. "I'm sorry, Billy. It's just that…this has been very difficult. I've had young men die before…before they were supposed to."

Billy wanted to leave. "Forget about it. It's been tough on all of us."

Remsburg shook his head as if to tell Billy he had no idea how much it had affected him.

"I'm sorry I can't tell you anything else, Mr. Remsburg. It's all in the past anyway."

Remsburg looked at Billy with the poker eyes once more and asked, "You can't tell me anything else, or you *won't* tell me anything else, Billy? Just tell me that."

Billy didn't answer. He just turned around and opened the door. Then he walked out of Mr. Remsburg's office for the first and last time.

forty-one

Shelby was waiting at a small table inside the East End Café. The weather had suddenly turned very cold and she was huddled behind a large cup of specialty brew coffee. She wore a beautiful light yellow sweater and blue jeans. As Billy approached her, he was in awe of her look, her sophistication, her presence, her beauty. In the chaos of the recent events, he had almost managed to forget how attractive Shelby was, and how lucky he was.

He smiled and leaned down to kiss her.

"Coffee?" he asked with a smirk, pointing to her steaming cup.

She smiled and kissed his lips. "I'll be in college soon. I have to get the look down, don't I?"

Billy sat and pulled a menu from the metal napkin holder. "You don't need to match anyone's look, Shelby. Other girls should be trying to look like *you*."

She blushed. "Did you meet with Mr. Remsburg?"

He nodded.

"How did that go?"

"Weird," he said in no uncertain terms. "It was weird."

"What did he say?"

Billy considered his answer carefully. "The guy has been through a lot. Those rumors about his being a war hero are true."

"He told you that?"

"In a way," Billy answered.

"What do you mean?"

"I don't know. He's just very upset about Noah, more than anybody, maybe. Except Noah's mother, of course."

"Of course," Shelby agreed with a frown. "He and Noah were very close."

"He was, but it's more than that," Billy said scratching his chin. "He thinks there is more to this case."

Shelby didn't say anything. They both knew that Billy had never revealed what was in the envelope that Noah had left in the back of her car.

Billy continued. "He thinks Noah *knew* he was going to die, the same way Ryan and Sam did. He thinks maybe he knew from the very start."

Shelby reached a cold hand across the table and took Billy's. "Did he, Billy?" she asked in a whisper. "Was he the 'captain of the ship'?"

Billy looked at the menu, trying not to get upset.

"Do you remember those drives we used to take Shelby? Those rides with Ryan and Sam?"

"Sure I do," she said sadly. A waitress had begun to approach the table, but seeing that she might be an intrusion, disappeared back into the kitchen.

"I remember feeling so lucky back then," Billy said. "Lucky to be in the same car with you and Ryan and Sam. I felt like a regular kid back then."

"What do you feel like now, Billy?"

Billy shook his head and looked at the floor. "I'm seventeen years old," he said. "And I don't even feel like a kid anymore."

"Me either," Shelby said.

They squeezed hands tightly.

"Can I get you two anything?" the waitress asked, sensing an opportunity.

Billy looked up. "Nothing for me, thanks." Shelby signaled that she was just having coffee.

"You don't want anything, Billy?"

He shook his head. "I've been such a jerk, Shelby," he said as if confessing.

"What do you mean?"

"I was jealous when you were talking to Noah," he said. "I treated you like I own you."

She took his hand in both of hers. "No you didn't, Billy," she said. "You were just overreacting."

"I've never had a girlfriend, Shelby. I've definitely never been with a girl who comes close to how great you are. And *that's* what I do? What is my problem?" Billy crumpled the paper napkin in front of him and threw it on the table in disgust.

"Stop it, Billy," she demanded.

Billy took a long pause and a deep breath. "You deserve better than me, Shelby. I still have a lot of growing up to do."

"What are you talking about, Billy?"

"I don't know, Shelby. I have to go," he said as he stood. "Can I call you later?"

"Yeah," Shelby answered, unsure how to react.

Billy turned to leave without kissing her. He was almost to the door when he heard her voice again.

"Wait, Billy," she called softly.

Billy turned around.

"What was in that envelope?" Shelby whispered desperately. "What did Noah tell you?"

Billy wiped his eyes. "It was private, between Noah and me. But I'm going to finish what he started," he said. "The truth is still out there."

forty-two

The jubilation in the locker room was a surprise. Of course any team would be happy about playing in the state championship game the next day, especially after overcoming the death of one of its beloved teammates.

Still, Billy was surprised at the mood before practice. He strapped on his shoulder pads and gazed across to the empty locker of Kenny Alvarez. He smiled to himself as he thought of the funny things Kenny used to say every day as they were prepping for practice. *But not today.*

Billy looked to his left and watched as players walked by Mike Drummond, slapping his hand and embracing him. Their friend and captain had returned. Even though he would not be playing, his presence in the locker room today was enough to lighten the mood. He had lost weight and his eyes looked older, sadder, but he was still the same old Mike.

Just four days earlier, Mike had drugged Kenny, thrown him into an icy lake and left him for dead. If it hadn't been for Noah, Kenny would have been the second fatality on this football team, and the school's third this year. But Mike was welcomed home as a hero. He had run away to avoid the wrath of teacher-gone-mad who had it in for any kid who was held in higher esteem than he. When the teacher's co-conspirator tried to deal the final blow, Kenny bravely fought him off, breaking the curse and freeing himself from danger. Every player was glad to see Mike's smiling face. All were glad that Mike would be stepping back into his old role as captain on Saturday when they played for the state championship. Even if he couldn't play, just being there would be inspiration for every player.

Every player but one.

Billy had made it a habit of being the first player out the door and onto the practice field. Every now and then Goodwin Cobb would beat him out the door and the two would race to the field, throwing elbows and insults the entire way. Of course, Billy always won.

But today when it was time to take the field, Billy stayed by his locker and watched as the others shuffled past him. Cobb stopped in front of Billy's locker and barked, "What's up, Wirth? We gonna' do this today, or what?"

Billy looked up at the huge man and said, "Go ahead, Cobb. I'll be right out."

And one by one the room cleared of players and coaches until it was just Billy and Mike. Billy had not spoken to Mike since his disappearance six weeks ago. He had thought about Mike every day, and hoped for the day when Mike would return. But to Billy, Mike Drummond's return was far from glorious.

Mike turned around to see Billy on the opposite side of the room, staring with an empty expression. "Hey, Billy," he said.

"Hey, Mike."

Mike acted surprised. "I guess I never got to thank you for coming up to the mountains on Monday," he said. "That was really great of you and Shelby."

"And Noah," Billy corrected.

Mike nodded. "Yeah. I never even knew that kid, but he went up there to save my life. Wow. And he ends up saving Kenny's instead."

"He saved Kenny from *you*, Mike," Billy said flatly.

Mike nodded slowly, considering his words.

"Yeah, well, he did come to *kill* me, Billy. What was I supposed to do?"

Billy looked at Mike with an expression that burned deep into him, an expression that let Mike know exactly what the score was. Billy knew everything.

"Why did you do it, Mike?"

"I told you, Billy," Mike said. "I was…"

"Why did you help Mr. King, Mike?"

Mike's eyes betrayed him, even if his words didn't. He knew that Billy had found out. Still, he played dumb.

"Billy, I don't know what you're talking about."

"No, Mike. *Kenny* didn't know what you were talking about. But you tried to kill him anyway. He went to that cabin to visit a friend, because that is all he ever wants to be to anybody. And now he's sitting in a jail cell trying to explain why his friend drugged him and threw him off a dock."

"Billy," Mike warned, "You don't know what you're talking about."

"You were supposed to be Ryan's *best* friend, Mike. You were closer to him than anyone. But you used that against him, didn't you?"

"What?"

"You knew his schedule at work, and he told you Sam's. You were able to disconnect his car battery so it wouldn't start. And since you took auto shop with Corey Curtis, it was pretty easy for you to drain Corey's brake fluid, then suggest Mike take his car from work when his wouldn't start."

Mike was silent. Beads of sweat began to form on his brow.

"You called Ryan at work that night, didn't you? You told him you had a flat and needed him right away. I'll bet you said, 'Just take Corey's car. He won't care.'" Billy could feel his stomach tightening. It suddenly occurred to him that he was confronting a killer. *Does this make me a hero?*

"And you did the same thing to Sam, right? You knew she was working, and she borrowed Phil Margiotta's car, who also happens to be in your auto shop class."

Mike was still silent.

"But I want to know *why* you did it," Billy said. "Was it for the grade? Was *that* how you got an A in King's class last year?"

Mike looked at the concrete locker room floor.

"So do you want to go tell Kenny all this, or should I? Because there is no way he is spending another night in jail because of you."

Mike closed his eyes and shook his head. "Kenny will be fine," he said quietly. "They can't connect him to any of this."

"Except the whole town will think he's a murderer for the rest of his life. You make me sick, Mike."

"Billy, listen to me. I didn't know anyone was going to die. You have to believe me," he pleaded.

"Why should I believe that?"

"King was crazy," Mike said. "He told me if I helped him, he would make sure I had the grades to get into any college I wanted. He told me he could make it so I could get a scholarship to anywhere. Do you know what that would mean to my family?"

Billy was enraged. "What does it mean to Ryan's family?"

"He was never supposed to die, Billy! It was supposed to be a small accident. King just wanted to prove he could make the predictions come true. First it was really small stuff, like grades that he could change himself, or he'd have me trip a kid in the hallway.

"But he wasn't happy with any of that. It wasn't *impressive* enough," Mike said. "He wanted something big. So, yeah, he had me tamper with Mike and Corey's cars. He figured it would be harder to figure out if he was driving someone else's car. It would seem like he just lost control."

"What about Samantha?" Billy asked.

"Man, after Mike's accident, King told me he could pin it all on me. He said if I didn't make the same thing happen to Sam, he'd make sure the police knew who did it to Mike. I was scared man. That's why I did."

Billy felt an enormous sense of relief mixed with exhilaration and anger. Noah's work was almost finished. Noah had saved Kenny because he knew he was innocent.

Mike continued. "Then when I got to the cabin, I kept checking my email and King told me there was still one more job to do: the *director*. I told him I didn't even know who he meant. I wasn't going to kill anybody else, anyway."

"He said the *director*?" Billy asked, his blood running cold.

"Yes! He said it would be either him or me who went down," Mike said. "I didn't even know who he was talking about!"

Billy was numb. He couldn't believe what he was hearing.

"He said he had someone else working with him, and that he was on his way to kill me. He even told me the day. So when Kenny showed – on *the day* - I figured it was him or me. I did what I had to do. I thought he was there to kill me!"

"And then what?" Billy asked.

"Well, then you showed up in the car with Shelby and Noah. I started to think maybe I had the wrong person. I thought maybe the police had come and were going to shoot me, or something. So I ran."

"What do you mean, you thought the police would shoot you?"

Mike was becoming crazed. His eyes were bulging out of his skull and his knee shook as he spoke, causing the rubber of his sneaker's sole to squeak against the floor. "Billy, he told me I would die that day. And he was *never* wrong! I knew I would die one way or another. So I ran as fast as I could."

"So why did Noah die instead of you?"

Mike sat on the closest bench and put his head in his hands. "He tricked us all, Billy. Everybody in the club thought I was the captain of the ship, but it could have been me *or* Noah the whole time. One of us was going to die that day. King didn't care which one. Either way, his big prediction would come true."

"And who else was in the club?" Billy asked.

"That's it," Mike said. "Ryan, Sam, Noah, and me. He invited us all to his chat room and made all these crazy predictions. And they always came true, whether I helped him or not. And then he told us all when we would die, and they all did. Ryan's accident wasn't supposed to kill him. But King got lucky and it did."

"Why Ryan and Sam?"

Mike answered as if it was obvious. "He couldn't stand them, Billy. They were popular, king and queen of the prom. He hated how the beautiful and popular got all the attention." Mike stopped, suddenly realizing something else.

"It was me he really wanted dead," he finally said. "But I guess he figured Noah would do if it wasn't me. We were both captains. The most important thing was to make the predictions come true." He looked up at Billy. "Just like in *Macbeth*. Man, I hate that play!"

"So what now, Mike?" Billy asked.

Mike wiped his tears away. "Well, I guess I have to talk to the police now, right?"

"That would be a good idea," Billy answered.

Mike agreed without any argument. "Do you have a phone," he asked. "I'll call them."

"Don't," Billy said. "I already did. He's probably waiting outside. I'll go with you."

Mike smiled. It was a smile that admitted defeat. It was a weak and pitiful smile that showed his life was never going to be the same.

"Damn you, Billy Wirth. You always were prepared for anything."

Hero's daughter had a 'guardian angel'

By Trudy Waters

Along with about four hundred classmates, Michelle Ramsey will receive her high school diploma from Newark High this spring. But over Christmas vacation, Michelle received a huge surprise in the mail.

On Wednesday, Michelle returned home from a church youth group retreat to find a letter in the mail. It is easy to imagine Michelle's astonishment when she read that she would be receiving a free college education, compliments of an anonymous 'guardian angel.'

"All the letter said was that someone who cares about me will pay for all of my college," said Michelle, who plans to attend the University of Delaware in the fall. "It said an account had been set up at the bank and that I don't have to worry about anything. It's like a gift from God!"

The surprise education fund had been arranged through the Newark Trust Bank, and was not to be revealed to Michelle until this Christmas. Bank officials refused to identify the anonymous donor.

"This person is someone who knew Michelle's father, and now wants more than anything to see her succeed," Bank Manager Christian Aument said. "I haven't spoken to this person in years, since the day he came in to set up the account. But he called me yesterday with instructions to get the money to Michelle."

Michelle's father was killed in action in Iraq twelve years ago. "I know my father would be proud," said Michelle. "The letter said that he has been watching over me, like a guardian angel. I'm going to make him proud. I just wish I knew who this person was so I could say thank you."

forty-three

It was snowing, and Billy decided to walk home from school. It was now late February, more than two months removed from the chaos that had consumed the teenager's life, but it was just as present as if it had happened yesterday. He walked slowly, enjoying the after-school daylight that seemed to disappear in the late fall. Without having to spend two hours at practice, he could walk home while the sun was still out, and today was a good day to be walking.

A strange peace follows a fresh snowfall, even in the busiest of towns and even under the most chaotic of circumstances. The snow seems to force tranquility upon an angry place and today Billy walked through Newark as if it were the first truly peaceful day in months.

He crossed the pedestrian bridge toward Main Street without stopping to look back at the school, the Bee Hive, or the football field. He proceeded slowly to the entrance of St. John's Cemetery, which was now the home of three of his friends. Before entering he stopped by a trashcan, which had filled almost halfway with snow. Too bad this is Friday; maybe school would have been cancelled tomorrow.

He reached for his wallet and dug out the folded newspaper clipping and opened it slowly. It was the story from the state championship game, the last game he would ever play. He looked at his name in the headline and shook his head. In one motion he crumpled the story and dropped it into the bin. He kept walking.

He stepped past the graves of Samantha Selby and Ryan Chambers, both graves standing alone, both with flowers that struggled to survive the snow. Billy stopped briefly to read the inscriptions, as he had done many times before, and kept walking.

When he arrived at Noah's grave he turned away from the stone and saw his footprints, many of which were already covered by fresh snow and had all but disappeared. A strange feeling came over him, as if he had been here all along. He looked at Noah's grave, his name inscribed next to his father's, but with a much shorter span between years. Billy closed his eyes and said a prayer for Noah. He finished by asking Noah to look over him and his friends, convinced Noah was in a better place and still acting as director. His eyes began to fill as he thought of something Noah once said: *"I'm glad you're not afraid to be the guy who comes and talks to the weirdo in the graveyard."*

Noah had been exactly the kind of student Mr. King had grown to love in his decades as a teacher: kind, introverted and brilliant. And he exploited Noah's talent and killed him for it. Noah had died stopping a madman, sacrificing himself for the lives that King had felt had no meaning.

He smiled to himself and asked the headstone, "Are you sick of seeing me here, Noah? Maybe I should leave you alone for a while." And he did.

He walked toward Main Street, his steps getting heavier. He was tired, hungry, and ready to go home now. But that would have to wait.

He turned onto North Chapel Street and walked into the Newark Trust Bank, just as Noah's letter had instructed him. He spent only a few minutes inside, despite the warmth and dry. He nodded to the teller and went back out into the cold.

He waited until he was standing at the mailbox before he pulled the beautiful sealed red envelope from his backpack. He looked at it for a moment and dropped the card in the box. Noah's mother would get her Valentine's Day card on time, as always.

Billy reached back into his backpack and retrieved a second sealed envelope, this one yellow. It was addressed to Shelby Cooper, whom he had not spoken to in over a month. Disaster can bring people closer together than they have ever been, but it can also drive them apart.

He took a deep breath, wondering again if he should send the card, which was more a friendly greeting than a Valentine. But his mind was already made up. He dropped the card in the box and thought of Shelby's beautiful smile as she opened her mailbox to find a card with her name on it. Maybe we'll work things out, he thought. I'm so much wiser now. *If it's meant to be…*

Finally, Billy turned to walk home. North Chapel was well out of his way and now he had a longer walk ahead of him, but he was looking forward to the walk again. He was sensing a new optimism he had not felt for a long time.

He quickened his pace but stopped when he heard the unmistakable chirp of his cell-phone. He fished into his pocket, pulled out the phone, and looked at the tiny screen. It was Kenny. Billy smiled and let it ring. He had a lot to say to his best friend, but nothing that couldn't wait until he got home. He silenced the phone and put it in his pocket. He was beginning to feel the cold, but it felt good.

He lifted his hood and kept walking.

Made in the USA